INNOCENT VICTIM

BRIAN CORNETT

ISBN: 978-1-09836-027-6

CONTENTS

Disclaimer

This is a work of fiction. While the cities of Muskegon, Muskegon Heights and North Muskegon are real places and some of the street names used in this story are real, the organizations, businesses and street addresses in this story are the products of the author's imagination. All of the characters are fictitious and any resemblance to real people, living or dead, is purely coincidental.

Brian Cornett

Acknowledgements

Many people supported me and helped significantly in the creation of this book and I can't thank them enough. Nor can I list all of them here, but I must gratefully acknowledge a few who contributed so much. First, my wife Pam who never failed in her support and encouragement. My critique buddies Mike and Tom who listened to and read early chapters and always offered helpful criticism. Tracie Carter, my editor, whose excellent eye saved me a lot of embarrassment. I also want to say thanks to the half dozen or so law enforcement personnel who patiently answered questions and lent advice, especially Ray, Mike and Jack. If I had chosen another path in life, it would have been law enforcement. Blue lives matter.

Books by Brian Cornett

Tales From the Brass Rail

ISBN 0-9720640-4-4

Swift Mission

ISBN 978-1-4620-0820-9 (sc)

ISBN 978-1-4620-0821-6 (hc)

ISBN 978-1-4620-0819-3 (ebk)

CHAPTER ONE

Catherine Hood turned another page of sheet music and quietly hummed the simple melody while tapping her fingers on the desk as if it were the baby grand piano in the studio across the hall. The music was only a series of exercises fit for beginning piano students. She was really looking forward to working with the two new students Jennifer had signed. They were young, with little experience with music and none with the piano, but they had seemed eager to learn when they came to the studio with their mothers yesterday. The two little girls would begin their lessons next Monday. Catherine enjoyed working with the youngsters. It gave her a sense of purpose now that she was retired, and they reminded her of the many students she had helped during her long years as a middle school music teacher. She was glad she had volunteered to help Jennifer when the young woman opened her piano studio. What had started as a one day a week volunteer job had turned into a three day a week paid position. Catherine was fond of Jennifer. Although they weren't really close, she looked on the younger woman as the daughter she might have had if she had chosen another path in life. She had no regrets about the time she had spent caring for her mother and sister until they both were gone. Now she was alone and had few close friends. She had already resolved to correct that soon. Catherine had made the decision to start traveling and was already studying the beautiful brochures for cruise ships that catered to single travelers. They were full of pictures of young, good-looking men and women having fun in the sun. Not that she expected to find romance at this stage of her life. Oh no, she was much too pragmatic for that. But a girl could dream a little, couldn't she? She was only a little overweight and she was only fifty-two so who could tell what might happen?

Catherine paused and listened carefully. She heard Maddy practicing in the studio across the hall from her small office. She winced involuntarily as the girl hit a wrong key and then winced again as she hesitated in a complicated passage. Maddy was working on "Fur Elise", a not too difficult piece the girl planned to play in an upcoming recital. Today, she seemed to be making more mistakes than usual. Catherine sighed and returned to the music before her. Madeline was a sweet girl but she had no real talent for the piano. She could read music and played adequately but there was no fire in her playing. It seemed to be mechanical rather than emotional. Catherine looked up suddenly, thinking she heard a muffled thud. Had something in the studio fallen? She listened for another minute or so but heard nothing more and once more went back to the sheet music on her desk. Another minute or more passed and she realized that Maddy was no longer playing. Catherine got up and left the little cubby-hole of an office, crossed the hall and opened the piano studio door.

The soft closing of the porch door at the far end of the studio caught her attention for a second and then she saw Madeline Straub lying sprawled on the carpeted studio floor.

Catherine screamed, "Oh, God. Jennifer, come quick. Oh, my God."

CHAPTER TWO

The dispatcher's voice blasted into my patrol car. "Any car. Code twenty-nine, possible thirty. Nineteen thirty-three Lakeshore Drive." As always, the dispatcher's voice was calm and controlled. I grabbed the mike and responded, "Makarios here. I'll take it. I'm on Lakeshore just past the country club headed into Lakeside." I had just driven past the entrance to the Country Club Golf Course, thinking of the last time I had played golf.

"Copy, Lieutenant. You got it." She gave me all the information she had. She told me a woman had called, given her address and reported a death. The dispatcher added that the woman sounded panicky, almost hysterical. The woman had blurted out: 'She's dead…strangled… there's a cord around…'. Then she repeated the address and hung up. The caller didn't give her name.

I said, "OK, got it. Send me some backup and notify forensics. I can be there in ten." I hit the switch for the patrol car's blue grill lights. I felt my excitement ramp up. 'Thirty' is police code for homicide. In the three and a half years that I had been a member of the Muskegon Police Department, I had handled four homicides. Three simple shootings and one stabbing. In every one of those cases we had the perp in custody within hours. I wondered what this one would turn out to be.

Brian Cornett

For late September it had been a beautiful day. Just a few minutes before the dispatcher's call, I dropped my partner, Detective Sergeant Sean Dunphy, at his house in Bluffton, an area of the city near Lake Michigan. Sean and I had arrested a suspected child molester several days before and we spent most of this Friday interviewing the suspect's neighbors and friends. I drove past the abandoned car ferry docks and the Milwaukee Clipper restoration site. This was where, in a small inlet just east of the docks, my dad established his first boat yard back in nineteen fifty-six. I came into the little business section of Lakeside and went past the theater and the drugstore and looked left, toward Muskegon Lake, the gateway to Lake Michigan for the port of Muskegon.

A little over a hundred years ago, the city of nearly forty thousand souls had been the primary lumber port on the Great Lakes. It boomed again during World War II and was still home to half a dozen major manufacturing companies. But its largest attraction was as a tourist center and the mecca for fisherman seeking the huge salmon that had been introduced into Lake Michigan to combat the lamprey eel infestation. Muskegon was home port for well over a thousand fishing boats and pleasure craft.

Traffic was picking up. I tapped the siren and quickly moved around a pickup that swerved abruptly toward the curb. The bed of the truck was full of teenagers. I hoped I hadn't scared the kid who was driving. They were probably headed somewhere for a burger before tonight's big game with Bay City, I thought. In the three years that I went to Muskegon Senior High School I never got to go to pregame parties like that because I was on the football team. The kids were dressed in T-shirts and light sweaters. Late September weather in Michigan wasn't usually this nice. This year September was all warm days and cool nights with no hint of frost. I really wanted it to continue but the forecasters were saying we were in for a change soon.

I punched Sean's speed dial number on my cell phone and, when he didn't pick up, gave him the address for the call and told him to meet me there ASAP. Lakeshore Drive led toward an area of large older houses that overlooked Muskegon Lake from across a wide, tree-lined street. During my school years, this was a high-class neighborhood and I had attended several boy-girl parties in a couple of the big houses. At that time this was a wealthier part of the city and a few of my classmates had lived up here. I've always thought it's a shame that many of these old places were remodeled and converted into apartments or low traffic businesses during the years I was away. But then, a lot of things changed in Muskegon in those almost fifteen years.

It was just past four thirty and the early dusk made seeing the house numbers difficult, but I looked for the stenciled numbers on the curb and soon found the house I was looking for. It was a big Georgian style set well back from the street in the block between Cascade and Piedmont streets. There were two cars in the double width driveway that led to a detached two car garage at the back of the lot. An older Honda Civic was parked next to a red '01 Ford Mustang convertible. I pulled in and parked behind the Mustang. The front door of the house was wide open and lights blazed from both the upper and lower floors. A woman stood on the wide covered porch that ran across the front and down the west side of the house. I heard the siren of my backup coming down Lakeshore. I knew the protocol was that I should wait for them but the woman was waving frantically. I got out of the car and ran across the lawn, loosening my Glock in its holster and pulling my badge from my belt as I ran. I took the steps two at a time and winced as stabbing pains ran up my left leg. I shrugged them off and found myself facing a short, middle-aged woman dressed in a dark skirt and blouse. She had a pale yellow sweater thrown over her shoulders and held a wadded up handkerchief in her hand. Her eyes were red and swollen and her tears had made faint streaks through the light coating of makeup on her cheeks. I showed her my badge. She barely glanced at it, looked up at me through tear-filled eyes and pointed to the open door of the house. She choked, took a deep breath and stammered, "Maddy's in there…on the floor…in the studio…the door on the right."

The patrol car skidded to a stop in front of the house, its siren dying to a low growl, and two patrolmen got out and ran to the porch. I told the first one to check the outside of the building and motioned for the other to come with me. I noted a small sign at the side of the entrance that read 'Jennifer Clayton' with the words 'Piano Instruction'. I stepped through the big front door and moved quickly toward the door the woman indicated.

I looked down the hall and saw that five doors opened into it. There were two on either side and one at the far end marked 'Private'. They were all closed. I pointed toward the doors and told Winters, the cop who had come in with me, "Check those out." Then I turned and opened the first door on the right side of the hallway. It was marked 'Studio'.

The studio was dark and in the square of light provided by the open door, I could see a woman sprawled on the floor in front of a white baby grand piano. A length of cord was wrapped around her neck. The young woman must have been very pretty before she was killed. She looked like she was probably in her early to mid-twenties with a good figure and a head of curly blonde hair cut short. Now, in death, with her face a choleric purple, her eyes bulging and her swollen tongue protruding between her even white teeth, she was not attractive at all. She lay on her back with one leg drawn up over the other. Her white blouse was pulled loose from the waistband of her grey slacks and she had kicked off her left shoe. There was a smear of blood on her cheek and I saw that her right earring had been torn from the lobe of her ear.

The overturned piano bench bore mute witness to the brief strug-gle the girl must have made. The piano was angled in the corner of the room between two large bay windows. Several pages of sheet music rested on the rack of the piano and a few more were lying on the floor. A small tape recorder was on the floor near the overturned bench. A standing floor lamp had also been knocked over. The studio lights were off and the meager amount of light filtering through the wide bay window, half covered by a heavy drape, was barely enough for me to continue my examination of the crime scene so I righted the floor lamp and switched it on.

I knelt beside the girl and reached down to touch her throat for a pulse and then realized there was no need. Her skin was cool but she had not been dead very long. I started to get up and then reached out again and gently closed the girl's staring eyes. I wondered if she had seen her killer.

I stood and looked around the studio. Other than the overturned bench and scattered sheet music nothing else looked out of place. I walked down the room toward the door at the far end. The studio was painted a light shade of green from the white ceiling down to the ash colored wainscoting. The carpet also stopped at the point where I could see a wall was removed to make one room out of what had probably been a living room and a dining room. Just past that point was a glass paned door that opened onto the side porch. I walked to it and saw that it was not locked. In that end of the room the floor was hardwood and the color of the painted walls was different, more blue–green. The wainscoting, although grey, did not match either. Neither did the drapes. A settee, five chairs and five music stands were the only other items at that end of the studio. A short stack of folding chairs was shoved against the wall under the window. I opened the door to the hallway and found myself near the closed door at the end; the one marked 'Private'.

Two forensic technicians came through the door from the porch and I went back up the hall and met them at the studio door. I knew both of the techs. Shirley Roberts and Jake Dahlgren. Both were long time law enforcement types. Now getting closer to retirement, they collected evidence for the lab, ran fingerprints and did other minor investigative stuff for the department. Despite what the crime shows on TV portray, most forensic techs are not young and good looking, nor do they chase bad guys with guns. I greeted them and said, "She's in the studio. Go on in. Don't move her until the ME gets here but dust everything for prints. Piano, bench and that tape recorder. And see if there are any prints on that door to the side porch."

"You got it, boss." Dahlgren and Roberts went into the room and I turned to Cameron, the cop who had come back up the hall to the studio.

"Find anyone?"

"Yes sir. The woman who runs this place is back there. I guess that's her apartment." He pointed the door at the end of the hall. He shook his head and added, "She doesn't seem very upset."

The other patrolman had come into the house and I asked her, "Where's the woman who met me at the door?"

"I don't know, L T. I didn't see her or anyone else around. There's no one outside but there's some lights on upstairs. Looks like it's an apartment, but I didn't go up there."

"All right. Check again to see if the other woman's outside some-place, maybe she went out to her car. Then take another look around the grounds and secure the house. I don't know if anyone besides the woman who let us in is around but if you find her or anyone else, bring 'em in to me." She waved and went back outside. I told Winters to stay at the front door and then I moved back to the open studio door and watched the techs as they laid out their gear and started to work. I had only been there a minute or so when I felt eyes on my back and realized that someone was standing behind me.

CHAPTER THREE

I turned around quickly and found myself looking into a pair of cool green eyes set in a beautifully shaped face with a peaches and cream complexion that was haloed by shining auburn hair. All of that capped a slender, athletic body with all the curves in the proper places. The lustrous green eyes were a scant three inches lower than my own. They were looking up at me inquisitively. I had never seen a more beautiful woman.

I managed to say, "And you are?" My voice broke a little on the 'you' and I know I must have been blushing. The vision standing before me had me dazzled. She didn't seem to notice.

"Jennifer Clayton. I'm the one who called 911." Her voice was low. She smiled, showing perfect white teeth, and extended her hand. "And who are you?"

I hesitated just for a second before I grasped the slim, tapered fingers. Her hand was as cool as her eyes but her grip was strong and confident. An athlete's handshake, I thought. After a moment I realized that I was holding her hand longer than was appropriate, so I released it, blushed some more and fumbled for my badge. "I'm Detective Lieutenant Alex Makarios." I groped in my jacket pocket and managed to drag my notebook and pen out without looking too much like a kid seeing his first ice cream cone. I opened the notebook and asked, "Ah…about what time did you make that call?"

"Madeline was practicing and I was called away to answer a phone call. I suppose I was in my apartment for twenty or thirty minutes and when I came back to the studio, I found her like that." She glanced into the studio. The techs were busily dusting the piano. I saw the young woman's beautiful face cloud with the memory and she looked away. "It's horrible."

"About what time was that?"

"I don't really know. Sometime after three, I guess. Maybe three thirty. Madeline's time was up at four."

I frowned and thought, yeah, but it looks like her time was up sooner than that. "The victim's name is…was …Madeline?"

"Madeline Straub. She was one of my students. I teach classical piano. Maddy was preparing for her performance at next week's recital." The young woman's eyes and voice remained cool and tightly controlled. I found myself getting lost in the infinite depths of those green eyes again but when I heard the victim's last name, I was jolted back to reality.

"Her last name is Straub? Like in Rudy Straub, the brewery guy? The girl was Rudy Straub's daughter?" I shook my head. Krystos, this was going to be some homicide investigation. Rudy Straub was one of the wealthier men in the city. A guy with his fingers in a lot of pies. He was a city councilman and a candidate for the US Senate in the upcoming off-year national election. A real big shot. Now his daughter was lying dead on Jennifer Clayton's piano studio floor.

"Yes. That's her family." She nodded and her lush auburn hair swirled over her shoulder.

"How long has she been your student?"

"About six months. When I opened the studio here, she was one of my first students."

"Isn't that a long time to prepare for a recital? That seems pretty unusual. Or were there others?" I didn't know a lot about classical pianists but six months seemed like a long time to practice for a recital in a small place like Muskegon. "What piece was she working on?"

"Fur Elise. It's a standard recital piece. Maddy didn't have an overwhelming talent and her progress was a little slow. For some reason she had a desire to perform as a pianist in a formal recital and she was trying very hard." She shrugged and turned away from the door. "Perhaps it was to please her father."

"Was today any different than her usual practice days?"

"Maddy did seem sort of distracted. When I first saw her today, I thought she might have been crying just before she came in. Her eyes looked red to me. I asked her if there was something bothering her. She assured me she was fine. But today she seemed to have trouble concentrating. I had to come in once and help her with some of the phrases she was working on."

"If she wasn't progressing, why did you continue with her?" My question brought her around to face me again.

"Money. Rudy...Mr. Straub...pays well. Maddy was his only daughter and I think he spoiled her a little." She turned away and crossed the hall to a small marble topped table. She took a cigarette from a silver box lying there. Facing me again, she struck a pose I had only seen in an old Humphrey Bogart movie. Something Lauren Bacall did. She held the cigarette in her right hand near her mouth, one hip thrust slightly forward and her left hand cupping her right elbow as she waited for me to offer her a light. Her eyes never left mine and I could feel the challenge in her posture and steady gaze.

"Sorry, Miss Clayton. I don't have a light. Quit years ago." I watched her eyes carefully and added, "It is Miss, isn't it? You're not married?"

She shook her head. "Not any more. I also quit years ago." She dropped the unlit cigarette into a spotless ash tray on the table and turned away. "I'll be in my office if you have more questions."

I touched her arm and spoke quickly before she could retreat down the hall. I really didn't want her to leave. "Sorry. I have just a few more. How did Miss Straub get here? Is that her car in the driveway?"

She turned back again. "No. The Mustang is mine and the other car belongs to my assistant. I suppose Madeline's brother brought her. He usually does. But I didn't see him."

"Which brother?" I knew the dead girl had three brothers. Damn, I was already thinking of the girl in the past tense.

"It's almost always Peter, the young one. I assume it was him that brought her today."

I glanced at my watch. "It's well past four thirty. No one has come to pick her up."

She frowned, "Yes. That's very strange. Peter quite often comes early and listens to her play. Sometimes he stays for the whole two hours but I don't think he's done that much in the last month or so. He's just been dropping her off and then coming back around four when her lesson was over. It's strange that he isn't here by now. Perhaps Gerd was supposed to pick her up."

I knew all three of the Straub brothers. Peter, the youngest, was a college drop out with no job and a bit of a drug and gambling problem. He was in his mid-twenties and was spoiled, but he wasn't really a bad kid. He occasionally ran with some semi-tough-guy wannabes. His rap sheet at police headquarters listed a DUI and a couple of misdemeanor drug possession charges. I'd arrested him a year or so ago for 'drunk and disorderly' after he and a couple of his friends had gotten in a brawl with some local college boys. He was never charged. His older brother, Paul, bailed him out and his father's position on the City Council pretty much ensured that he wouldn't spend any time in jail.

I went to Muskegon High with both of Peter's older brothers. Paul and I were in the same graduating class. All through high school he was a stuck-up, arrogant kid who believed he was better than anyone else. We'd both played football: he was a second string running back and I was the starting wide receiver the year we won the state championship. Paul never got to carry the ball much. While he was fairly fast and a shifty runner, he was afraid of taking a hit so our coach didn't play him very often. Now Paul Straub was an up-and-coming attorney, but he was still arrogant.

Gerd, the oldest of the three boys, worked with his father as Assistant Manager of the Alt Zeit brewery. He was two years ahead of us in high school. I knew him back then, but not very well, and now I saw him around town occasionally.

"We'll see what's up with Peter. One more thing. You live here in the house, don't you?"

She gestured down the hallway. "Yes. My apartment is back there."

"And what's upstairs?"

"There's another apartment. It's fair sized and a young couple and their little boy live there."

"All right. I have to ask you to come down to Central and give us a written statement. It looks like our forensic guys will be here for a while so please stay here until they finish." I put my hand out first this time. "Thanks, Miss Clayton."

She took my hand and smiled up at me. "Then I'll see you later." I watched her walk away down the hall. The crisp white blouse and form fitting grey skirt she was wearing showed her slender, curvaceous figure to full advantage. I guessed she was about five –seven and her three-inch heels brought her up to within three inches of my own height. She was graceful as a cat and I was wishing we had met under more pleasant circumstances. She looked to be only a year or so younger than I. If she had been in town for six months, why had I never seen or heard of her? I was thinking that I missed the boat there somehow. But she seemed too cool; too detached from what had happened here in her studio this afternoon. I found myself asking 'why'? Roberts, the forensic tech, interrupted my musings.

"There's a ton of prints in there. It'll take a week to get 'em all. Oh, and we found this under the piano bench." She held out a small red leather wallet.

I took it from her and opened it. Inside were a couple of credit cards, some cash and Madeline Straub's driver's license, issued last June. According to the State of Michigan she was born on the twenty-second of July, nineteen-eighty, was five feet four inches tall, weighed one hundred and twenty-two pounds and had blonde hair and blue eyes. There was also a student ID card from Western Michigan University in the wallet. "Okay, thanks. Concentrate on the piano and bench...and the tape recorder. I want to know who handled that stuff last." I pointed to the hall table. "And dust that cigarette box, please. There should be a good set of prints on it."

I put the wallet in a plastic bag and the tech and I went back into the studio. "Do we know where the cord came from?" I gestured toward the body on the floor.

Dahlgren looked up from where he was busily chalking the girl's outline. "Looks like it came from one of the drapes. I won't take if off her neck until the ME says I can. She should be here soon."

A silken cord that matched the one around the victim's neck held one of a pair of heavy drapes back from the window beside the piano. The other drape hung straight down across one half of the window and fully to the floor. I walked around the piano to where I thought the killer might have been standing, behind and slightly to the left side of the victim as she sat at the keyboard. I stretched my hand back. The drape was within easy reach.

"Hey, Alex. What have we got?" Doctor Chris Karras breezed into the studio and bent over the body on the floor. The Muskegon County Medical Examiner always seemed to be in a hurry. I remembered that she had been the same at Muskegon High School when we had dated and suffered through a teen-age on-again, off-again romance. Her name had been Christine Pappas back then and we were never a serious couple.

I smiled, "Well, I don't think it was suicide, Chris. But it's your call."

"Guess you're right. I really don't think she could have done this to herself. Or would have." The ME knelt beside the body and gently turned the victim's head from side to side. "She's still slightly warm and rigor hasn't started so she hasn't been dead long. Maybe no more than two or three hours. I'll be able to get the time closer when I do the internal liver temps." She looked up at me and grinned. "So at first glance, I'd say the cause of death is strangulation by a person or persons unknown. Or do you already know who did it."

I shook my head. "Not yet. We're good, but not quite that good. We don't have any real suspect in mind at this point." I pointed to the vic. "Can you get that cord off her neck?"

Chris turned to Roberts, "Got all your pictures, Shirley?"

The tech nodded, "Yes, Ma'am. I think we're finished with her. You can take her away now if you want."

Chris carefully loosened the silken cord and unwound it from the girl's swollen neck. Once it was free, she placed it in a plastic bag and handed it to me. "There's your murder weapon...I think. I'll put that in writing when we get through with her downtown."

I handed the bag to the forensic tech and looked up as the ME's people came in with a gurney followed by Sean Dunphy, my partner. I made a show of looking at my watch.

"Get lost, Sean?" I was still getting used to Sean. We had been partners for only a little over six months. He became my partner when I was promoted to lieutenant and named to head one of the department's two detective squads. Sean was a long timer on the force but I had been back in Muskegon for only four years and on the police force for about three and a half. I knew he resented that a little. I was willing to put up with his habits and occasional fits of attitude because he was a good, solid policeman and I valued his abilities and street knowledge. He was sometimes sloppy and habitually late and that pissed me off. Once in a while my military background showed.

"Nah. Got stuck in traffic."

Chris stood up and peeled off her latex gloves. She grinned at Sean. "There hasn't been a traffic jam on this street in years. Come clean, Sean. You were screwing off somewhere." She also knew him from high school. He had been a year behind the two of us. While she and I had gone off to different colleges, Sean stayed in Muskegon, worked for a couple of years and joined the police force as soon as he was old enough.

Now he smiled back at Chris and put on his Irish brogue, "Aw, come now, lass. You know I'm always on the job. How could you possibly accuse me of goofing off? Sure now, you know I'm the hardest working cop on the whole force."

"Yeah. And the biggest story teller, too." Chris turned to me. "We'll take the body down to the morgue and go through the routine. When I'm finished, I'll give you a call." She motioned for her team to pick up the girl and they quickly placed the body on the gurney. "See you later, guys."

I turned to Sean. "Take a good look around here and then go to the apartment upstairs and see if anyone there saw anything we can use. I need to talk to the Clayton woman again so if you need me, I'll be in her office."

The hallway was carpeted in a tan, cut Berber that absorbed the sound of my footsteps. When I suddenly appeared in the doorway of her small office, Jennifer Clayton stood up quickly. Her abrupt move forced the expensive leather chair back from the the large mahogany desk so hard that it slammed against the paneled wall. She dropped her cell phone in the middle of the desk blotter.

"Sorry. I didn't mean to startle you." I apologized. "I do have a few more questions before I'm finished here. Where's the woman who was waiting on the porch when I got here?"

Still standing, she answered, "Isn't Catherine in her office?" When I shook my head 'no', she looked down at the desk. "Perhaps she went home. She was terribly upset." She paused, "But I guess she shouldn't have done that. You probably need to speak with her, don't you?'

"Definitely. Tell me who she is." How had I let the older woman get away from the crime scene? I should have taken her into custody immediately. How dumb was that? I was sure I'd hear about that from the chief.

Jennifer Clayton leaned forward and placed her hands on the desk. "Her name is Catherine Hood. She's my assistant and secretary...part time. She only comes in on Monday, Wednesday and Friday each week. She takes care of the books and handles some of the paperwork. Catherine's also a retired music teacher and helps out with some of the younger students." She shrugged, "I really don't know her very well. Catherine came to me and just sort of volunteered last spring at the end of the school year. Now I pay her for her time."

I wondered how much paperwork there could be for such a small piano studio but didn't ask. "I'll need her address. Was she here all afternoon?"

"Yes. Today she came in around one and was working in her office until I found Madeline's body."

"Right." I gestured toward the cell phone on the desk. "Have you called the Straub family? Or anyone else since I've been here?" I watched her closely as I asked the second question.

She looked away before answering. "No. To both questions, lieutenant"

I nodded. "Okay. That's all I need from you for now. As I said, we'll need a written statement from you and Ms. Hood. My partner will drive you down to police headquarters as soon as the ME and her crew are finished. We'll notify the Straubs…unless you want to do it." I waited for some kind of reaction from her but she showed none and remained calm. "I assume you know all of them pretty well."

She shook her head and looked away again before she answered. "I really don't know the family that well. I've met Mr. and Mrs. Straub and Madeline's brothers only a few times. Except for Peter, of course." She sighed, "But I really would prefer that someone else tell them what happened. Thank you."

"Fine, I'll take care of it. I'd like Ms. Hood's address and phone number, please." She quickly wrote the information on the back of one of her business cards and handed it to me. "I'll see you at headquarters later, Miss Clayton. Thanks."

Sean was still in the studio talking to Shirley, the woman on the forensic team. I told him to contact Catherine Hood and gave him the business card with her address. I also told him to bring Jennifer Clayton to Central when he was finished with the people upstairs. I looked around for a minute or two and then headed for the front door. Jennifer Clayton's composure and coolness in the aftermath of the murder confused me. She was a beautiful woman, and I felt an attraction to her but warning bells were ringing loudly in my head.

CHAPTER FOUR

Sean Dunphy walked up the driveway toward the stairs at the back of the house. A dim yard light, its protective screen half obscured with the bodies of dead insects, shone down on the concrete pad next to the detached two car garage. Sean peered through the dirty window and saw an older Ford pickup truck up on blocks. The hood had been removed and lay in the bed of the truck. A tarp was draped over half of the empty engine compartment. He walked around to the side and saw that an alley ran behind the building. Sean aimed his flashlight through the side garage window and could make out engine parts scattered on the floor and work bench. Restoration project, he thought.

The lights were on in the upstairs apartment and he climbed the wooden stairs to the second floor and knocked on the door. A young woman carrying a baby on her hip pulled the door open and stood silently. Sean's badge was in his hand and he saw the quick look of apprehension cross the woman's face. She can't be older that twenty-one or two, he thought. "Sorry to bother you, ma'am. I'm Detective Sergeant Dunphy. There's been an incident downstairs and I wonder if you would mind answering a couple of questions for me?"

The girl took a deep breath and seemed to relax. "Sure. I was afraid you were here to tell me something happened to Joey...my husband. He works out at Century Foundry. Should be home anytime now." She shifted the baby to her other hip. "I guess you can come in."

"Yes, ma'am. Thank you." Sean moved into the kitchen of the apartment. A pot of what looked and smelled like vegetable beef soup was simmering on the stove and he remembered that he hadn't eaten anything since breakfast. The rich aroma of the simmering soup was almost more that he could bear. He looked around the small kitchen area. The table was set for two and the whole place was neat and clean, unlike his house in Bluffton. "Could I have your name, please, Ma'am?"

"I'm Emily...Mrs. Joey Walton, I mean." She blushed and looked down at the baby, "And this is little Andy. He's almost one."

Sean smiled at little Andy who immediately screwed up his face and started to cry. I always have that effect on kids, Sean thought. What is it with me? He heaved a sigh and said, "Ms. Walton, have you seen any strange cars around here this afternoon? Or anyone walking around that isn't normally here?"

"No. But I've been inside with the baby almost all day. I did go down to the trash barrel and I think there were a couple of cars in the driveway. Miss Clayton parks there and sometimes Miss Hood does too. But I think there was another one down at the end today. I thought it was probably the Straub boy's." She paused, "I think he usually brings his sister here on Friday."

"That the only other car you saw? Do you know what kind it was or can you describe it?

"Oh, I'm not sure. It was some kind of a dark color...black or maybe blue. I don't know what kind it was but I think it's been here before. There weren't any others that I know of."

"About what time was that?"

"Oh, golly, I don't know. Maybe around two-thirty or three." She played with the baby's fingers. "Little Andy goes down for his nap around two usually."

"That your husband's truck out back? Looks like he's taken on quite a project."

"Yeah, Joey spends all his spare time...and money...on that thing." She smiled, "But it keeps him home." She sighed, "He really loves that old truck. He got it from his grandfather just before he passed away."

"Well, tell him I wish him luck with the restoration. Thank you for your help." Sean handed her his card and added, "If you think of anything, else please give me a call."

He left the apartment and started down the steps, the aroma of the soup still making his mouth water. Damn, he thought, that was a god-damned waste of time. Now I've got to take the Clayton woman downtown while the hotshot lieutenant goes off and does whatever the hell he thinks he should be doing. He didn't even tell me where he was going. Sean kicked a rock off the driveway. Dammit, he shouldn't be telling me what to do like that in front of other people. He's not an officer in the goddamned Air Force anymore. I'm his partner and besides, I should be a lieutenant, too. I almost passed the exam last time and I've got 'way more time on the force than he does. And to top it off, now I've gotta work tonight and miss the high school game. And I've got five hundred bucks riding on those kids in this one. Then he straightened up and smiled to himself. Well, I should clean up on this one. Those kids should beat the spread; they've won twice already and Bay City's hasn't got much this year.

Jennifer Clayton was waiting for him at the front of the house. She had changed into jeans and a bulky sweater that did nothing to disguise her figure. She looked hard at the wide yellow crime scene tape that festooned the porch and now also stretched across the front of the lot and up the driveway. She turned to Sean and gestured toward the young policeman standing by the front door. "Will he be here long?"

"I'd guess most of the night…at least until the forensic crew finishes up. I imagine you'll be the only one allowed in and out of this place since you live here. But I don't know that for sure. I'll talk to Chief Bauer and let you know." He opened the car door for her. "We're going to take a little detour and run over to your secretary's place. She's got to come in too, so we might as well pick her up and do it all in one trip. Shall we go?"

* * *

Jennifer settled into the passenger seat of the detective sergeant's Chevy. She took a long look at him, mentally comparing him to his boss. They were about the same height but the lieutenant was less beefy. This one needs a haircut, she thought, and he hasn't shined his shoes in a while. She decided his sports jacket was also in need of a good cleaning. He looks like the proverbial Irish beat cop who made good, she mused. She relaxed and looked out the window as Sean pulled away from the curb. She thought, this one is not much like his boss, Lieutenant Makarios. I think I would like to get to know the lieutenant better. I'll bet he could be really interesting when he's off duty and if he relaxed a little. I know he's single but I wonder if he's in a relationship right now. Guess I could ask Dunphy here. No, I'll ask the lieutenant myself when I get the chance. She heaved a frustrated sigh and shook her head. But I think that before I get in too deep with any of these people, I'd better find out how much I can tell them. Wish I could have reached Frank again after poor Maddy was killed. Jennifer straightened up in the seat and decided that she would try to call him later when he might be back in his office.

CHAPTER FIVE

"Who's dead? Was it a homicide?" Danny Gordon, the hot-shot reporter for the Muskegon Journal, grabbed my arm as I came down the steps of the house. "What's happening, Alex?" He was almost hysterical with his need for information.

"No comment, Danny. You'll get your info when the Public Information Officer at headquarters gets a statement ready for release." I pushed past the reporter. Danny was nearly fifty and slightly smaller than average. He was slowly working his way down from the big city daily he worked on in Chicago to a small town weekly somewhere in the boondocks. I'm sure he realized that's where he would eventually finish his career. The Muskegon Journal was just an intermediate stop on his slide downhill. Danny always reminded me of a weasel but he was really a cross between a bloodhound and a bulldog. He earned a couple of National Press Club awards when he worked in the big city but he was still chasing that elusive Pulitzer he thought he deserved. I liked him as a person and respected his talents as a reporter but he could be a real pain in the ass when he smelled a headline and a front page story.

"Hey, you know I heard the call you got from the dispatcher. I heard her say it was a possible homicide. C'mon, Alex, don't shut me out here. You owe me one for the tip on that pervert you and Sean collared last week." The little bulldog was persistent and he was right. I did owe him one.

I stopped and faced him. "Look, Danny. You know I can't give you anything specific right now but I'll tell you this much. It looks like a homicide. We don't know by whom or why at this point. I won't tell you who the victim is…you'll have to get that from the PIO at Central. They'll release the name of the victim after the next of kin have been notified. You know how that works. If you can sit on this until tomorrow, you'll get the full story from the PIO. But that's all I can give you for now."

The little reporter shrugged. "It's too late for tomorrow's edition and our rag won't publish again until Monday anyway so I guess I can wait until you guys get something to hand me. Thanks for the scraps." He pointed to the van belonging to the local TV station. "Those clowns probably will have it all on the late news tonight anyway." He grinned and then said, "That gal who runs this place is a real looker, ain't she? When she opened this studio, Lucille interviewed her for our artsy-fartsy page. Musta been about six months ago." His forehead wrinkled with concern. "She's not the victim, is she Alex? That would be an awful waste." When I didn't answer, he went on, "Maybe I'll see if she'll talk to me." He pulled a pack of cigarettes from his pocket, shook one out and stuck it in the corner of his mouth and started to turn away.

I grabbed a handful of his sports jacket and pulled him up close. "Get out of here, Danny. Miss Clayton's not the victim. I don't want you interfering. This is a crime scene under investigation. Now I'm telling you to stay away from her and don't try to talk to any of our people. No one here can tell you anything right now. You hear me?"

I shoved him away and watched him as he straightened his jacket. He bent down and picked up the cigarette he had dropped. When he stuck it back in his mouth, I turned and headed for my car. He called after me, "Yeah. I got you, Makarios. But I'll see you and Dunphy again at Central in the morning."

Brian Cornett

I eased myself into the car and sat back. My leg hurt and I rubbed it for a minute and tried to relax. It had been a long day and it looked like it was going to get longer. I saw that Catherine Hood's Honda was gone from the driveway. Sean's Chevy along with two patrol cars and Danny's car were in the street but the driveway was clear behind me. A few curious citizens, attracted by the police cars, were standing on the sidewalk. I realized I was stalling because I really didn't want to drive all the way out to the Straub estate and tell the family that their daughter had been murdered. I tried hard but I could think of no reason to avoid it. My watch indicated that it was a little after six. I figured the drive wouldn't take more than thirty minutes so I probably could be back at Central by seven thirty or eight at the latest. I started my patrol car and pulled out of the driveway and around the EMS van parked in the street. I went up Lakeshore until it turned into Michigan Avenue and then joined US 31 Business through the heart of Muskegon. The route took me through the downtown area and then out to the causeway spanning the two channels of the Muskegon River. A mile or so beyond the causeway I turned left onto Lake Avenue in the city of North Muskegon but that didn't matter. Although they were three separate cities, Muskegon, North Muskegon and Muskegon Heights operated with a consolidated police department. I was still in my jurisdiction. Twenty minutes later I was among the mansions that lined the north side of Muskegon Lake.

It was full dark now and the big piles of brick and stone that passed for houses in this neighborhood were nearly invisible. Almost all of them were hidden from the road by small forests of evergreens broken only by the entrances to the circular drives that led to three and four car garages. Even though it had been about fifteen years since I had been to the Straub home, I easily found the right driveway and pulled into it. Two cars were parked in front of the porte-co-chere that jutted out from the imposing grey stone façade of the house. A light tan Cadillac that I knew belonged

26

to Paul Straub was parked in front of a silver Mercedes sedan. I went to the cars and put my hand on their hoods. Both were warm and I could hear the soft ticking sounds of the engines as they cooled. Neither car had been there for very long.

I walked around the attached garage to the back of the big house. While it was screened from the road, from the rear, the mansion provided an open view of the lake and the city a mile or more away on the other side. Some of the homes on the lakefront had small private docks on channels that the owners had paid to have dredged. The spoil from all the dredging created mud bank islands that provided homes for opportunistic grasses and small trees. There was no such channel or dock at the rear of the Straub mansion. A path paved with interlocking bricks and lighted by solar powered spike lamps every twenty feet or so led from the rear of the house. I walked down it to the narrow strip of beach that lay along the edge of the lake. The beach was at least fifty yards from the patio across the immaculate lawn. Several beach chairs, a weathered picnic table and a torn umbrella rested on the grass near the sand. I went back up the path toward the house. A large garden area that looked as though no one had bothered with it since the last carrot or radish had been pulled lay forlorn and abandoned on one side of the spacious yard. On the other side was a long, low structure. I moved closer and saw that it was a fiberglass Quonset-style cover over a swimming pool. Then I realized that it was actually a lap pool about three lanes wide and twenty meters long. The far side of the pool covering was concealed by a thick stand of bushy evergreens which separated the Straub estate from the neighboring one. At the other end of the pool there was a small clapboard building with a ten or twelve foot mast with a spinning anemometer on top. I didn't remember any of that being there the last time I had been at the Straubs. On that occasion, a party for the football team to celebrate our state championship, we boys and girls hadn't spent much time outside. Our season ended on Thanksgiving Day and Rudy had thrown the party the following Saturday. That was the last week of November and it was cold with a couple of inches of snow on the ground that night. I and about twenty of my teammates and our girlfriends spent the entire evening in the warmth of the house.

I moved over to the garage and took a quick look through the side window. There was just enough light spilling from the rear windows of the house for me to see the single car parked inside, a silver Mercedes convertible. It seemed Rudy was consistent with his vehicle choices.

I walked back to the front door and mounted the steps slowly, favoring my leg. I raised the heavy brass door knocker and heaved a sigh. Reluctantly, I let the knocker fall.

CHAPTER SIX

The big, ornately carved oak door opened on the fourth knock. Paul Straub pulled the door wide, "Come in."

"Paul, I've got some bad..." Straub put up his hand and stopped me.

"We already know. Jennifer Clayton called me. She told me what happened." He hesitated and then said, "I assume she is a suspect. Of course, I'll represent her as her attorney."

I stood silently for a moment and then said, "I don't know that she needs an attorney but that's between you and her. Right now I need to talk to you and your family. Are they all here? I only have a few questions so this won't take long." I asked myself, when did Clayton call him? She told me she hadn't made any calls. Maybe she called after I left. I really hoped she hadn't lied to me. "What makes you assume Ms. Clayton would be a suspect, Paul? Were there problems between her and the victim?"

He shook his head, "No. no. No problems that I'm aware of. I just thought that since she was at the studio you'd automatically suspect her of having something to do with the murder. That's all." He backed into the hallway. "My mother is in the family room and Gerd's on his way. I don't know where Peter is." Paul turned and headed down the spacious hallway, knowing full well that I would have to follow him. He'd always been condescending toward anyone he felt superior to. And I believed that included everyone he'd ever met. I guessed it came with the territory. I followed him down the hall without comment. Paul stood aside at the doorway to what I remembered was the family room and I went into the huge room at the rear of the house. A fieldstone fireplace took up the whole wall opposite the floor to ceiling windows that overlooked the rear lawn and the lake. Comfortable chairs were arranged in front of the fieldstone hearth. The whole room was done in old English style with horse prints and hunting scenes in ornate frames on the walls. An antique silver tea service sat on a chiffonier against one side wall and a small bar was located across from it on the other side of the room. Karla Straub, the victim's mother, sat in an embroidered wing chair to the right of the fireplace. I approached the woman. "I'm sorry for your loss, Mrs. Stroud. I'm sure Madeline will be missed."

The woman looked at me with cold, dry eyes. "Thank you." Her mouth was set grimly in a straight line. She folded her hands and rested them in her lap. She had black hair that was flecked with grey and was perfectly done. She wore no makeup. As far as I could tell, she had not been crying.

Paul moved to stand beside his mother's chair. "You said you had some questions."

"I know this is an awkward time but I have to do this." I pulled out my notebook and turned to Paul. "What time did Ms. Clayton call you?"

"She called me at my office about twenty-five minutes ago. I called mother and Gerd and then came right here. I got here just a few minutes before you did."

"You were at your office pretty late. Were you there all afternoon?"

"Yes, I was there all day. I stayed late because I have a very tough case on Monday and need to prepare for it."

"Anyone else there with you?"

"No. We only work half days on Friday and I give my staff the afternoon off."

I looked at Mrs. Straub. "Ma'am, can you tell me where you spent the day?"

"Here." Her answer was quick and abrupt. Stone-faced, she looked down at her hands which she held perfectly still in her lap.

"Was there anyone else here with you? A maid or cook perhaps."

"No."

"Did you see your daughter today? Or Peter?"

"Peter and Madeline had lunch with me here at the house and then he took her to her piano lesson. I spent the afternoon here at home…I worked in my garden for a while." Her voice was rock steady. "And then I took my daily swim."

"About what time did you do that?"

"Maybe it was three or three thirty…I do not keep the time." She looked down at her hands.

Nice alibi, I thought. I wondered what she did after that so I asked. "Where did you go after your swim?"

Her head came up and she frowned. "I did not go anywhere. I told you. I have been here."

I decided not to mention the warm car hood until we knew more about what the rest of the family was doing.

I turned to Paul and asked, "Paul, have you called Peter?" I was perplexed. Neither Paul nor his mother showed any emotion over the murder of Madeline. Maybe Germans aren't very emotional, I thought. No, that's not right; they're people just like everyone else. Something's very wrong here. Both of them are way too calm and composed.

"No. I couldn't reach Peter. I haven't seen him in a couple of days so I have no idea where he might be. I did call Gerd. He was at the brewery and he's on his way." He shrugged. "And you know my father is in Grand Rapids at a dinner with some of his supporters and fund raisers." He looked down at his mother. "Mama told me she called him while I was on my way out here. He's driving back tonight right after the dinner." He stepped away from the chair and asked, "Can I get you something, Mutti? Tea, maybe? Or a drink?" She shook her head 'no'. He didn't offer anything to me. I didn't expect him to.

I faced Paul and asked, "Your father didn't skip the dinner and come back immediately?"

Karla Straub spoke quickly, "No. He could not do that. He has the senate campaign to win. It is very important to him. It is important to all of us. He must win."

Paul added, "It's a very tight race and he needs all the help he can get. The money papa raises at tonight's dinner will buy him some significant media time." He moved over to stand in front of the massive fireplace. "Has Jennifer Clayton given you a statement?"

He seemed awfully concerned about Ms. Clayton but I assumed it was because they knew each other. Somehow that bothered me, so I said, "My partner's bringing her in to Central this evening to do that. So far all I have is her oral version of what happened but we need a written one to go with it. I need to be sure we have everything she remembers."

Paul straightened up, "I want to be there when you interrogate her." He pointed his finger at me. "In fact, I insist that you allow me to be there."

I looked at him and said, "Paul, she's not going to be interrogated. We just need a written statement of what she saw or heard. Unless she says she wants you to represent her, you have no right...or need... to be present when we talk."

He began to bluster, "I don't care what you call it; I must be there if I'm to represent her."

"Relax, Paul. She's not a suspect. I'm sure she'll appreciate you representing her but I really doubt that she'll need a lawyer. She's not under arrest." I wondered why he was so insistent on representing the Clayton woman. I knew Paul was a real hound when it came to women. He'd been that way when I knew him in school. He'd dated most of the girls in our class and the one behind us at least once but he never had a steady girlfriend that I could recall. One or two dates and then he would move on. But maybe he had a romantic interest in Jennifer Cllayton. I hoped not or at least that if he did, it was only on his side.

I turned back to Mrs. Straub, "Can you think of anyone who would want to hurt Madeline?"

Her head snapped up and she said, "No, of course not. That is a very stupid question. No one would want to harm her. She had no enemies."

I tried again, "Did she have a boyfriend? Or are there some close girl friends that she ran around with?"

"She had no boyfriends. She was a good girl. Why do you ask such stupid and rude questions of me?"

The door opened and I turned as Gerd Straub came in. He was a carbon copy of his father. About five ten or eleven and stocky with wispy blondish hair. He was two years older than Paul. I remembered that Gerd joined the army about a year after he graduated from high school. He spent his three years in the army driving trucks in Japan. Leave it to the army to send a kid who speaks fluent German to a motor pool in Japan. After he came back to Muskegon he started working at his father's brewery. Now he was the assistant manager. Most people thought that it was in name only. Rudy still ran the whole show. I had talked to Gerd several times in the past year or so. We were both members of the yacht club and had shared a beer or two. He still had the habit of dropping German words into his conversation.

He came through the door and rushed to his mother's side, dropped to his knees beside her chair and reached to put his arms around her. "Mutti, I'm so sorry... so sorry." He had been crying. His eyes were red and swollen and I could see faint tear streaks on his cheeks.

His mother pushed his arms away and stood up. Karla Straub was tall and looked like what she was: an athlete slightly past her prime. I had heard somewhere that she was on the East German swim team in the '64 Olympics. She gestured to Paul, "I will now have a drink. You will make me a vodka." Gerd slowly got to his feet and stood awkwardly beside her chair nervously clasping and unclasping his hands while his brother stepped over to the well-stocked bar. Paul half-filled a tall grass with vodka, dropped two ice cubes into it and brought it to his mother.

She turned to Gerd but didn't touch him. "These things happen. It was not our fault. We have no responsibility for her. Das macht nichts, Liebchen."

I stepped back. What the hell was going on here? What did she mean 'it didn't matter'? And 'no responsibility'? Responsibility for what? She was her daughter for Christ's sake. I tried something else. I said, "Mrs. Straub, she was your only daughter. You and Paul know she was brutally murdered only a few hours ago. I'm sorry to say this, but I can't believe none of you except Gerd seem to care very much."

Karla Straub turned on me, eyes flashing. "It is none of your business whether we care very much or not. Or whether you believe it or not. It does not matter to me. We are finished with your questions. You will go now." She turned away from me and took the glass of iced vodka from Paul. Raising it to her lips, she drank nearly half of it in two swallows. She turned back to me, "My husband will speak to you tomorrow at police headquarters." She left the room without saying anything more. She did not look back at me or either of her sons.

Gerd wiped his eyes with the back of his hand. "She's gone, Pauli. Maddy is gone."

Paul moved over to him and put his arm around his older brother. "It will be all right, Gerd. You'll see. All of this will all turn out all right." He turned back to me, "Like my mother said: we're through here, Makarios. I'll be downtown soon to meet with Jennifer. You can see yourself out."

I cut him off, "Not so fast, Paul. I'm not quite finished yet. Gerd, where were you today?"

"Where I am every day. I am at the brewery. That's my job if you didn't know." Gerd was built differently than Paul and Peter, more like his father. He had been a lineman in high school a couple of years before Paul and I played. He wasn't as smart as Paul but he got through high school all right. He was born in Germany and still spoke the language now and then. He did that in high school, too and it had earned him the nickname 'Kraut' but he never minded when kids called him that. Now he had composed himself and seemed to be fully in control. "Why do you want to know?" He went to the bar and and reached for the vodka bottle.

"Just gathering information, Gerd. That's my job." He missed the point. I went on, "What exactly do you do at the brewery"

"I am the manager and I do whatever papa needs me to do. Mostly I do the paperwork and sometimes work in the laboratory or help on the bottling line." He puffed his chest out a little. "But when he is gone, I am the manager." Then he turned back to the bar and filled his glass.

"Was anyone with you at the brewery this afternoon? Anyone see you there?"

Gerd jerked around, nearly dropping his drink. "No. No one was with me. No one."

"Are you telling me that the brewery shuts down on Friday too? There must have been workers there. I know beer doesn't brew or bottle itself. Who was there with you?"

"Oh, Ja. Of course, the people were there. I thought you meant upstairs in the office with me." He took a long drink from his glass. "Sure. Maybe some people saw me sometime during the day. I don't know. I was in the laboratory or in the office most of the time. Around four o'clock this afternoon we had a problem on the bottling line. I worked with them on that until Paul called me. That's why I am coming so late here."

"Did Madeline work with you at the brewery or was she still going to school?"

Gerd moved back to his mother's chair. "Sometimes she worked at the brewery. Mostly in the laboratory with me or papa. But she did not work today." He looked as though he was going to cry again.

I said, "I know, Gerd. Friday is the day for her piano lesson and practice. Was she still going to college?"

Gerd shook his head and sat down heavily. "Last spring she graduated. She has a degree in chemistry." He looked away. "It was papa's idea. So she could work with him in the laboratory."

"OK. Do you know where Peter is? Paul said he couldn't reach him."

"No. I do not know where he is. I have not seen him since Tuesday morning here at breakfast. We were going to take Paul's boat out and fish for a little in the afternoon." He took a long pull at his vodka. "But he didn't come to the club to meet me. So I took one of the boat boys from the yacht club out with me."

Paul turned to him quickly, "You didn't tell me you took my boat out." He raised his voice and pointed his finger at Gerd, "I hope to hell you refueled it when you got back. You left it damn near empty the last time."

"Ja, ja. I took care of it. You don't have to worry." He took a big gulp from his glass. "If you don't want me to use the verdammt thing, why do you give a set of keys to me?"

Paul shook his head, "Ah, it doesn't matter. You don't know where Peter is, either?"

"No, I told you that already." Gerd finished his drink and got up and headed for the bar again. "I'm through with the questions." He turned back to face me. "Mutti told you to get out. Why are you still here? You will leave now."

"Just a couple more questions. What kind of car does Peter drive?"

They looked at each other for a moment and then Paul said, "It's a new Dodge Challenger...black. He got it a month or so ago."

"Who belongs to the car in the garage?"

Gerd was busy at the bar but answered, "That one is Maddy's."

"I take it Rudy drove to Grand Rapids in his own car. What time is your father due back? Did he tell you?"

Gerd turned around with another drink in his hand. "He did not tell us. You know he has a very important campaign to run so he must be there to talk to people, however long that takes. Anyway, that is none of your concern. The campaign has nothing to do with Maddy's death."

I turned to Paul, "Who all lives here in the house? I know you have your own place but how about the rest of you."

"Peter and Gerd still live here." He stopped for a second before adding, "And Maddy did too. Their rooms are upstairs."

I closed my notebook. "We'll have to take a look at Madeline's room. I'll have someone from Forensics come out and do that as soon as I can. In the meantime, don't touch anything in there. Lock it if you can. Paul, as an attorney and officer of the court, you know what we have to do so I'm counting on your cooperation. I'm going back downtown to meet with the Clayton woman. I expect I'll see you there shortly. I'll show myself out." I turned and headed for the hallway. The sooner I got out of there the better, I thought. Something was really wrong with this family but I didn't know what it was. I let myself out through the big oak door and took a huge breath of fresh air. Gerd's car was parked behind my patrol car on the circular drive. Another Mercedes. This one was dark blue.

CHAPTER SEVEN

Central Police Headquarters was housed in the main building of a two square block complex on Clay Street in the middle of downtown Muskegon. The building was a big gray, one story fortress. A forbidding place, all it lacked was a moat filled with alligators. The middle section had an arched roof like an aircraft hangar and the wings on either side had flat roofs: one of which sported the helicopter pad which was seldom used. The whole building was about a hundred and twenty feet wide and eighty feet deep with the main section, the part with the curved roof, about half of the width. Sean and I shared a cubicle in that middle section near the back left corner of the big open squad room. Detective Lieutenant Jim Richards and his partner had the corner cube and ours was the one next to it, just a little closer to Chief Jack Bauer's office.

The Muskegon police department wasn't very large; about a hundred and twenty patrolmen and detectives worked out of Central and there were two sub-stations manned by around twenty men – and women - each. We only had two detective squads. Richards headed one of them and I was in charge of the other. There was supposed to be a Captain of Detectives over us but that position was unfilled. Richards and I reported directly to the Chief of Police. Besides Sergeant Sean Dunphy, I supervised four other officers, all detectives first grade. They did a lot of the leg work and interviews. Before I was promoted to Detective Lieutenant, I had put in two years doing that sort of scut work in Lieutenant Richards' squad.

The flat-topped wing on the right side of the building contained six holding cells and a locker room for the patrolmen and women. The holding cells were only used for keeping prisoners for short periods of time. Only hours in most cases. Once they were booked, they were usually transferred to the County Detention Center – a nice term for 'jail' – which was just across the parking lot. Occasionally we let a drunk sleep it off in one of the cells before we turned him loose. The wing on the other side housed the interrogation rooms and our IT and computer center. The two secretaries who transcribed our reports had an office next to the computer room. There was a conference room in the center section just to the right of the chief's office.

When I got to Central, I mounted the wide outside steps and went through the big double doors that fronted the Desk Sergeant's domain. Sergeant Sally Murchison was on the desk this Friday night and I waved 'hello' at her as I went around the desk, past the waiting room area and through the door into the open squad room.

Although it was a little too early for the usual Friday night fighters and the serious drunks, there were already a couple of each in residence when I came through the squad room door. The big grey painted room contained twenty desks and a small bank of computers with attached printers. One of printers was spitting out sheets of 'wants and warrants' as I walked past. I smelled the rank odor of stale beer and cigarettes given off by a man sprawled in a chair next to one of the desks. He was drunk and I thought he must have started early in the day to get that stoned by now. The officer sitting with him was trying to get his name and address but was making no headway. I grinned at the cop and gave him a thumbs up. He shrugged and shook his head. At a desk across the room one of our female officers was taking a statement from a young hooker. The girl looked like she'd been in a cat fight and lost. Her scarlet mini-skirt was smeared with dirt and her black net stockings were torn. The black eye and messed up hairdo added to the effect. Detective Lieutenant Richards was at his desk in his corner cube across the room and I waved at him as I headed for Chief Jack Bauer's office. Sean wasn't back yet with the two women we were going to interview.

I reached the chief's office and knocked on the glass pane of the door. Hearing a gruff 'Come', I went in. Chief Jack Bauer was seated behind the desk and was leaning over it like a bear with a fresh caught salmon. Bauer was six five and weighed something north of three hundred pounds. When he was a street cop he had been known as 'Bull' Bauer. His massive arms and shaven head made me think of one of the villains from a James Bond movie. But I knew my boss was much smarter than any of Ian Fleming's Bond characters.

"Makarios, what have you got on the Straub thing? I need some answers. That clown from the Journal has been sniffing around and one of the TV stations showed up a little while ago. Richards sent 'em away. I've already heard from the mayor – twice. Give me some good news." He settled back in the oversized chair that had been built especially for him and put his fingertips together.

I cleared my throat and fished my notebook from my jacket pocket. I flipped it open and began to brief the big man. When I finished, Bauer squinted his eyes and heaved a sigh. "You're telling me we got nothin'. How does the Clayton woman figure into this? Or the other one? Hood, was it?"

"Dunphy is bringing them in to get their statements tonight. In fact, they should be here now." I hesitated and then went on, "I don't think we'll get much from them. Clayton sort of covered for her secretary but I don't think either one had anything to do with the murder."

Bauer scowled at me. "Maybe I should give this case to Richards and Davis. He's got more experience than you. Maybe he can turn something up."

I moved closer to the desk and looked directly into the chief's eyes. He had been reluctant to promote me back in March and had made that clear a couple of times. I took a breath and said, "Chief, I was the first one on the scene. This is my case. Let me and Sean work it through." I continued, "I know you weren't too keen on promoting me but I think by now you know I'm more qualified than any other man on the force. I worked the streets here for almost three years and you know what I did in the Air Force."

"Yeah, I know all about that. You got promoted over Davis because you grew up here and know most of the people we deal with. Davis is a newbie and doesn't know the city as well as you. You did well in the P.O.S.T. course even though you've got a physical problem. I'm just not convinced you're ready to handle this. We haven't had a high profile murder case since you've been here. And, trust me, this will be a high profile case and people will want answers from us." Bauer turned away and looked at the plaques and certificates that covered one wall of his office. He was the most decorated policeman in the history of the department. Finally he turned back and growled, "All right. You and Dunphy stay on it. But I want you to brief Richards and Davis and keep them up to speed. They'll back you up on the investigation. And I want some results. Understood?"

I mumbled "Yessir'" and turned for the door.

Bauer spoke again, "Is Dunphy all right? Do you want someone else as a partner?"

I turned back and said, "No, Chief. Sean will be fine. I'm watching him pretty closely and he hasn't been drinking like he did before. I'm sure I can keep him on track." During his twelve years on the force, Sean had been disciplined twice because of his problem with booze.

"Okay. I'll leave it up to you. He's your responsibility. Now go bring me the killer."

I was almost to the door when the phone rang and Bauer growled, "Wait." I turned back and watched as the big man answered whoever was on the other end. He finished with "OK, Rudy. I'll see you in the morning at ten." He hung up and glared at me. "In case you haven't guessed, that was Rudy Straub. He is somewhat upset and demanding action. He's in Grand Rapids right now but he'll be here at ten in the morning. I want you and Dunphy here at nine. With some answers. 'Cause Rudy's gonna have some hard questions. You got it?"

"Yes sir. I'll see what else we can get from Clayton and Hood." I left the office and was nearly at our cube when Sean came through the squad room.

"Hey. I put the Clayton dame in the conference room. You gonna take her statement now?"

"Yeah. Where's the Hood woman?"

He shrugged, "Damned if I know. We went by her place on the way in. Her car's in the driveway but the house was dark and no one answered the door when I knocked. Maybe she went to stay with a relative or something. The Clayton woman said she was pretty shook up."

"All right. We'll try her again in the morning. Bauer wants both of us here at nine. Rudy Straub is coming in. So we better be sharp. Understand?"

Sean looked away for a moment and then back at me. "Yeah. I understand you."

"OK, let's go see what the piano lady has to say now."

CHAPTER EIGHT

Just as Sean and I reached the conference room door, Paul Straub caught up with us. "Has Jennifer made her statement?"

He was wearing a tan camel hair topcoat and carrying a briefcase. I couldn't understand why he was so eager to represent her. I answered him, "No, Paul. We just got here and I haven't had a chance to beat a confession out of her yet...but I'll get right on that." He didn't smile.

The conference room was next to Chief Bauer's office and took up the rest of the back wall of the main part of the building. It was furnished with a mahogany table that would comfortably seat ten and an additional dozen chairs were arranged against the walls. There were no windows and the walls were decorated with framed old photographs of the city in its past glory days; pictures of old ships loaded with lumber, the car ferries which used to run across the lake to Milwaukee and scenes of the downtown area.

Jennifer Clayton was sitting at the end of the table when we walked in. She looked comfortable, relaxed but alert and interested. The slacks and sweater did nothing to diminish her good looks. She smiled at me. "Lieutenant Makarios. Nice to see you again." She nodded to Straub and then said "Hello, Paul."

I pulled out the chair opposite her and sat down. "Thanks for coming in this evening, Miss Clayton. I know this has been a difficult day for you."

Paul took another chair two places to my left and butted in, "I'm here to represent you, Jen. That is, if you want me to do that."

She looked at me and asked, "Do I need an attorney, Lieutenant?"

"You have not been charged with a crime, Miss Clayton. I think Mr. Straub is being a little over-eager."

I turned to him, "Straub, I've told you this before. Miss Clayton is not under arrest and doesn't need a lawyer to represent her. However, she can ask for one at any time if she wants one. But, as I told you before, if you interfere with me, you'll find yourself outside. Understood? We're only here to get a written statement." I pushed a yellow legal pad and a pen across the table. "Just write out as much as you can remember about what happened this afternoon, Ms. Clayton. If there's anything you remember in addition to what you told me, put that in your statement too."

She nodded and picked up the pen. It took her less than five minutes to write out her statement. She slid the pad back across the table to me. "I think that's as accurate as I can recall."

I scanned the single page. It read like the reports I used to prepare when I was assigned to the Air Force Office of Special Investigations. It was clear and concise, with no wasted words. Jennifer had traced the whole afternoon, putting times in as nearly as she could recall. But there were two discrepancies between what she had told me earlier and what she had written now. I fished my notebook out of my pocket.

"We've got a little problem here, Ms. Clayton."

She looked at me calmly. "What do you mean?"

I consulted my notes. "This afternoon you told me that you found the body and made the call to nine eleven. Here you've stated that Ms. Hood made the discovery and the call. Which one is the truth?" I locked eyes with her, looking for the tell-tale signs of lies.

"What I wrote here is the truth. Catherine found Madeline in the studio." Jennifer's eyes never wavered from mine. They didn't shift around in the way they do when people are lying. "I wanted to spare her from having to go over all of that with you this afternoon." She looked at Paul for a moment and then back to me. "When she found Madeline, she called me and I came back to the studio from my apartment. I had been on the telephone. Madeline was lying on the floor. I saw the cord around her neck. I could see she wasn't breathing but I checked for a pulse anyway. She was already dead. Catherine was in the hall and was quite upset and crying. She really liked Madeline. I asked her to make the call to 911. She also told me that she thought she had seen the other door to the studio closing just before she found Madeline."

I nodded. "The dispatcher did say that the caller was nearly hysterical, and you don't strike me as being the hysterical type. We'll see what Ms. Hood has to say when we bring her in." I reread her statement. In it, she wrote that Catherine Hood made the call. OK, I thought, so she lied this afternoon to protect Hood. Was that the only reason? Why did she think Hood needed to be protected? I decided to let that go for now. Everything else in the statement jibed with the notes I had taken earlier. I looked over at Jennifer again. She was relaxed and poised; her hands folded on the table in front of her. I really didn't want to let her leave just yet. I was beginning to enjoy looking at her but I was running out of reasons to keep her there.

Another odd thought was bothering me, so I asked, "Paul told me you called him after I left your office. Why did you do that? You knew I was going to notify the family."

She sat up straight. "I didn't call him. He called me about fifteen minutes after you left and I took the opportunity to tell him of Madeline's murder."

I looked at Paul and he shrugged and spread his hands as if to say 'so what'.

I could let that wait for a time too, so I said, "Ms. Clayton, you are free to go. We may need to see you again after we talk to Ms. Hood so please don't leave town." I got up and turned to my partner, "Sean, would you check with Chief Bauer to see if she can go back to her apartment tonight?" Dunphy left and I turned back to woman. "I'll have a patrolman take you home or to wherever you're going to be staying."

Paul Straub spoke up quickly, "That's not necessary. I'll take Jen home."

She shook her head. "No, Paul. You need to be with your family. Your mother must be terribly upset. I don't need you here and I'm sure she could use your help at this awful time. Please go home." She came around the table and stood next to me.

He waved his hand, "Oh, my mother was fine when I left her. Gerd is there at the house and he'll probably stay up with her until Rudy gets home. He should be back from Grand Rapids before too much longer. Who knows, maybe Peter will turn up. They don't need me out there."

As I watched and listened to Paul, I wondered, where is the grief? His sister has just been brutally murdered and he shows no emotion at all. No anger. No sorrow. None of the usual emotions one would expect. Why not?

Sean came back in with an attractive young female patrolman. "Chief says it's OK for you to go back to your place, Ms. Clayton. The forensic people and the ME are through for tonight." He nodded toward the young woman with him. "This is Officer Haynes and she will drive you."

Jennifer stood, "Thank you, sergeant." She turned to me, "I was hoping you might give me a ride back to my apartment, lieutenant. And please stop calling me Ms. Clayton. My name is Jennifer."

I looked into those bottomless green eyes and had the urge to wrap my arms around her right then and there. I felt I owed her more of an explanation so I said, "Ms. Clayton...Jennifer, you are still a person of interest in this case and I'm still the investigating officer so I don't believe that would be appropriate."

She nodded and said, "I understand." Then she smiled up at me, "But maybe another time. Call me if you need me for anything else." With that, she turned and followed Officer Haynes out into the hall.

I watched her go and my blush must have betrayed my thoughts because Paul snapped at me. "Don't get any ideas, Makarios. You just stay the hell away from her. I think Jen likes to flirt sometimes but she's not the kind of woman for anyone like you. She's way out of your class." He stopped for a beat and then gave me a wolfish grin. "Besides, you should know that Jennifer and I have been dating for a couple of months."

"Why did you tell me she called you? And why did you call her?"

He gave me that grin again and said, "I called her to ask her out…as if that's any of your business. I guess I told you she called just to see what you'd say. She's mine, so just stay away."

His comments were way out of line and I snarled, "Get the hell out of here, Straub." Sean grabbed him by the arm and pushed him through the door. When Paul was outside, Sean slammed it shut and, when he turned back, my partner muttered, "What an asshole." He looked at me and finished with, "Ah, what can we expect? He's a fuckin' lawyer."

CHAPTER NINE

It was eight thirty on Saturday morning when Sean walked into the squad room. As he passed by her desk, Officer Sandra Haynes looked at him, smiled and said, "You all right, Sarge? You don't look like you feel very good this morning."

He slumped into the chair next to her desk. "Nah, I'm fine. Was a late night. You get the Clayton woman home alright?"

"Sure. No problem. She seems like a nice lady. You don't think she killed that girl, do you?"

"No. We talked about it last night and neither of us can think of a motive. But she does seem to be pretty calm about the whole thing. Alex told me the whole Straub family is taking it the same way...they're all very calm. Seems pretty strange to me."

Haynes smiled and said, "What did your wife say when you came in so late last night?"

Sean looked over at the young woman, "I don't have a wife. I never found anyone who would put up with me." He smiled back at her and then his head pounded again and the smile turned to a grimace.

* * *

Sean followed Lieutenant Richards and I over to our cube and greeted us, "Morning. Guess it's almost time for us to see the chief."

"Yeah, but we've got a few minutes yet." I stared at him for a long minute. "You okay? You don't look so good. What did you do after we left here last night?" The bags under Dunphy's eyes looked packed for a long trip.

"Stopped at the Lakeside Inn for a drink on the way home. Stayed a little later than I planned to." Sean watched Richards wander over to his own cubicle. "You brief the lieutenant this morning?"

I nodded, "Yeah, I wanted him to be up to speed on this before we talked to Bauer again. I went by the Hood woman's place on my way in. Her car's still there and the door's locked like you said. I'll ask the chief to get a warrant for us so we can get in the house and take a look around. Richards said he and Davis could do that tomorrow morning if we don't get the warrant early enough. I think you should go along with them if they do it tomorrow. I'll be tied up for a while."

"Okay, I can do that. What'll you be doing?"

"It's Sunday and it's also my niece's birthday. I promised Theo I'd go to church and then have breakfast with the family." I shrugged, "It's a Greek thing. I promise I'll catch up with you early in the afternoon at Hood's place if you're still there."

The door to Chief Bauer's office opened and Danny Gordon sauntered out. He spotted us and came over to the cube. "Hey, Makarios. I told you I'd see you guys today." He smirked, "Chief Bauer gave me everything I need for Monday's edition. I'll punch it up and make it a real good story. This'll be front page stuff with the girl's old man running for the senate and everything." He sighed, "We don't get many nice juicy murders like this out here in the sticks very often." He grinned and said, "But I sure saw a lot of 'em when I was on the paper in Chicago. I know how to really work 'em. See you guys later." He headed for the door at the other end of the squad room whistling to himself.

"Makarios. Get in here." The chief's deep voice boomed through the squad room and we quickly made our way to his office. The big man was leaning back in his chair, an unlit cigar clamped between his teeth. It looked like a Churchill, probably a sixty ring from Nicaragua since the embargo against Cuban cigars was still on. A Churchill is a big cigar but it looked natural in his huge hand. He gestured for us to sit and then took the cigar from his mouth with a disgusted look on his face. "Damned 'No smoking in public buildings' law." He started to drop it into the hubcap-sized ashtray on his desk and then thought better of it. He leaned forward and pointed the cigar at me like it was a pistol.

"You know anything about baseball, Makarios? I mean, you do know that you only get three strikes before you're called out?" I nodded, unsure about where this was going. The chief leaned back in his chair again and barked, "Yesterday you whiffed twice."

"I don't know what you mean, chief." I still didn't have a clue.

"What I mean is that strike one was when you let a material witness in a capital murder investigation get away from you." He pointed the unlit cigar at me again. "What the hell were you thinking and where the hell is the Hood woman?"

I knew this was going to bite me but I stammered, "We don't have her yet. She disappeared sometime yesterday afternoon. Her car is at her house. The house is locked up tight so we need a warrant to enter and search the place. We were hoping you could get it for us right away so we can do that today or tomorrow morning at the latest. Richards and Davis are going to help."

He grunted, "All right. I'll call the DA and ask him to try and find a judge today." The big man leaned forward again. His voice was soft and low, "Do you want to know what strike two was?"

I fumbled with my notebook and then said, "No. But I guess I'm going to find out anyway."

Bauer scowled at me and lifted a plastic bag from the top of his desk. I saw that it contained Madeline Straub's red leather wallet. He dangled it in front of me. "According to forensics, the only prints on this thing are the dead girl's…and yours. Now how do you suppose that happened?"

I looked down at my hands. "Oh Christ. Gloves. I didn't use plastic gloves. When the tech handed the cell phone to me, I didn't take time to put 'em on before I took it from her."

Bauer barked, "A goddamned rookie mistake. With all your experience you're supposed to know better. That's what you told me yesterday." He leaned back, "You are just about one strike away from walking a beat up in the Heights. I've still got a good mind to turn this whole investigation over to Richards and see what he and Davis can do. But I told you it was your case so I'll give you and Dunphy a couple more days to straighten it out. You're still up to bat but you better not whiff again. Understood?"

I nodded and said, "I understand, Chief. And thanks."

"Don't thank me yet…this case could turn into a real bitch." The chief turned to Sean, "Dunphy, you don't look good. Are you drunk this morning or just hung over from last night?"

Sean coughed and said, "I haven't been drinking, Chief. I'm just a little tired from a long night."

"Celebrating our big win over Bay City, were you? I heard it was a good game. What was the score? Twenty-six to fourteen or something like that? That's pretty good for the kids."

Sean nodded and looked away. "Yeah. That was the final." He didn't look very happy about the score and I wondered how many points he'd been forced to give in order to get decent odds. I also wondered how much he had put down on the game.

"Okay. Get out of here for now. Rudy Straub is due in a little while and I'll call you if I need you. Both of you stay close."

We went back out to the squad room and when we got to our cube, I asked Sean about his bet.

"I had to give thirteen and a half goddam points to get three to one. And the kicker misses two extra points so they win by only twelve. Goddamnit. I dropped five hundred bucks on that goddamned game." For a minute I thought he was going to cry. "That fifteen hundred was going to be my stake for the college and pro games this weekend. Now I'm down the five hundred and won't be able to get any action with any of the books. They all know I don't have any cash." Sean was a gambler: He wasn't really addicted to gambling but he liked the adrenaline rush of the risk. He'd bet on baseball and basketball once in a while but he loved football. Particularly the college and pro games. And of course, he had to bet on the local high school team. I knew he sometimes won but on average, I believe he lost more often.

"Who'd you place the bet with?"

"You know Fumbles Cernak? He handles the local stuff. Especially the high school games."

"Yeah, I know Fumbles. We're going to go see him later today."

Sean jumped. "What the hell for? I don't want to see him. I owe him a grand besides what I dropped on last night's game. He'll want the whole fifteen hundred bucks and I haven't got it. Any of it."

"We have to go see him. I think he might have a lead on Peter Straub. The kid also gambles and he's probably doing business with Fumbles...just like you." I was needling Sean a little to show him I knew he had a problem. Personally, I'm not against gambling. I've been to Vegas and contributed my share to pay the Strip's light bill and I played some poker when I was in the Air Force but I just can't make myself lay big bets on a bunch of high school kids. We were saved from discussing it any further by Rudy Straub's entrance.

Rudy, followed by his son Paul and his gofer, a young man who carried his briefcase and ran errands for him, went through the squad room like a bull coming out of the chute at a Texas rodeo. He didn't bother to knock on Chief Bauer's closed office door. He jerked it open and stormed into the office; leaving Paul to close it behind them. Sean and I looked at each other for a moment and I'm sure we thought the same thing: the chief was going to get an earful and then we would probably be on the carpet again. I hauled some reports out of my IN basket and tried to kill some time by proofreading and signing the ones that had been transcribed over the last few days. It didn't work. I couldn't concentrate and I fervently wished we could hear what was happening in the chief's office.

CHAPTER TEN

"Bauer, what the hell is going on? Who killed my daughter? Why haven't you arrested anyone yet? Was that piano teacher involved? Tell me what you know. I want some goddamned answers. And I want 'em now." Rudy Straub's face was red and twisted with anger and he slammed his fist down on Chief Bauer's desk. Rudy had a well-deserved reputation for being all bluster and threat. He had bullied his way onto the city council in ninety-eight and wielded what little power he had with a heavy hand. His son, Paul, sank into one of the chairs against the office wall and Rod Ashley, a long-haired, pasty faced young man who trailed Rudy around and did whatever he was told to do, sat stiffly on the office sofa, a briefcase on his knees.

Chief Bauer cleared his throat and began, "Rudy, I can't tell you how sorry I am about Madeline's death. She was a sweet girl."

Straub shook his head impatiently, "Yeah, yeah, enough of that bullshit. I don't need to hear it. Just answer my goddamned questions. I don't have time for a lot of crap." He turned to his errand boy, "Ashley, when's our next meeting?"

The pale young man jumped to his feet and answered, "You've got a fund raiser dinner in Lansing on Tuesday evening and a lunch down in Detroit at the Press Club on Wednesday, Mr. Straub."

Straub looked at the young man like he had just crawled out from under a rock. "No, you damn dummy. I meant today."

Ashley fumbled with the briefcase and finally pulled a typewritten schedule out of it. "There's an interview at three with Channel Eight and that reporter from the Journal wants to talk to you after that."

Straub turned back to the chief. "See, Bauer. I told you I've got a busy campaign schedule and I can't afford to screw around with this shit. Give me some answers."

Bauer tried again. "Be patient, Rudy. We just started our investigation. I'll tell you what we know for sure. We know your daughter was killed sometime Friday afternoon at Jennifer Clayton's piano studio. She was strangled." He paused but Straub gestured for him to get on with it. "The Clayton woman and her secretary, a woman named Hood, are both persons of interest but right now we don't believe they had anything to do with the murder. One of them may have seen the killer and we're looking into that. That's all I can tell you at the moment. Of course, we'll keep you informed as our investigation develops".

Straub stepped back from the desk and sat down. "You're damned right you'll keep me informed. I want to know everything that's happening. Who's heading the investigation?"

"Detective Lieutenant Alex Makarios and his partner are the lead on the case."

Straub turned to his son, "That the guy you went to school with? He the one that was out at the house last night?"

Paul sat up, "Yes. He questioned the three of us last night. He also interviewed Jennifer Clayton here at the station after that."

Straub turned back to the chief. "I want to talk to him."

Bauer leaned forward and said, "Rudy, you and I go back a long way. I helped you get acquainted when you first came to Muskegon. Right now

I'm asking you not to interfere with our investigation into your daughter's death. We know what we're doing. Let my people do their jobs. Please stay out of it."

Straub's eyes narrowed and he lowered his voice. "Bauer, did you forget that I am on the city council? That makes me your boss. If you want to keep this nice office and the fat salary you collect, you'll do what I tell you and you'll be goddamned quick about it." He sat back in the chair. "I've dealt with your kind of police official before. Now, I'll say it again. I want to talk to this Makarios kid. And I mean right now."

CHAPTER ELEVEN

Even through the closed office door, Sean and I heard Chef Bauer's shout of summons and were quick to respond. We went in and stood to the side of the chief's desk. We had no clue about what we were in for.

Rudy Straub pointed at me and opened with, "Why haven't you found out why my daughter was murdered and why haven't you arrested whoever killed her?"

I looked at the chief, hoping for either guidance or interference. I got neither. He was staring at the top of his desk, clenching and unclenching his big hands. He looked as though he wanted to kill something…or someone. I turned back to the murdered girl's father and said, "Mr. Straub, I'm sure that Chief Bauer has told you everything we know at this point. It's an ongoing investigation and we will answer those questions and arrest the killer as soon as we can."

"Bullshit. You know damn well you don't have any leads and you don't even know where to start. I remember you from when you played football on Paul's team, Makarios . You went off to the army or something and came back a cripple. I don't understand how in hell you got on the police force. I certainly didn't have a say in it. You upset my wife and son last night with your stupid and intrusive questions. I don't want you talking to her or my sons again." He turned and looked at Sean. "And I know you, too, Dunphy. You're a drunk. Typical of your kind." He stood up and put his hands on the chief's desk. "Is this the best you've got, Bauer? A Greek cripple and an Irish drunk?" He turned back and pointed at us. "Bauer, I want you to fire these two and get someone on this case who knows what the hell they're doing. Someone who can produce results. And I want that done immediately."

I started for the arrogant, insulting bastard but Sean grabbed me from behind. I was trying to wrestle free when the chief slapped his hand down on the desk. We all froze. The sound his hand made was like a blast I once heard in Iraq.

The chief stood up and leaned over his desk. The big man towered over Rudy Straub even though the German was no midget. The chief spoke very softly. "Hear me, Straub, and hear me good. You have gone too far." He swept his arm toward Sean and me, "These are my men and I will tell them what to do and when to do it. I don't care if you are a city councilman, a United States Senator or even the goddamned President of the United States. You do not tell me how to run this police department. We will do our jobs and we will find your daughter's killer. But we will do it our way and without any interference from you. We will talk to whoever we want to, whenever we want to, in order to get whatever information we need. That includes you and your family. If we ask you, your wife or your sons to come in here, you will all do it." He stopped, took a deep breath and raised his voice a little, "But I don't ever want to see you in here again unless I call you. Is that clear?" He took another breath, "Now, get the fuck out of my office."

Paul had grabbed his father by the arm and was pulling him away from the desk and toward the door. The young campaign worker had already fled from of the office. The elder Straub's face was crimson and the veins of his neck stood out like cables. He sputtered and struggled to put words together but Paul succeeded in pulling him out of the chief's reach.

I realized Sean was still holding me by the arms and I shook him off. The Straubs went out the door and Chief Bauer turned around and resumed his seat behind the desk. He picked up his cigar, jammed it into his mouth and sat quietly, looking at the stuff on the office walls. Finally he motioned for Sean and me to sit down and he swiveled his chair around to face us.

A few more silent minutes passed and then I cleared my throat and said, "Well, that was fun." I was still pissed and trying to make sense of Rudy Straub's tirade. I knew I would never forget nor forgive his insult of me and Sean. Bauer began chewing on the unlit cigar and seemed to have regained his composure. I decided I needed to know more about the Straub family so I asked, "Chief, how did you and that bastard get mixed up together? I think it would help us to know more about that family. That is, if Sean and I are going to stay on this case."

He took the cigar from his mouth and smiled at us like a wolf smiles at a sheep. "Oh, you better believe you two are going to stay on this case. You will be on it until it's finished. And I expect that to happen pretty damned soon. Understood?" We both nodded and he continued. "I can't tell you a lot about where the Straubs came from. Someplace in West Germany. I think they were in Canada for a while and then showed up here in seventy-two or thereabouts. I met them through the pastor at St. Peter's, the Lutheran church we all go to. Helped 'em get settled during the first few months they were here. I was still a street cop back then. I didn't make sergeant until seventy-four." He paused and looked at his cigar for a moment. "Then Rudy bought the old Lake City Brewery. I think that was about five years later. Maybe in seventy-seven or eight. He told me once that he worked for a brewery someplace in Germany for a while. No one knew where he got the money to buy the old brewery and upgrade it but I heard that he was hooked up with a banker back east."

Sean spoke up, "Are the Straubs all citizens? Rudy would have to be if he is running for the Senate, I think."

"Yeah. Somehow Rudy got a work visa or green card or something from the government and they applied for naturalization. That seemed kind of strange at the time but they all became naturalized citizens in eighty-five or six." He paused and thought for a minute. "Except for Rudy's wife, Karla. He and the boys went through the process but she didn't. So I guess she's still a German national. I don't know why she'd want to do that. Keep her German citizenship, I mean. Karla's a tough one to figure out. Maybe she just doesn't like us." He thought some more. "They've traveled back to Germany a half dozen times that I know about. I don't know what they do over there when they make those trips. Some of those visits lasted for a couple of months. I think the daughter was born over there on one of those trips." He paused, "I wonder if she is…was… a citizen?"

I chimed in, "Chief, I don't think Straub's wife likes anybody. She seemed awfully cold last night. How'd he get into politics?"

"After he bought the brewery he joined the Chamber of Commerce and then a couple of service clubs and pretty soon he'd made a name for himself around town. Volunteered on some civic stuff and made some hefty donations. Got elected to the city council four years ago but he's never done very much. He throws his weight around when he thinks it's to his advantage." The chief hesitated a moment. "I expect that to change. In fact, after today I think he will be gunnin' for us…or me at least."

I said, "You don't seem too concerned about that, Chief."

"I'm not worried. I've probably got more clout with the council than he does. I don't think anything he tries to do to me will get very far."

I continued, "Good. You know, Chief, I've got a couple of problems with the way Straub acted and how he talked in here." Bauer nodded so I went on, "Not once did he ask about when they could have the girl's body for services or burial. I've told Sean this and now I'm telling you. None of the Straubs have shown any sorrow or grief over their daughter's death. I find that a bit unnatural to say the least."

Bauer nodded. "Yeah, that is strange. Straub does seem to be more concerned with his campaign than what to do about the girl. It's almost as if they've already forgotten about her or like she was never part of their family. Like I said, I think they went to Germany on a long trip and she was born over there. Anyway, she came back with them when she was a month or so old. They had her christening at St. Peter's."

I nodded and said, "Another thing I've got a problem with is the way he speaks English."

"What's wrong with his English?" The chief looked puzzled by my statement.

"Nothing, and that's the problem. It's too good. He didn't learn it like Gerd and Paul. The boys picked it up in school and from their friends. Gerd still makes occasional mistakes in putting his words together and he still mixes German into his speech. Paul doesn't do that so much. Perhaps because he was a little younger when he came here. Paul's also trained himself better. Peter was born here so he never was a German speaker. Karla and Rudy speak very precisely. I think they had to have been taught to speak that way by professionals. I wonder where and when would they have done that?"

"Not since they've been in Muskegon. They spoke perfect English when they got here."

"Chief, I spent some time in Germany. The only people that speak English as well as Rudy does are government officials and diplomats. They are schooled. The average working man over there maybe learns some English in high school and then picks up some more from TV and movies. I'm pretty sure Rudy didn't learn the language that way. He's too good."

Bauer smiled, "I'm sure he's been vetted by the party or they wouldn't have endorsed his candidacy for Senator Markham's seat. The boys at city hall tell me that he's got a fairly good shot at winning, even though it's a close race and the senator refused to endorse him." He chewed on the cigar for a minute or so and then pointed it at us. "Perhaps we should do some sniffing around in Rudy's background and see what we come up with." He frowned at us. "Not 'til we get this murder solved, though. I'll get that warrant for you so you can run down the Hood woman. She might have seen something that will help."

We got up and were starting for the door when Chris Karras breezed through it. Bauer looked at her and grumbled, "Don't you ever knock?"

She laughed, "Hardly ever, Chief." She had a folder filled with papers in her hand and she dropped it on the big desk in front of him. "There's the autopsy report on the Straub girl."

Bauer didn't touch the papers. "Karras, you know I'm not gonna read that stuff. Tell me what you found and give the damn papers to Makarios. He can read, I think."

She picked up the folder and handed it to me. "All right. The victim was a twenty-two- year-old female. Cause of death was strangulation. Time of death was sometime between three and four o'clock yesterday afternoon." Chris paused, "That's plus or minus fifteen minutes or so. No evidence of sexual assault. There were no bruises or other defensive marks. Whoever killed her probably stood behind her, pulled the cord from the drape and dropped it around her neck. She must have struggled some but there was no skin beneath her nails. We did find some fibers and a few grains of dirt. The perp might have been wearing gloves but, of course, we have no way of knowing. The dirt and fiber could have come from something like that. If we find him…or her…and the gloves, we can try and get a match. One of the victim's earrings was torn off during the struggle but that was the only other injury." She took a deep breath. "Now for the really bad news.

The victim was pregnant. About six weeks along." She sighed. "You've got a double homicide, Chief."

Bauer swore and banged his fist on the desk. Sean and I looked at each other and he made the sign of the cross. I shook my head and muttered, "We have to get the son of a bitch."

Chris stood up and asked "Any more questions? I've got things to do."

While she talked, I had been looking at the photos included with the report. One of them caught my eye. It was of the girl's buttocks and lower back. "What are these marks in this picture, Chris?"

"Alex, I haven't figured that out yet. They appear to be old scars. Probably from when she was a child. It looks like they were made with something about an inch in diameter and jagged. Some of the scars are full circles and others just arcs. We found them on her lower back, upper legs, belly and butt. Places where they wouldn't show when she was fully clothed. She couldn't have done it to herself. It looks like the girl was abused when she was quite young. The scarring varies in depth and texture which indicates the abuse occurred over a substantial period of time. Possibly over several years." She looked at the chief and said, "And we know that usually means someone in the family or close to it, doesn't it?"

He sighed, "Yeah. It almost always comes out that way." He looked at me and Sean. "Take it and run with it. Do whatever you have to…and if that means dragging the whole damn Straub family down here and putting the screws to 'em, you do it."

Sean reached in and took the photos from me. "Ahh, how could anyone do that to a girl like her?" He stared at the picture of the scars for a long minute, his hands shaking. "We'll get the filthy bastard who did this. I promise you that." I knew where he was coming from. He once told me about the abuse he had enduresd when he was growing up. His father suffered from the 'Curse of the Irish'; he was a drunk and abused his wife and his two children. No one did anything to stop it and Sean's older sister ran away from her home and family at sixteen. Sean stayed to try and protect his mother but hadn't been able to help her very much. That was one of the reasons he became a cop. His mother died while he was in high school and his dad disappeared shortly after, leaving Sean to fend for himself. He handed the photos back to me and turned away, wiping his eyes.

Bauer waited a moment and then said softly, "You're right, Sean. We'll get whoever did it. Now go find who killed her."

CHAPTER TWELVE

We drove up Peck Street toward the Heights and Sharkey's, the run-down pool hall Fumbles Cernak owned and managed. Sean was still suffering from his self-inflicted hangover and was crowded over against the passenger door with his head resting against the cool glass like he was trying to get a nap. I made sure that didn't happen by asking him about last night's high school football game. "So tell me about the game, Sean. When did we score?"

He came alive, sat up straighter and stretched. "I guess it was a pretty good game." He cut his eyes toward me. "Shame we had to miss it. The guys I met at the bar told me the kids scored twice in the first quarter. Our kicker missed the point after on the second touchdown, so it was thirteen zip at the half. We scored again early in the third and then our dumbass coach put all his second stringers in. Bay City scored twice in the third against those hamburgers. Hell, they got one on an interception. We got the final touchdown late in the fourth quarter and then that kid missed the fuckin' point after again." He looked out the window and sighed, "I don't know what I'm going to tell Fumbles. He'll want his money."

"That he will, my friend, that he will. Fumbles isn't known for his charity." I really did feel sorry for Sean but even if he asked, I was not going to lend him any cash. He would just have to work it out with the bookie.

Sharkey's pool hall is in a rundown old red brick building on Broadway in the Heights. It was a good-sized building that had once been a store of some kind but now it housed a short four-stool beer bar and eight pool tables. Those tables also had seen better days. The walls and ceiling of the big room were grimy with the residue of countless cigars and cigarettes, but it was quite possible they had been some shade of white at some time in the past fifty years or so. Behind the big fly-specked windows that flanked the front door were displays of old and well-worn sports memorabilia: an old football helmet along with a half-deflated ball, a couple of baseball bats and gloves and three signed jerseys from past stars of the Muskegon Heights Tigers, the high school football team.

I made a U-turn in the wide street and pulled to the curb in front of the place. I could just barely make out Fumbles Cernak through the dirty front window. He was behind the bar just inside of the front door. We went in and the smell of old beer and cigarette smoke nearly caused me to gag. The interior of the building was so gloomy that I could barely see the half dozen guys shooting pool or sitting around in the back by the tables. One of them looked up and saw us when we came through the door. He said something to the rest of them, dropped his cue on the table and made a beeline for the back door. A couple of the others were carefully looking away from us and intently studying the balls on the dirty green felt covering the tables.

Fumbles recognized me, grinned and stuck out his meaty hand. "Did you have to park right in front of the joint, Alex? You're going to ruin my walk-in business."

I shook hands with him and then said, "We don't mean to cause you any problem, Fumbles, but we're looking for Peter Straub. I thought you might be able to help us out. You seen him lately?"

He shook his head. "Not this week. He dropped two large last weekend and hasn't come around yet to tell me when his old man's gonna make it right."

I watched the rest of the pool players rack their cues and quietly leave by the back door.

"Geez, Fumbles, I'm sorry we're chasing all your paying customers away like this. Looks like a couple more of them just found something else to do this afternoon."

"Ah, those bums wouldn't pay me if they had the money. They come in here, read the papers and maybe try to con each other into paying for a table for an hour so they can hustle a buck or two. They don't very often pay their debts." He turned to Sean, "And speaking of paying debts, what are your thoughts on last night's game, Sergeant Dunphy?"

I watched as Sean tried to think of some excuse Fumbles might possibly believe. Finally he just blurted out, "I haven't got the five hundred, Fumbles. But I'll get it for you. I promise."

Fumbles Cernak had been two years ahead of me at Muskegon high school. His senior year he was the top running back in the state of Michigan. He was selected as All Conference and All State and he was cinch to get a scholarship and go on to college and maybe the pros someday. For a couple of reasons none of that happened and now, eighteen years later, he was running a second-rate pool hall and making a little book on the side. He'd put on a few pounds in the years since high school but he worked out and was in good shape. Fumbles outweighed Sean by nearly fifty pounds and probably had thirty on me. I'm a couple of inches taller at six one, but he looked big as a house when he came around the counter and stopped in front of me. "Sorry I can't be of more help on the Straub kid. If there's nothing else, I think you and me are through here, Alex." He cut his eyes toward the door and continued, "Would you mind waiting outside while Sean and I have a little chat?"

"No problem, Fumbles. I need to check with Central anyway." We shook hands again and I went out. I knew he wouldn't physically hurt my partner but I suspected that Sean's debt was going to grow like flowers in the springtime. I got into the patrol car and waited. Sean came out of the pool hall a few minutes later. His face was the color of freshly washed bedsheets. He got into the car, wiped the sweat from his face and sat staring at his hands for a moment before he spoke.

"Fumbles says I got a week to come up with the two grand." He looked back at the pool hall. "Where the hell am I going to find that kind of money in a week?"

I started the car and pulled away from the curb onto Broadway. "I don't know, Sean. Maybe you could sell your car. Or borrow against it at one of those title loan outfits. But that probably would cost you more, I guess. Could your sister help you out?"

He looked at me like I was nuts. "Nah. She and that bum she married are on welfare most of the time. He can't, or won't, hold a job. I don't know how they survive down in Detroit. I try to help them sometimes but it's a losing proposition. When she ran away and married that clown she was way too young to know what she was doin.'"

I was out of advice. "You'll think of something, I'm sure." I wondered what the unsaid 'or else' would be if Sean didn't make the payment. The added five hundred dollars didn't surprise me. That was just interest and was to be expected. I knew Sean wasn't in any physical danger. Fumbles was sometime a little rough on his customers but he knew better than to go after a cop. Still, he could cause him a lot of trouble. Trouble that could cost Sean his job.

He brightened a little, "Yeah. At least he gave me a week. I'll think of somethin'. He looked through the windshield. "Where we goin'?"

"'Smokin' Joe's'. Maybe Buddy's seen the Straub kid this week."

"All right. It's way past lunch time and I could use some of Joe's barbequed ribs." He looked at me and added slyly, "You are buying, aren't you?"

I laughed, "Yeah, but just this once."

CHAPTER THIRTEEN

'Smokin' Joe's' is a Texas style rib and brisket joint a couple of blocks off Marquette Street close to Four Mile Creek. That property had once been a substantial farm. The restaurant itself wasn't much to look at from the outside. The big building had once been the hay barn and milking parlor. Now it was home to a dozen oilcloth covered tables and an eight-seat counter in one half of a huge main room with a modern open kitchen in the other half. The real magic took place in an open area out back, behind the main building.

Out there, a coffee-colored genius named Buddy Miles oversaw the cooking of the ribs, brisket and chicken that brought people from all over western Michigan to eat at the place. Joe Carter, for whom the joint is named, is an ex-NBA power forward who played eight seasons with the Spurs. While he was in San Antonio he discovered, and fell in love with, true Texas hill country barbeque. In eighty-eight he blew out his knee and retired from the hardwood. Joe persuaded Buddy, who had been working his sorcery up in Fredericksburg since he was a little boy, to come north to Michigan with him. Joe played his college ball at Wayne State but didn't care much for Detroit. He liked Muskegon, so in eighty-nine the two of them opened a small rib joint in a downtown storefront. They soon outgrew that location and moved to the old defunct farm. It needed a great deal of renovation but eventually they got it together and made it into the best Texas barbeque restaurant in western Michigan, maybe in the whole state.

The parking lot was nearly full when we pulled in and it looked like the late Saturday lunch crowd was out in force. We went in and found Joe sitting in his usual place by the cash register at the end of the little counter. He saw us and waved us over. "Hey, fellas. Good to see you. How's it going this beautiful day?" Joe was always the upbeat, happy type. I had never seen him any other way.

"Doin' great, Joe. Thought we'd grab some ribs to go while we were out here. Can do?"

"Sure, Alex. Comin' up." He stopped one of the busy waitresses and we told her what we wanted. She hustled into the kitchen where the customers could watch a couple of chefs prepare the cornbread, coleslaw, beans and potato salad that went with most orders. Joe served draft and bottled beer but no hard liquor. I believe a cold beer along with the fixin's makes true Texas barbecue the best thing that's ever come out of that great state. It was a shame we had to pass on the beer this time.

I moved toward the back door. "Goin' to talk to Buddy for a minute, Joe. That okay?"

He nodded and I went out the door. Out back was the barbeque pit. Open sided but covered with a galvanized roof and built of concrete above ground, the pit was waist high, about four feet across and twenty feet or so long. It was a full-time job to keep it filled with wood and that was usually done by some kid Buddy hired cheap. The pit was covered by mesh grates and a couple of sections of iron grill, the kind that puts the marks on steaks. There were also some warming racks above part of it and on one end there was a hand cranked rotisserie rig where chickens basked in the heat and smoke. A row of six gas fired smokers stood against the back wall of the main building. That's where the brisket came from. When I got closer to the pit, the smell of the oak and hickory wood mixed with the pungent odor of Buddy's spicy barbeque sauce was almost more than I could take. It had been a long time since breakfast.

Buddy was mopping smoky, sticky sauce from a galvanized bucket onto a half dozen decks of ribs with one hand and turning the hand-cranked rotisserie with the other. I counted six golden brown crispy skinned chickens on the spit. Buddy's bucket was about half full of the sauce that he made fresh every morning before he put the ribs and chickens on the grill. He swore that it was his own secret recipe, but I was sure he 'borrowed' it from his former boss in Texas. The skinny black man's apron and tee shirt were sweat stained and covered with splotches of sauce and grease from the ribs. Buddy was a world class barbeque cook and a sometime marijuana dealer. I stepped up beside the huge charcoal pit and got his attention. "How you doin', Buddy?"

He stopped cranking and mopping and turned to face me. "Jes' fine, Mistah Alex. Kin ah hep you? Ya'll want a chunk a' this rib?" He pointed to a six-rib slab that was ready to come off the grill and go to the kitchen.

"No, thanks, Buddy. We're gonna have some for lunch in a minute. I'm lookin' for Peter Straub. You seen him this week?"

He looked over my shoulder and off into the middle distance somewhere and in a moment said, "Yah,sir. Ain't been around all week 'til yesterday."

"He get some stuff from you, Buddy?"

The black man turned back to the pit. He stirred the bucket of sauce with his mop and turned the chickens a couple of times before he looked back at me. "You workin', Mistah Alex?"

I shook my head, "Not today, Buddy. I'm just looking for the Straub kid. That's all."

He nodded and went back to mopping on the ribs. In a little while, he said, "He got some weed from me way las' week. Sunday, mebbe Monday. He come back here yesterday evenin' sayin' he wanted more. Din't have none to give him. Reckon he mighta gone someplace else to find some. Don' know fo' sure." He stopped mopping the ribs and turned to face me. "But that boy was sho hurtin' some 'bout somethin'. Ah ain't seen him since."

CHAPTER FOURTEEN

It was nearly three o'clock when we got back to our cube in the squad room. As was usual on a Saturday, it was crowded with patrolmen and people who had run afoul of the law themselves or who were complaining about someone else who had. I made my way to my desk, stopping at Richards' cube to speak to him. He told me they had the warrant to enter the Hood woman's home. Chief Bauer had apparently strong armed an assistant district attorney into running down a sympathetic judge. Richards and Davis were planning on going to Hood's place around ten the next morning. I asked him to get with Sean and set it up and he said he would. I looked around for Sean and saw that he stopped to talk to Officer Haynes for a moment. She was a nice-looking young woman and I knew she had been on the force for a couple of years. I guessed her to be somewhere in her late twenties. Sean seemed to be paying a lot of attention to her lately. When I got to our cube, I found the forensic and ME's reports on my desk. I figured Chief Bauer had dropped them there when he quit for the day. I called Sean over and we went through both carefully.

The forensic report detailed what the techs had found at the crime scene. There were several sets of identifiable fingerprints on the piano and bench. They belonged to Madeline Straub, Jennifer Clayton and Catherine Hood. The prints had been run through the NCIC data base. Neither the Straub girl nor Catherine Hood had anything against them. There was no record at all for Jennifer Clayton. The report indicated that there were many other partials, but they were not identifiable because they were too smeared or too small. We decided they probably belonged to kids who were not in the system. The door to the porch had yielded a couple of partials but they were badly smudged. They were either wiped or they were made by a gloved hand. In any case, they couldn't be used. Only Jennifer Clayton's prints were on the cigarette box. A copy of the tape from the recorder was included with the report. Only the victim's prints were on the machine itself. I took a recorder from my desk drawer and put the copy in.

Sean and I listened to several minutes of piano scales and chords. That was interspersed with some passages that sounded like they might belong to something we should know. There were a lot of missed notes and hesitations. Pretty soon we heard a voice we recognized as Jennifer Clayton's say 'No, it should be a little faster, Maddy. More like this.' The passage was repeated several times. It sounded a lot better. We heard more chords and scales for the next eight minutes and then something I recognized as being from a piece by Shubert. Then a woman's voice from somewhere farther away called, 'Telephone. It's Mister Duncan.' Jennifer Clayton's voice came again 'Tell Frank I'll call him back. I'll do it from my apartment, Catherine.' And then, 'Keep repeating those phrases, Maddy. You're doing fine.' The piano continued for another twelve minutes and then a woman's voice said 'Oh, it's you' and two minutes later the voice said 'Stop.' That was followed by a choking sound and a muffled thud. Another two minutes and forty-five seconds of silence and then Catherine Hood's voice 'Oh God. Jennifer, come quick. Oh my God' followed by a scream 'Jennifer.' Within a minute the tape ran out. I sat back and looked at Sean. "Well, we just heard a murder being committed." We played it back again and I thought that a little bit before Hood's voice, I heard two very faint footsteps on a hard surface and a door closing. The forensic report indicated that the tech had heard the same thing. I had been hoping that Madeline had cried out or said a name but we had no such luck. The girl must have known her killer since she spoke to whoever it was and didn't seem alarmed even when she said 'Stop'. The tape did corroborate Jennifer Clayton's story about the phone call and her being absent from the studio for a long period.

We went through the rest of the report. It didn't tell us anything we didn't already know. The cord she was strangled with came from the drape by the piano. There were no fibers or other detritus under the victim's nails except for the few strands of fiber and dirt. Chris had mentioned that. In short, there were no startling clues we could hang our case on. Our two major gaps were the Hood woman and Peter Straub. I reminded Sean about the search of the Hood home the next day and told him to coordinate with Richards and Davis. He said he would and that he'd see me sometime the next afternoon. He left, stopping to speak with Officer Haynes again on his way out, and I went over the forensic report and Chris Karras's autopsy report again. Chris's report said that Madeline Straub had eaten a light lunch a couple of hours before she was killed. There were no traces of drugs or alcohol in her system. The old scars on her body still bugged me. Who had done that to her and why? Her brothers had been children when they came to Muskegon and Peter was born here. Chief Bauer told us she probably was born in Germany on one of their trips and brought here as an infant. Could Paul or Gerd have abused her like that? Or was it Rudy?

There was a big whiteboard on the wall next to our desks and we had listed all of the principals in the case. In the column labeled 'Alibi' beside each name we'd written out their supposed alibi. None of those alibis were very strong but we hadn't dug into them very far yet. I knew that we would be able to confirm or refute them in another twenty-four hours. The spaces under the column headed 'Motive' beside each name were blank.

CHAPTER FIFTEEN

I turned into the parking lot of the Muskegon Yacht Club and looked for a place to park my Rover. The lot was fairly full and I saw that Paul Straub's Cadillac was tucked into his usual spot near the entrance. I parked and went up the steps and on to the veranda that looked out over the yacht basin. Most of the boats had been pulled and stored for the winter. I figured that our yard at the marina probably had a good number of them. I went in through the big double doors and saw the ell-shaped bar was quite busy but I found an empty stool right at the corner of the bar and sat down, grateful to be off my leg for a while. It didn't usually bother me much but on long days like this had been, it made me aware that it wasn't exactly right. I knew I needed to go get it fixed. When Chuck, the bartender, finished serving a customer down the bar and looked my way, I just nodded. He reached for the bottle of Jim Beam, poured a generous shot over two ice cubes in a rocks glass, added a little water and slid it to me across the polished mahogany bar.

I said, "Thanks, Chuck." I took a sip to get the good whiskey taste before the ice melted and diluted it too much. "Looks like the usual suspects are here tonight."

"Yeah. It's been pretty good. Most of the regulars are here. The mayor and his gang were in but left after a couple of rounds. Judge Whiteman and a couple of his lawyer buddies came in early. The only ones missing are the

Straubs. They aren't at their usual table. Guess that's understandable what with Rudy's campaign and Madeline being killed. Paul is the only one of them to come in tonight."

I took a healthy sip of my drink and swiveled the stool around to see who was out on a Saturday night. The members of the club were faithful in supporting the facility and there were quite a few of them in the room. The bar and dining room were open to the public and even though the drinks and food were a little pricey, quite a few of Muskegon's non-boating citizens frequented the place on the weekends. The dozen tables in the room were occupied by couples and foursomes while the bar was full of singles and small groups. The salmon charter boats were through for the day and there were three little groups of fishermen who were either celebrating their catches or commiserating with one another about the ones that got away. It was a little after seven o'clock so the club was still serving dinner and I considered looking at the menu but decided to just have my drink and then go home to my apartment although I didn't have the faintest idea about what I would find to eat there.

Even though I don't own a boat, I knew several of the club members and quite a few of the local businessmen who were in attendance. I nodded 'hello' to some of them and then I saw Paul Straub at his favorite window table. Jennifer Clayton was sitting with him. Damn, I thought, what's she doing with him? I turned back to the bar and picked up their reflections in the long mirror above and behind the stacked glasses. As I watched, Straub leaned in close to the Clayton woman and put his hand on her arm. I took another long pull at my drink and scowled at the mirror. Why did what Paul was doing bother me? Who she goes out with was no concern of mine so why was I getting all worked up? He's her attorney. But it didn't look as if he was acting much like an attorney at the moment. I remembered he did say that they were dating. I looked at them in the mirror again. They got up from the table and I saw that Paul probably had a couple too many.

He started walking unsteadily through the tables, occasionally bumping a chair back or someone's shoulder and mumbling his apologies. Jennifer Clayton followed him with a slightly amused smile on her beautiful face. I turned my stool around to face them just as they got to me.

Straub spoke first, slurring his words a little, "Well, if it isn't Mr. Makarios. Off duty and out on the town tonight, officer?"

"Hello, Straub. Ms. Clayton." I stood and faced him. "It's Lieutenant Makarios, Paul. And it might surprise you to learn that even detectives get some time off now and then."

"Well, I think you should be out there somewhere trying to find Madeline's...uh, my sister's killer." He waved his arm in the general direction of the door and nearly hit a waitress carrying a tray full of drinks. "Oops, sorry," he mumbled.

"Watch yourself, Paul." I looked at Jennifer Clayton. "Have you two been here very long? It looks as if Paul has about had enough for this evening."

Before she could answer, Straub put his hand in the middle of my chest and leaned his weight into it. "You playing at being a cop, Makarios? I'm not drunk so knock it off."

I batted his hand away and he staggered, catching the back of a bar stool to keep from falling. I grabbed his arm and said, "I didn't say you were drunk. But I think you've had more than enough. I wouldn't try to drive if I were you." I turned to the girl. "And I wouldn't ride with him either."

She smiled up at me, "I'm sure you're right, Lieutenant, but I've already called a cab. It's probably outside by now."

I had a sudden brainstorm and said, "Why don't we let Paul take this one and we'll get another one for you?" There were those eyes again, green and deep as the ocean. I listened to my heart pound for a minute, waiting for her reply.

She looked at Paul, who was still leaning on the bar stool and staring at the floor as if he'd lost something down there. Then she smiled at me and said, "I think that's a good idea. Paul does look as if he could use a ride."

Straub straightened up and squared around to face her. "I'm not drunk and I'll take you home. You came here with me." He reached for her arm but she pulled away and took a step back from the bar.

I stuck my arm out between them and said, "Take it easy, Paul. No need to make a scene here at the club."

"Still playing the hero, aren't you?" His voice was ragged and he reached out for my jacket. "Big man with a badge and a gun. I don't care. I can take you any time." Paul is almost as big as I am…within five pounds or so…but there is no way he could 'take me'. I really wanted him to try someday but not right now nor here at the yacht club.

So I put my best command voice on and said, "Stop it right now, Straub." I forced his arm down and held on, putting pressure on his elbow. "This has gone far enough. Take the cab and get out of here now." I saw Richie Stevens, who drove for Red Top Cab, come through the door. I waved him over and said, "Richie, Paul needs a ride to his place and then I'd like you to come back here and pick up Ms. Clayton. Can do?"

"Sure. No problem. I can be back in about thirty minutes if that's all right."

I said that would work and let go of Paul's arm. He collapsed into himself and stood there, rubbing his arm. All of his usual arrogance and bluster had disappeared. He looked lost for a minute. But there was anger in his eyes when he raised his head and looked at me. "I won't forget this, Makarios."

I gestured to Richie and he took Paul by the arm and guided him toward the door.

Jennifer looked at me silently for a moment and then shrugged and said, "Well, since you've appropriated my cab, the least you can do is offer me a drink." She slid onto the bar stool I'd vacated and asked Chuck for a glass of Moscato. I watched as she crossed her long, shapely legs and made herself comfortable. "Did he say thirty minutes?"

"Yes. Paul doesn't live that far away."

She sipped a little bit from the glass of wine that Chuck had placed on the bar and said, "I know."

I drained what was left of my drink and pushed my glass across the bar. Chuck picked it up and quickly fixed me another. Jennifer watched him pour the Beam and then turned to me. "Do you always drink your bourbon like that?"

I smiled down at her, "A wise old colonel taught me to drink whiskey neat or with water. He told me water's almost always available when mixes aren't and besides, it's the sugar in the mixes that give you headaches."

She nodded. "My father drinks it the same way. Nothing but water."

"Good for him." I thought I'd try to get a little more information from her and about her so I asked, "Where does he live?"

"He and my mother are in Texas. Corpus Christi."

"Nice area. Is he retired like my dad?"

"No. He's a judge and still working every day. Have you ever been to Corpus?"

"Several times when I was in San Antonio on TDYs...temporary duty assignments. Did some fishing off Padre Island and down along the intercoastal canal. I like the area."

"Me too, but I've been back East for the last few years. Until I came here, that is."

We sipped our drinks in silence for a little while. I was watching her in the back-bar mirror and she was looking pensive, as if she was thinking about something from times past. I started in again. "Whereabouts back East did you live?"

She shrugged, "Oh, here and there, mostly in the Washington area. This past spring I decided I'd had enough of the traffic and people so I moved out here. This is much better."

"Yeah, I think so too. 'Course, I was raised here so I'm a little bit prejudiced. Have you and Paul been dating long?"

She turned quickly and looked straight into my eyes. "Who told you we were dating?"

"Paul told me last night after you left Central. He said you'd been dating for a couple of months." I watched her carefully. She never lost eye contact.

"He lied." She still didn't look away. "Yesterday afternoon he called to ask me out. I turned him down…again. He's asked me out several times and I've always refused. He's not my type. That's when I told him about Maddy. But you knew that already." She finally broke eye contact and picked up her wine, took a sip and looked at our reflections in the mirror. "My dealings with the Straubs have been with Rudy and Madeline. I've been to the house a couple of times to help her with piano exercises and to talk to Rudy. I don't know why Paul would say something like that." She turned back to me and went on, "He called me again this afternoon and suggested that we have dinner and discuss my participation in whatever hearings Madeline's case might bring about. I really didn't know what that would involve so I agreed. He picked me up and we got here about four thirty." She looked at her glass. "This is my third glass of wine. Paul had a few more drinks than I."

I nodded. "Yeah, that was easy to see." Richie Stevens came in and waved at me. I said, "Here's your cab. I'll walk you to the door."

She slid down from the bar stool gracefully and started for the door. I looked at our reflections in the back bar mirror. I thought we looked very good together. We walked to where Richie was holding the door open and she stopped and turned to me. "Thanks for the drink…and taking care of Paul the way you did. I don't think he's really a bad person."

"No. I've known him since we were sophomores in high school. He's arrogant and selfish but I agree that he's really not such a bad guy. Just a little full of himself and sometimes he pisses people off."

She smiled, "I think that's accurate. But it probably doesn't matter much. He told me he was leaving Muskegon soon."

"Really? I hadn't heard that rumor. Did he tell you where he planned to go?"

"Washington, I guess. He said Rudy was going to make him Chief of Staff after he was elected in November."

"What about his law practice/? He's built up quite a nice little following here. Local boy making good and all." I thought for a second or two and then went on, "Although I guess he could still manage that from DC. Other people have."

"I guess we'll just have to wait and see what happens with the election in November." She reached out and put her hand on my arm. "Thanks again, Alex." I watched appreciatively as she turned and followed Richie to the cab. And again I wondered: who is this woman? She seems too tightly controlled, too aloof and uninvolved in what has been going on. Why is that?

I paid my tab, tipped Chuck and headed across the parking lot to the Rover. It's only about a ten minute drive from the yacht club to Makarios and Sons Marina where I live. I parked on the side by the man-gate, unlocked it and made my way across the paved boat lot to the stairs up to my apartment. I took time to stop and say hello to Dusty, the big German shepherd guard dog who spent his nights under one of the boats in the yard and his days on the couch in my brother's office. Some dogs have it made. It took a few minutes for me to convince the big dog that he should stay on guard down in the boatyard and not come upstairs with me.

The apartment the folks and Theo fixed up for me is quite large with two bedrooms, a generous living area and an excellent kitchen. I like to cook when I have the time and I've fitted it out with top quality equipment and cookware. Unfortunately, on this night my cupboard was pretty bare so I fixed a quick grilled cheese sandwich, washed it down with a beer and headed for bed.

Sleep eluded me for quite a long time. I kept turning the case over and over in my mind. Who had a motive to kill Madeline Straub? Who would profit in some way from her death? Who had abused her when she was a little girl? I had the nagging feeling that it was someone in that strange family. But which one of them? And why would they do a thing like that? When I finally did drop off to sleep, I dreamed. Mostly about beautiful green eyes and lush auburn hair.

CHAPTER SIXTEEN

Our beautiful Indian summer weather held into Sunday. My brother Theo and I sat on the deck behind his house enjoying a cup of coffee and a piece of Patricia's homemade Baklava. Barbara, my only niece, was busily getting dolls from her bedroom and bringing them to me so I could tell her how pretty they were. Today was her sixth birthday and I had given her a new doll. Naturally, it was a Barbie. This one came complete with a dog and a whole bunch of other stuff. The little girl loved it. My brother managed the Makarios and Sons Marina and boat yard. When our father retired and moved to Tampa two years before, I had been back in Muskegon for only two years and on the police force for just one. Theo earned a BS in Marine Engineering at Texas A & M so he was the logical one to assume the responsibility for the family business. I was perfectly happy with that decision. I wanted to stay in law enforcement. I fell in love with police work, especially the investigative side of it, when I went through the Office of Special Investigations training at Quantico in Virginia. I never want to do anything else. Besides, Theo is three years older than I am, so as the eldest son, it was only right that he take over managing the business when dad retired. Theo and his four-man staff ran the yard and boat dealership very efficiently. I sometimes helped out on my days off. I like boats. When I was discharged from the VA hospital in Seattle in '98, I expected to move in with the folks when I came home. But they and Theo surprised me. They built a great two-bedroom apartment over the office at the boatyard for me. I even had my own private man-gate through the chain link security fence that surrounds the marina and boat yard and could come and go as I pleased.

That morning we all went to services at St Basil's, a very ornate Greek Orthodox Church out on Highland. I sort of got out of the practice of going to services regularly during my time at the Air Force Academy and later while I was on active duty. There weren't many Greek Orthodox churches in some of the places where I spent my six years in the Air Force. But I was enjoying today with the family and it was nice to see Patricia and Barbara. We talked about what was going on in our lives. Theo told me about Steve Karras's new boat, a '67 Bertram Bahia Mar with twin diesels. Theo found it for him in Florida and refitted it after it was shipped up to Muskegon. Steve had two well-equipped fishing boats now and was doing well in the salmon charter business.

"Alex, I've got just the boat for you. It's a Luhrs 29 and it's only three years old. I'll fit it out for you any way you want it." Theo has been trying to sell me a boat ever since I came back from Seattle. We both knew he'd do it eventually, but I wasn't quite ready yet.

"Bro, I think I'll pass on that for a little while. Not sure I can afford something that new. Or that big." I grinned at him. "Maybe I'll get a little sixteen-foot runabout come spring. Maybe a Whaler. I've always liked those." I was pulling his chain a little.

"C'mon, Alex. You can't go after the big ones on Lake Michigan in something that small."

"Why not? I remember that you and I used to do just that when we were kids. Little boats were all we could beg, borrow or steal back then. Of course, we weren't going for salmon in those little boats, but we caught a hell of a lot of perch." I drank some of my coffee.

Theo laughed, "Yeah, and dad made us scale every last one of them with that old fish scaler he made...three bottle caps nailed to a piece of wood. That piece of crap was crude but efficient. I still have a scar on my knee from that time I slipped with it."

I almost kissed him.

Bottle caps.

I realized that it was bottle caps that made the scars on Madeline Straub's body. I needed to call Chris and tell her and then we would go from there to find out who had done it.

Theo bugged me again, "You really need to look at this boat, Alex. It'd be a great one for you. Plenty big enough for parties and maybe sleepovers." He winked. My brother had an exaggerated idea of my sex life.

"Not just yet, Theo. But speaking of boats, what does Paul Straub have now?'

"It's a Bayliner Avanti. Nice outfit. Thirty-four-footer with all the bells and whistles. We've done some work on it a couple of times. Really fancy boat but she's not as fast as Steve's new one. Paul keeps it in his slip at the yacht club. The boys and I are going over there tomorrow to haul it out and put it on the lot for the winter."

Patricia joined us on the deck and I complimented her on the Baklava. For an outsider, she had almost mastered Greek cooking. Theo had gained about thirty pounds since they'd been married. These days he wasn't nearly as slim as he was when he was running the eight hundred meters down at the Texas A & M. After a few minutes, Patricia asked if I ever heard from my ex-wife, Cathy.

I stuffed the last bit of the sweet, gooey pastry in my mouth and shook my head. "No. I think she and her colonel are still somewhere in Japan. One of my classmates told me he ran into her at Tachikawa Air Base a month or so ago."

"Well, are you still dating that girl from Grand haven, Alex? I think she's very nice and you two seemed to be getting along pretty well. What was her name again?" Patricia sipped her coffee and smiled at me. She thought I should get married again. So did my mother.

"Her name is Janine. And no, we're not still dating. We haven't seen each other in a month or so." I laughed, "You know how summer romances go."

"What happened?" Patricia was all but holding her breath: wanting the sordid details.

"Nothing happened. She was looking for something...or some-body...that I'm not. So we just sort of called it quits. No problems. We're still friends I guess." Patricia frowned and looked disappointed but didn't ask anything more about my short fling with Janine, a nice girl looking for a husband. We had gone out a few times and we did get along well but I was not in the market for a wife. At least, not yet. I figured the right woman would come along someday if it was meant to be.

Theo asked how the case was going and I told them that since it was an open investigation, I couldn't say much. "Danny Gordon will probably have all the details in tomorrow's Journal. He's been hounding everyone in the department for two days. And of course, the TV people were all over the story last night."

Theo changed the subject, "I almost forgot. Uncle Demo called this morning before we left for church. Said he'd like you to drop by today if you can. He had heard about the murder and that last night he heard some-thing about one of the Straub boys that might interest you."

"Sure. I'll stop in at the restaurant when I leave here. I guess it's been over six weeks since I've seen him. He's always fun to visit and he does pick up some interesting information now and then." I finished my coffee and Theo refilled the cup. I said, "I need to keep in closer touch with all you guys. Sometimes the job gets in the way. Sorry." My cell phone went off just then and I dug it out of its holster on my belt. It was Richards. I listened for a couple of minutes and then said, "I'll be there as quick as I can." I turned to Theo and Patricia. "Sorry. I've got to run. They found Catherine Hood."

CHAPTER SEVENTEEN

Catherine Hood's neighborhood looked like the parking lot at police headquarters. Besides the Honda parked in the driveway, there were three patrol cars, a forensic team van and Chris Karras' ME van crammed into the drive or on the street in front of the neat white bungalow. I swung in and parked facing the wrong way on the other side of the street from her house. It was typical of the neighborhood, a white-painted, single-story frame with an attached two car garage. The lawn was neat and had recently been mowed. A few people, apparently her neighbors, attracted by the activity, unusual for a Sunday, were standing on the sidewalk in groups of two or three. Winters, one of my detectives, had his notebook out and was talking with one of the couples. I went up the walk and through the open front door and found myself in the tidy living room. Richards and Davis were in there with the forensic guys. Richards looked up when I came in.

"Where was she?" I asked.

Richards pointed at his partner, "Davis found her stuffed in the freezer out in the garage. Karras is back there now trying to figure out how long she's been crammed in there. There's no sign of forced entry. We don't see any evidence of a struggle either. It looks like she must have known whoever killed her."

I nodded. "How was she killed? Do we know that?"

"Yeah. Looks like she was choked to death. Chris said she thinks there are some bruises on her face and neck and that she'll be able to tell us more pretty soon."

I walked into the kitchen of the small house, assuming it would lead to the garage. Behind me, Richards said, "By the way, Dunphy didn't show."

I turned back into the living room. "What time was he supposed to be here?"

"We all agreed on ten o'clock."

"Shit." I turned around again and went on out into the garage.

There was a large chest-type freezer against the back wall and one of the forensic techs was dusting the edges of the propped-up lid for prints. I could see several packages wrapped in butcher paper and some frozen dinners in the bottom of the freezer. A plastic-wrapped butterball turkey, the kind with the red pop-up button, was slowly thawing in a puddle of water on the floor of the garage. I pointed to it and suggested that the tech see if she could raise any prints from the plastic. She said she'd try but it looked too wet.

Chris and her people had already pulled Catherine Hood's body from the freezer and placed her on a gurney. The dead woman was bent almost double. Chris was having a difficult time moving the victim's head so she could examine the dead woman's neck and throat. Catherine Hood's face was grey and set in a grimace of pain. I came up beside Chris and watched as she tried again to move the woman's head. She wasn't having much luck with that.

"Frozen stiff." The ME stepped back and peeled off her gloves. She looked up at me and smiled, "Well, the only thing I can tell you for sure is that she's dead. She was choked to death. I can tell already that her larynx is crushed. I think she's probably been in that freezer for at least two days. I won't be able to tell you anything else until we get her thawed out a little so we can open her up and get some internal temps. Sorry, Alex."

"I understand, Chris. You know she's been missing since late Friday afternoon. I guess it's possible that she was killed sometime that evening. Would that be about right, time-wise, for her to be frozen this completely?"

"I think so. When I get a look at her insides, I'll be able to tell more. That tissue should be less frozen and may give us a better sense of the time of death." She signaled to her crew, "Let's take her downtown so we can get to work." They began to roll the gurney to the front of the garage. She turned to me. "Steve and I saw you in church this morning, but we didn't get a chance to say 'Hi' to you or Theo and Patricia." She walked out to the van and I followed her outside. "Steve didn't have a charter this morning so he could attend services with me."

"Too bad we missed each other. Theo tells me Steve's got a new boat and is doing well."

"Oh yes. He's been awfully busy with his charters but he's happy and doing what he wants to do. We're doing fine. You need to go with him on one of his charters." She grinned, "Maybe he'll let you be the bait boy."

I laughed, "Not anymore. I did that for my dad twenty years ago. But I'll call Steve and go for a ride with him soon if the weather holds." I had been out on the lake with Steve a couple of times a few months before and we caught some nice salmon. He was a good charter captain and knew where the big fish were to be found.

"Good. He'd like that. I'll tell him you're going to call." She watched as her crew closed the door of the van. "See you later at Central when I know more about Ms. Hood." Her crew was ready to roll. She climbed into the van and waved at me as it pulled away. Then I realized I forgot to tell her about the bottle caps.

Richards and Davis came out of the garage and I told them what she had said about the estimated time of death and we agreed that it fit the scenario. We stood there for a minute or two and then I said, "Any idea why Sean didn't show up this morning?"

Davis shook his head. "Nope. Tried to call him but never got an answer on his cell or at his house."

"Did he check with you on the time yesterday?"

"Yeah. We coordinated that last night at Central. Like I said, ten o'clock was the meet time. He agreed to that...but he never showed up."

I nodded and said, "Let me take care of it. But do me a favor: don't put anything about it in your report. I'll tell the chief personally."

Richards looked doubtful and shrugged. "All right. He's your partner. If he was mine, I'd have the chief suspend his ass again...or fire him."

"I'm considering that but I want to see what Bauer has in mind first." Sean had already been suspended twice and I knew that a third time could cost him his job. While I was pissed because he'd blown his assignment today, I wanted to hear his side of the story before I recommended anything to Chief Bauer. I knew the chief was pretty well fed up with Sean and wouldn't hesitate to take his badge permanently. I really didn't want that to happen. Sean was too good a cop.

When I went back into the house, the forensics crew was finishing up. "We haven't found anything unusual in here yet. There are a lot of prints but look like they're all the same and probably belong to the victim. She kept a neat house." The tech pointed to the garage. "Can we go out there and help her finish up now? She already got some prints from the freezer but we need to dust the doors."

"I doubt if you'll find much out there. I'm guessing the killer wore gloves but maybe you can get fibers or something." I went back to the garage with them and then walked outside with Richards. "When you brief

Chief Bauer this afternoon, tell him I'm following up another lead. Don't even mention Sean. I'll take care of him when I find him."

"OK, Alex. I don't know where he could have gone off to. Is that dumbass in some kind of trouble?"

"No more than usual. He owes his bookie some gambling money but it's not enough to get him beaten up or killed over. I'm sure I'll be able to run him down before morning. Maybe I'll see you guys at Central later." I left him there and went back across the street to my car. Most of the neighbors had gone home and Winters came over to speak to me. He told me that one of the neighbors had been walking his dog at the end of the block and had seen a car parked close to Hood's house, but he couldn't identify it. I thanked him and headed downtown to the Olympus restaurant to visit with my Uncle Demo.

CHAPTER EIGHTEEN

There's not a lot of traffic on Western Avenue on Sunday afternoon so I didn't have a problem finding a parking space close to the Olympus restaurant. It was a couple of hours too early for the dinner crowd and there were only a few people in the main dining room and bar when I walked in. A couple of guys sat on the padded stools at the near end of the bar and there were only three couples seated at the four tops and booths in the big dining area. The Olympus was decorated in a Cretan motif. Lots of rectangular maze-like murals and fake upside-down cedar pillars painted in the brownish reds like the palace at Knossos adorned the walls. Uncle Demo, like my father, came from Crete. He was in his accustomed place at the far end of the bar. Gus, the regular bartender, waved 'Hi' at me as I went past. He had been a bartender at the Olympus since I was in grade school and knew me well. Uncle Demo looked up, saw me and shouted, "Alexiou…my boy. Where have you been hiding? I miss you." The few people in the place were startled by his shout but then they smiled and laughed as he came off his bar stool to give me a bearhug. The top of Uncle Demo's head barely cleared the breast pocket of my sports jacket. He stands about five foot five with shoes on and weighs a little something over two hundred pounds. Very little of that weight is fat. Demo is built like a wrestler. He has a barrel chest and massive arms. Even at age sixty or so, I believe he could hold his own in a Graeco-Roman match.

Demosthenes Kavelakos is not really my uncle. Demo is a few years younger than my dad and came to the States in '56. My father sponsored him and he worked at the boatyard for a year or so before he began working in restaurants. When he wanted to open his own place in '71, my dad lent him the money to buy the building and equipment he needed. The venture was an immediate success. It was still flourishing. Demo has always run the place with an iron hand, so the service and food are both excellent. The sign out front reads: 'Olympus Restaurant. Where Mortals Dine Like Gods.'

He pulled me onto the stool next to his and then went around behind the bar to get a glass for me. Gus stayed at the other end of the bar. He knew Demo wanted me all to himself. "Ouzo," he said as he poured double shots of the clear liquid for both of us. "Ya Mas." We touched glasses and I took a healthy swig of the anise based Greek liquor and coughed as it burned its way down. I like Ouzo but it's an acquired taste.

When my throat returned to normal, I said, "Uncle Demo, how've you been? I think it's been over a month since I've been in to see you. What's going on with you?"

"Everything is good, Alex. We are doing fine." He put his hand on my arm and a concerned look swept over his broad face. "But you...you are busy with a murder. How does that happen in a city like this?" He poured some more of the clear liquor in my glass. I slid off the stool to go behind the bar and get an ice cube. I dropped it in the drink and watched the ouzo turn milky white. It's better chilled.

Back on the stool again I said, "I don't know what to tell you. We've got a tough case on our hands." I sipped some of the drink. "Theo told me you might have some information that would interest me. What have you heard?" I knew Demo heard a lot of things at the bar and in the dining room. He had very good ears.

"Ya. Last night I heard a customer say he saw Peter Straub get in a fight out at Colletti's. It was just about closing time and this fellow had just come in and was talking to one of his friends here at the bar. He told him he wasn't sure who the other guy in the fight was but he thought it might have been Fumbles Cernak." He cocked his head and looked at me. "You know this Fumbles?" I smiled and nodded, and he went on, "He said the boss out there hollered at them and the Straub boy left." Demo shook his balding head. "I thought you should know. I think that Straub boy should have been home with his family. My God, it was only one day after his sister was killed? Such a terrible thing. Why was he out at a place like Colletti's so soon after?"

"I don't know, Demo, maybe I'll go out there and see what I can find out."

"Out where? And find out what?" Jennifer Clayton was standing just to my right and her entrance had caught both Demo and me by surprise. Neither of us had seen her come in. I got off the bar stool as quickly as I could. She was dressed in workout clothes: a pale green warm-up suit of running pants and matching jacket with Asics running shoes. Her auburn hair was pulled back in a ponytail. She looked wonderful.

I finally managed to say 'Hi' and then went tongue-tied again.

Uncle Demo, always the gracious host, bailed me out. He was off his bar stool and looking up at her before I could say another word. "Good afternoon, Miss. Won't you join us for a glass of ouzo? I was telling Alex here all about what I have been doing since he left us." That, of course, was a blatant lie but he went right on. "Did you know that he used to work here? No? Sometime you must ask him to tell you about his days in the kitchen here at the Olympus restaurant." Uncle Demo was having a grand old time with all of this but I finally came to and jumped in and introduced them.

"Ms. Clayton...Jennifer, this is my Uncle Demo. He owns the place. Will you have a drink with us?"

She put out her hand and Demo took it gently in both of his, smiled up at her and said softly, "It is a very great pleasure to meet such a beautiful woman as you Ms. Clayton". He could be very courtly when the situation called for it. She smiled and said, "Thank you. What are you drinking? I've just come from working out and I took a long run on the beach afterwards." She smiled up at me, "I saw your Rover out in front so I thought I'd just stop and say hello and see how things are going with the investigation."

Demo went behind the bar to get her a glass and some more ice for me and I helped her onto the stool I had just vacated. I decided not to tell her about Catherine Hood right then. I didn't intend to keep the information from her but I didn't believe this was the time or the place. Demo came back to us and I waited until he had poured the drinks. He picked his glass up and gave the traditional toast 'Ya Mas'.

Jennifer took a little sip of the clear liquid in her glass, coughed and said, "What does that mean?" She looked down at her drink and added, "And what is this stuff?" Demo and I laughed.

I told he, "'Ya Mas' means 'I drink to our health'...kind of like 'cheers' or 'prosit'. And this stuff is ouzo. It's a Greek national drink."

"Tastes like licorice. But stronger." She made a face and put her glass on the bar. Turning to me, she said, "So where are you going, Alex?"

"Uncle Demo told me something that might give me a lead on where we can find Peter Straub. I'm going to check it out." Suddenly I had a brainstorm. "How would you like to come with me? It shouldn't take us more than an hour or two." If she agreed to go with me to Colletti's, I'd have the opportunity to tell her about Catherine Hood's murder in private. And I wanted to spend some time alone with her. A lot of time, I thought.

"Can I go dressed like this? Or should I go home and change into something else?"

I thought she looked absolutely perfect. I'm a sucker for the athletic type: especially when they dress the part. She could have posed for a Nike ad in Sports Illustrated. I finally managed to say. "No problem, you look great in that outfit." Demo beamed at me and nodded his head in approval. I said, "Colletti's is a restaurant and bar out in the county a little north of here. It's possible that Peter was out there last night and, if he was, I want to know what he was up to." I took another small sip of ouzo. "There's no rush, though. Enjoy your drink."

She hesitated and then picked up the glass and took another small sip. Demo watched her make a face again and then he broke in, "Perhaps you would prefer something else? A glass of wine? Retsina, maybe?" He started for the back bar.

Jennifer looked at me, "What's that? Another Greek national drink?"

"Sort of. It's a kind of wine. Tastes a lot like a pine tree." Another acquired taste.

Demo came back to us with a bottle of Retsina and prepared to open it. I stopped him and said, "Uncle Demo, I don't think we have time to try that today. I think we should get going after all. I promise I'll come back to see you when we get this case wrapped up. It probably won't be tomorrow but maybe sometime before next weekend. Maybe I'll come for dinner. That all right with you?"

"Yes, good." He put the bottle of Retsina on the bar and said, "We will have this bottle next time." He looked hard at me and said, "You will bring this young lady with you. I will have something special prepared for you both when you come back." Then he turned to Jennifer and took her hand again, "It is a pleasure to meet you…and I hope Alex brings you back here many times."

I was hoping the same thing but I didn't know what Jennifer was thinking. She blushed a little and thanked him for the drink. Turning to me, she grinned and said, "Shall we go? I want to hear about your days in your uncle's kitchen. Can you really cook?"

CHAPTER NINETEEN

We said goodbye to Demo and went out to my Rover. Her Mustang was parked about four spaces down the block. I opened the door for her and she settled into the passenger seat. I thought she looked good there; like she belonged. We pulled away and started down Western, turning right off the avenue onto Fourth and then picking up Muskegon Avenue, the north bound lane of Business 31. Neither of us said anything for a few blocks and when we reached the Causeway and the first bridge over the river, I said, "Jennifer, I've got some bad news to tell you. I'm going to pull into that little parking area on the right so we can talk."

She looked at me and nodded as I turned into the graveled area near the two small picnic shelters on the bank of the South Channel of the Muskegon River. Turning to her, I said, "I guess there's no way to soften this. We found Catherine Hood's body at her home this morning. I'm so sorry I have to tell you this." She clenched her hands into fists and turned away from me toward the side window. I saw her shoulders heave once in the convulsion of a sob. There were tears in her eyes when she turned back to face the front. I went on. "She was murdered. We think it probably happened sometime late Friday afternoon or evening. Most likely before you and Sean went to her place to pick her up.."

"How was she killed?" Her voice broke as she stifled a sob.

"She was strangled."

The tears spilled over. "Oh God." She fished in her jacket pocket for a tissue without any luck and I handed her my handkerchief. She dabbed at her eyes and nose and then faced me. "Do you think it might have been the same person that killed Maddy?"

"We believe it probably was. We can't come up with anyone else who would have a motive. We think Ms. Hood may have seen whoever killed Madeline, but we'll never know for sure." I put my hand on her shoulder. "I'm sorry, Jennifer. I know you cared for her."

She wiped her eyes again and balled my handkerchief up in her fist. "I really didn't know Catherine that well, but she was a sweet person." She raised her head and looked straight into my eyes. "You're going to find whoever did this, aren't you, Alex?"

"Yes. We'll get the killer…and soon. We think we're getting closer but there are still some loose ends and a lot of questions." I waited a minute and then said, "Do you still want to go out to Colletti's with me or would you rather I take you home now?"

She gave me a half smile and dabbed at her eyes and nose again. "I think I'll stay with you for a while. I really don't want to be alone right now." She looked through the window at the picnic tables. "Maybe if you find Peter, he'll be of some help."

"I'm sure of that. He's the last one of the family who saw Madeline. He's one of the loose ends we need to tie up."

I pulled back out onto the highway and we headed north across the Causeway again. Jennifer stared out through the windshield at the gathering darkness and after a few minutes she said, "You didn't answer my question."

"What question was that?"

"I asked if you can really cook. I'm sure the answer is yes, what with all your experience in your uncle's restaurant."

I laughed. "Uncle Demo was putting you on. First of all, Demo is not really my uncle. He's just a close friend of the family. It's true that I did work in the kitchen of the Olympus when I was twelve or thirteen. But that was because when I got into some sort of trouble, like staying out past curfew or not doing what my mom or dad told me to, my dad would send me down to Demo's for a day or two. I'd live in the back room at the restaurant and wash dishes for my keep. Eventually Uncle Demo let me help with some of the food prep and I did learn quite a lot. I believe the most important thing I learned was that I didn't want to do that for the rest of my life. I still believe that was my dad's point."

She laughed a little bit and then asked, "What do you expect to find out at this place?'

"Demo heard that Peter was out there last night and had a tussle with someone. Could of been a bookie named Fumbles Cernak. The owner, Gino Colletti, broke it up." I shrugged, "But maybe Gino knows where Peter is holed up. We'll see."

She had turned in the seat so that she was almost facing me. She was more relaxed now and had composed herself. "Fumbles is a funny nickname. Not very positive, is it?"

I had to agree. "No. The guy's real name is Anton Cernak. In '83, his senior year in high school, he was the top running back in the state. He made 'All Conference' three times and 'All State' his junior and senior years. He was a cinch to go to college on a full ride and then maybe on to the pros. But he blew all of that. Now he runs a second-rate pool hall and does a little bookmaking on the side."

"How in the world did that happen?" She seemed genuinely concerned.

"It happened during his senior season. In the conference championship game against Benton Harbor, he fumbled the ball three times. Twice on the same series. We were three yards away from the goal line the second time. We lost by less than a touchdown." I still felt the pain of that loss. I was a sophomore and played wide receiver on that team. "The next week someone at school called him 'Fumbles' and everyone took it up. It really got to him. He dropped out of school after Christmas and never graduated. He started drinking and then he got into some serious trouble. Car theft, petty larceny and things like that. When he was about twenty, he got in a fight one night and nearly killed a guy. He did three years for aggravated assault down in Jackson. After he was released, he managed to straighten himself out. He got past the nickname and doesn't seem to mind that everyone uses it." I smiled at her, "Other than being a bookie, Fumbles keeps his nose clean and really is an okay guy. I know him pretty well."

Jennifer shook her head. "What a tragedy. That's a terrible waste of a life. And all because of a nickname."

"Yeah, words can hurt worse than bullets sometimes." I was thinking of Rudy Straub calling me a 'Greek cripple' in Bauer's office. I promised myself he'd pay for that someday. I pulled into the black-topped parking lot of Colletti's and we got out and went in.

Colletti's was a big place. All one big room with a long bar on the wall to the left of the entrance and two dozen six-top tables in a horseshoe around a medium sized dance floor. There were quite a few people in there for a Sunday evening. I guessed that most of them had spent the day outdoors taking advantage of the beautiful weather, probably they'd been on the lake or just driving around, enjoying the day. Gino and his wife, Angela, were sitting at a table back in the corner near the bar. A bottle of some sort of Italian red wine and a stack of upside-down glasses were in the center of the table. It looked as though they were expecting company.

We walked past the bar and and over to Gino's table. I didn't know him as well as I knew most of the bar and restaurant owners in Muskegon. Gino Colletti had come to Muskegon from the Boston area while I was away. He bought an old roadhouse named the 'Copper Kettle' shortly after he arrived and remodeled it, turning it into a nice restaurant and bar. Of course, Italian food was the specialty of the house and it was excellent. There was a small dance floor and Gino brought in live music on the weekends. It was popular with the younger crowd and there was seldom any trouble. There was a rumor that Gino was in the Witness Protection Program, but I doubted that. He was too visible. Gino weighed about three hundred pounds and some people referred to him as 'Fat Gee' but no one ever called him that to his face. I thought it probably wouldn't be a healthy thing to do. Everyone else just called him 'Gee' or 'Big Gee'. His wife, Angela, was a buxom blonde who was just a little overweight. She had obviously been a real knock-out when she was younger and she still looked pretty good. I stuck out my hand and said, "Hello, Gee... Mrs. C. How are you tonight?"

He remembered who I was after a minute and reluctantly shook hands with me. "I'm fine, Makarios. What brings you way out here to my place? This is county, not city."

"I'm not working, Gee. But, if you don't mind, I would like to ask you a question or two. I'm just looking for some information."

"No, I guess not. Sit down. Have some wine." He took two glasses from the stack and turned them right side up on the table. Angela poured them full. Gee sat back and said, "I won't answer the questions if I don't want to... you know that, don't you?"

"Sure. That's fine with me." I introduced Jennifer and we sat down. I took a sip of the wine. It was good. The label on the bottle told me it was a Barbera and I made a mental note to get some. I said, "Gee, I heard a rumor about Peter Straub getting into a beef with Fumbles Cernak out here last night. Any truth to that?"

He took a big swallow of wine and looked into the glass before he said, "Yeah, they were here. Fumbles and me was havin' a couple of drinks and talking and the Straub kid comes in and sort of wanders around over there by the bar." He waved his big right arm in its general direction. "Fumbles says 'I gotta see that jerk' and went over to him. I couldn't hear what they was sayin' 'cause the band was kinda loud." He turned to Jennifer. "We gotta band comes in on Saturday nights. You should come out sometime." Gee took another swallow of wine and came back to me. "Pretty soon Fumbles grabs hold of the kid and slaps him across the face two, three times. Then he kind of lifts him off the floor and shakes him like a dog with a rag doll. He shoved the kid toward the door and started to follow him. I know Fumbles has kind of a temper sometimes and I figure he's going to mess the kid up so I get up and holler at him. Fumbles kinda shrugs and lets the boy go outside. Then he comes back to the table and we drink some more." He turned to his wife, "That about right, Ang? You was here."

She refilled Gee's glass and nodded. "Yeah. I think that Straub kid was kinda out of it. Acted funny."

"What do you mean 'funny'?" I asked. "Was he drunk?"

She shook her blonde head. "No. Not exactly drunk. I watched him when he came in. I think he mighta been high on something. Didn't seem to know where he was. Just walked back and forth in front of the bar for maybe like ten minutes or so. Didn't order anything and then Fumbles went up to him." She shrugged. "Maybe he was coked up. I heard he uses that crap sometimes. I seen guys on that before. That hard stuff is murder."

"You have any idea where Peter's staying or where he was going when he left here last night?"

Gee and Angela both shook their heads. Gee said, "Not a clue. Last I hear he lives with his old man. The only time he comes out here is to lay a bet, collect if he wins something or pay me if he loses."

"He owe you any money now, Gee?"

He looked at me, stone-faced. "That's one of those questions I won't answer."

"I got that." I shrugged and smiled at him. "Just asking."

Jennifer turned to me wide-eyed. She had a 'He just admitted that he's a bookie. Aren't you going to arrest him?' look on her face.

I smiled at her, shook my head and drank some more of the good wine. "Thanks for the information, Gee. You know the kid's sister was killed last Friday." He and Angela both nodded. "Heard anything about that from anyone coming around?"

"Not a peep. I don't understand why anyone would want to whack that kid. She was a smart girl and pretty good lookin' too."

I jumped on that. "You knew her? Did she come out here very often?"

Angela spoke up, "She was here maybe three, four times with a couple other girls and her brother once or twice. We knew who she was 'cause of her old man. Nice kid. Behaved herself."

"Which brother was with her when she came here?"

She thought for a minute. "I think it was the kid once and the lawyer the other time. She was always kind of quiet. Would have a glass or two of wine. Never caused a problem."

I finished my wine and looked at Jennifer. She had only taken about four sips of her wine and the glass was still over half full. I saw Gee looking at her glass too. He spoke, "What's the matter? You don't like my wine?"

"No, it's not that. This is a very good one. I'm just not into wine tonight." She smiled at him and continued, "Maybe I'll come back some time and drink some grappa with you and your wife."

The big man's eyebrows shot up and he leaned forward. "You know about grappa? How come?"

Jennifer laughed, "When I was in college, I had a roommate who was from Baltimore. She was second generation Italian and every time she came back from visiting her folks up there, she would bring a couple of bottles of good wine back to the dorm. I went to Baltimore with her on a few breaks and was introduced to real Italian food and fine wine when I was pretty young." She smiled at him again and said, "And that included grappa."

Gee beamed at her and turned to me, "You got to bring this girl back out here, Alex. We'll have some dinner and a little party." I thought, so now he calls me 'Alex' like I'm a good friend. A little while ago he barely recognized me. Man, that is a big step forward.

"I'll do that, Gee, if she'll ever go out with me again." I glanced at Jennifer and she smiled and nodded. "But now it's getting late and we've got to get out of here. I appreciate the information...and the wine. I'll probably talk to Fumbles again tomorrow. We really need to find Peter."

"When you do find the kid, tell him to come and see me...and tell him to make it soon." Gee smiled like a shark eyeing a surfboarder.

CHAPTER TWENTY

We were on our way back into town when Jennifer asked me, "If you know this Fumbles guy and the fat man back there are bookies, why don't you arrest them? Gambling is still against the law in the state of Michigan, isn't it?"

"Yeah, it is, except for the lottery, church bingo and the Indian casinos. But Gee and Fumbles are small timers. They provide an outlet for working people to bet on football games or whatever sport they want to without getting tied up with the organized crime guys out of Chicago or Detroit. Most of the bets they handle are pretty small and there's only about five of these bookies in the county. We watch all of 'em pretty closely to see that no one gets hurt. I mean physically. That's why Tony called Fumbles off the Straub boy last night. All the books know that if someone gets beaten up or killed because of a gambling debt, we'll shut all of them down." I smiled. "Besides, we get a lot of information from these guys."

"But it looks like you're not enforcing the law of the state. Does your chief know about all this?"

"You bet he does. Chief Bauer was a street cop when the Chicago and Detroit mobs were in deep here. They were running numbers, high stakes crap and poker games and some betting parlors with terrible odds. All of that besides controlling the sports betting. Some people got hurt pretty badly. Bull Bauer helped clean that bunch out. He knows that some of us are looking the other way on the small stuff. And he also knows we're keeping close tabs on it so no one gets seriously hurt." I looked over at her. She didn't look convinced that it was all right. I continued, "We would rather deal with the locals that we know as opposed to the unknowns that would come in here from outside. Muskegon is too close to the big cities and those guys have been here before. We don't want 'em here again."

We were almost into the city and I said, "Let's pick up your car so you can get on home."

She glanced at me and said, "No. I think I'd rather get it in the morning. Could you just take me home, please?"

I looked over at her and nodded, "Sure. I'll be happy to do that." Really happy. It meant that I would get to spend a little more time with her. I couldn't help myself. I really wanted to know her better and I was hoping that we would find that we enjoyed each other's company and would continue to see one another when these cases were closed.

I turned off Webster onto the north end of Lakeshore, drove down the wide street to her house and pulled into the driveway. The yellow crime scene tape was gone from the front door and the neighborhood was quiet. Lights were on in the upstairs apartment but the ground floor of the house was dark. I said, "Here you are. Safe and sound." We didn't think Jennifer was in any danger but we had set up a patrol of the area just to be safe. I knew there was a black-and-white prowling around somewhere close even if she didn't.

Jennifer didn't make any move to get out of the Rover. She was looking straight ahead through the windshield. Then she turned to me, "Alex, Would you come in for a minute? After what happened to Catherine, I don't want to be alone just yet."

I said 'Sure', opened my door and got out. She had the passenger door open and was out and walking to the porch before I could get around the car. She unlocked the front door and hit a switch, flooding the hallway with light. The doors to the studio and the offices were closed and the yellow cop tape still covered all four of them. She led the way down the hall to her apartment door. Unlocking it, she said, "It's not much but it's convenient to the studio. Come in, please."

She went in and I followed her into a large living room. It was furnished in what I thought of as 'model home chic'. The furniture was good but it had the look of being temporary. It appeared to be comfortable enough for someone who didn't expect to use it for very long. Pointing to the marble topped counter that separated the kitchen area from the living room, she said "Fix yourself a drink if you want one. I'll be right back." She disappeared into what I supposed was a bedroom.

I walked over to the counter and looked at the small array of bottles. There was a nice variety of liquor but most of the bottles were unopened. I really wasn't sure I wanted a drink but the open bottle of Jim Beam tempted me and I poured an inch or so into a rocks glass. I turned around and surveyed the room. There were only a few decorations. Five framed prints of New Yorker covers were arranged on the wall over the sofa and the opposite wall was dominated by a large monochrome oil painting. About two and a half by three feet, it was a portrait of an elderly Asian woman facing slightly to the left. Done entirely in shades of brown that picked up the color of the massive frame that surrounded it, the painting would have overpowered a smaller room. It seemed to fit its allotted space perfectly. I went closer and saw that it was signed C. Yonaha and dated nineteen seventy-one.

Jennifer came out of the bedroom and I pointed at the painting and said, "That's impressive. Where did you get it?"

"My ex found it in Okinawa and brought it back. He was in the Marines and was stationed at Camp Hansen for a while. Do you like it?"

"Yeah. A friend of mine in Virginia has the mate to it. It's the old man and he's facing right. He found it in Okinawa too. I've always liked the way the artist got the details of the man's facial expression even though it's only in shades of brown. I tried to buy it from him once."

She picked up a pack of cigarettes from the coffee table and drew one out. "You still don't have a light, do you?"

I shook my head. "You know you should quit."

"Yes, you're right. It's a habit I picked up a couple of years ago." She played with the cigarette but didn't light it. "Please sit down, Alex. Unless you're in a hurry."

"No. I'm in no rush. This is nice." I raised my glass in salute, "Thanks for the drink. It's been a long day." I moved to an embroidered wing chair that looked uncomfortable and out of place with the rest of the furniture. When I sat down, I knew my assessment of the chair's comfort was correct. I would much rather have sat on the couch next to her but I didn't think this was the right time.

She sat down and pulled her legs up underneath. She dropped the unlit cigarette into the spotless ashtray on the coffee table. "Do you have any real suspects in Maddy's case yet? Or in Catherine's?"

"We've got some ideas but you know I can't discuss that with you." She nodded and didn't seem concerned. I sipped the bourbon and smiled at her. "You know, Ms. Clayton, while you're not exactly a suspect, I guess you are a 'person of interest' as the newspaper put it."

"Please call me Jennifer. You don't have to be quite so formal after today." She picked the cigarette up again and toyed with it for a moment but put it down. I noticed that there was a lighter on the end table, but she was obviously ignoring it. I realized then that she didn't smoke at all. There was no smell of cigarette smoke in the apartment or anywhere about her. The cigarette business was an act of some sort. She changed the subject.

"From what I saw at the yacht club last night, I would guess you and Paul Straub have of history of some kind."

"Yeah. You could say that. We go way back to our high school days. Just the usual competition. Sports, girls, that sort of stuff. But I doubt that you ever had to worry about anything like that. I can't think of any way another girl could compete with you."

Jennifer laughed and said, "Well, aren't you the gallant one. I'll take that as a compliment, and I thank you."

I blushed and gulped at my drink. "Maybe I went too far. Sorry."

"Oh, not at all. But I'm thinking that if I am still a 'person of interest' we probably shouldn't be seeing each other socially, should we?"

"Good point. And you're absolutely right." I stood and put what was left of my drink on the coffee table. "Again, thanks for the drink." I hesitated a moment. "I really enjoyed being with you today, Jennifer. Perhaps I'll see you tomorrow." I opened the apartment door and stepped into the hall. "Maybe when this is all sorted out we can do this again. We have been invited to dinner twice today."

She followed me into the hallway and we walked to the front door side by side in silence. At the door she turned and smiled up at me. "Yes, that's true. We have. I'm sure we should take them both up on their invitations. I'd like that. Good night, Alex…and thank you."

I closed the door behind me and walked across the porch and down the steps. Yeah, I said to myself, I'd like that too. Very much.

CHAPTER TWENTY-ONE

When I got to Central early on Monday morning Sean was waiting for me in the parking lot. He looked good. His jacket was clean and pressed and his shoes carried the gleam of new polish. When I got closer, I could see that he was clean shaven for a change and he even had a touch of cologne or aftershave on him somewhere. I cut him off before he could start to explain. "Don't say anything, Sean. We're going in with Richards and Davis to brief the chief on everything we found out yesterday. All you have to know right now is that Catherine Hood was murdered. You just listen and learn what you missed. And keep your mouth shut. I'll do the talking for us. When we get through with that, you and I will have a sit down where no one else is around. Got it?"

He nodded and said "Yeah. I can explain…"

I grabbed him by the shoulder and spun him around to face me. "Did you not hear me? I said keep your mouth shut. You and I will talk later." I let him go and headed for the entrance to Central. "C'mon. We don't want to be late."

Richards and Davis were almost at Bauer's door when we came into the squad room. I pushed Sean ahead of me and gave a brief wave to Richards as we went past Officer Haney's desk. She looked at Sean and then at me with real concern in her eyes. I tried to smile at her but I don't think it was one of my better efforts. I wondered if maybe she had something to do with Sean's disappearance on Sunday or his appearance today. Richards gestured toward Sean and asked if everything was all right. I told him we were fine and we went into Bauer's den.

The chief was not in a good mood. He had two murders on his hands and no suspects in custody for either one. He glowered at the four of us for a long minute, picked his cigar out of the ash tray and said, "What have you got that's good?"

Richards looked at me and I shrugged so he started. "Chief, the only things we know for sure is that the Hood woman was choked to death, probably sometime late Friday. We couldn't find any prints in that house that didn't belong to the victim so it's likely the killer wore gloves. None of the neighbors saw or heard anything out of the ordinary on Friday. No one knew the vic well. She was a retired teacher and kept to herself." He looked at his notes. "No family and no known relatives here or anywhere else that we've found so far. We're following up on her employment." He looked up in frustration, "There has to be someone, somewhere."

Bauer looked at me. "You think these two killings are connected?"

I'd given that some thought but had nothing solid, so I said, "They almost have to be. We don't have a clue as to motive for the Straub girl's murder but maybe Hood saw the killer when she went into the studio. Or maybe the killer just thought he was seen. That would be a reason for him to go after her. The killer might have gone out of Clayton's place through the front door and maybe she spotted him from her office. Or maybe he or she came in and out through the other studio door. We don't know. I'm just guessing here. But I do think that Madeline Straub knew her killer. She didn't seem alarmed or surprised when whoever it was came into the studio."

He pointed the cigar at Richards. "That make sense to you?"

Richards and Davis both nodded and mumbled 'yes'.

Bauer turned to Sean, "You got anything to add, Dunphy?"

Sean looked at me and then said, "No, Chief. I don't have anything to add. I agree with them."

Bauer sat back and chewed on his cigar for a little bit before he came back to us. "I don't know what to tell you guys except get your asses out there and find someone who knows something about one or both of these murders. You need to find someone with a motive for the girl's murder." The cigar came my way, "You're lead on the Straub girl." The cigar migrated to Richards, "You've got the Hood case." The cigar went back to the ash tray. "Both of you keep me and each other in the loop on what you're doing." He sighed, "I'm getting a lot of flak from the mayor and the media on this. I expected that. But Rudy Straub is high profile and a candidate for senator, so the party has been all over me about how this will affect his chances in November." He looked at us with a sheepish grin, "How the hell am I supposed to know anything about that? I got no crystal ball. In my opinion, he should drop out and take care of his family." We all nodded in agreement and I started to ask if that was all when Chris Karras came through the door with the inevitable sheaf of papers.

Bauer looked at her and said, "You didn't knock…again."

"No, Chief, you're right as usual; I didn't." She dropped the papers on his desk and sat down, waving a cheerful 'Hi" to the four of us still standing. "That's the Hood autopsy." She smiled at the chief, "I know you won't read it so I'll just tell you what we found."

Bauer picked up his cigar again and sat back. "Fine. Give the paperwork to Richards this time. Hood's his case."

Chris must have been up all night doing the autopsy but she looked as though she had gotten a full night of beauty sleep. She took a small notebook out of her scrubs pocket and faced us. "She was strangled…or rather choked to death manually. Her jaw was broken…left side. There were no defensive wounds on her hands. No bruising anywhere else. The broken jaw happened immediately before she was choked. The contusion from that had barely started to form before she died." She looked up at us. "It looks like the killer struck her once and knocked her out. Then he or she immediately choked her. It must have been a surprise blow and very hard. Forensics found some drag marks on the carpet in the living room. They led to the kitchen." She glanced at Richards, "Although the area was pretty well walked over by your search team before forensics got there."

I asked, "How much did Ms. Hood weigh?"

Chris looked at her notes, "One fifty-seven. With her clothes, she probably weighed one sixty-two or three."

"So our killer dragged her across the living room and the kitchen into the garage and then picked her up and stuffed her into that freezer. It would take a strong man or woman to do that." I didn't have a formal list of suspects but was mentally reviewing the physical capabilities of the Straub family. I didn't eliminate anyone.

Chris continued, "That sounds right. There was nothing else of significance. The killer came in, hit her, killed her and froze her. Took us six hours to get her thawed out enough so that we could do our jobs."

Bauer growled and pointed his cigar at Richards, "Who's on your suspect list?

"Right now, the whole Straub family. Do we know if Rudy stayed in Grand Rapids all day on Friday?"

"Not yet. Chief Lyle is supposed to call me this morning. His guys were checking on Straub and that kid that drives him around."

I spoke up, "We've got another lead on Peter that we'll follow up on when we leave here. He's the missing link in this thing and until we talk to him, we're still sort of blind."

"Could he have done it?" Chris's question caused us all to think for a minute.

Richards answered, "Hell yes. Any one of them has the capability. But what's the motive? Why would a parent kill their child? Or a brother kill his sister?" He stopped. "Is there anyone else we've overlooked?"

The chief took his cigar out of his mouth. "Winters found some of her girlfriends and talked to three of them." He shuffled through the papers on his desk and finally came up with the ones he wanted. "They all said she was pretty shy. Kept to herself a lot. One of the girls was in school with her down at Western. Seems she lived in the dorm down in Kalamazoo her freshman year but her family made her come back here for the second year." He read for a minute. "That's odd. She went back to Kalamazoo for her junior year and then came back here again to finish. Her girlfriend said she thought her father made her come home." He finished reading Winters's report and handed it to me. "The girls say she didn't go out much and they don't know of any serious boyfriend. That looks like kind of a dead end but keep asking around."

We all agreed with that and stood there for a couple of minutes trying to think of something useful to add. Bauer broke it up saying, "All right, get back to work. Makarios, you stick around for a minute. We need to talk."

The others filed out, Richards giving me the eye and nodding toward Sean. Chris smiled and rolled her eyes as she passed me. Then she stopped and said, "Bottle caps."

I looked at her. "The marks on Madeline's body? The circles? I figured that out, too. Forgot to tell you yesterday."

"I think someone put a bottle cap on her and smacked it hard or ground it in. I tried it and beer bottle caps will cut into the skin if you hit 'em hard enough. I'm pretty sure that's what made those marks." She went on, "We counted the scars. There are twenty-three separate marks. We can't tell for certain when they were made but there are no recent ones. From the amount of healing tissue, it looks like the latest ones were made maybe ten or more years ago. The earliest look like they go back to when she was six or seven years old." I didn't want to know how she had tested her theory or what she had tested it on so I just thanked her and motioned for Sean to go out. I turned to face the chief.

"Sit down." Bauer's tone was not friendly. He put the cigar away again, folded his hands and leaned forward. "You really screwed up. You know that, don't you?"

I knew where he was going with this. It had been bugging me since yesterday and I had lost sleep over it last night. I nodded and looked him in the eye. "I know. Catherine Hood is dead because of my mistake. If I had kept her at the crime scene on Friday, she would still be alive."

He leaned back. "Possibly. I think if the killer thought he'd been seen, whoever it was would have found a time and place to silence her in any case. But you're right. You do bear some responsibility for her death."

"It's something I'll never be able to let go, Chief."

"Yeah. I'm sure that's true. Whenever someone dies or is killed and you have some part in it, it is pretty hard to forget. But I wouldn't dwell on it too much. Like I said, I think the killer

would have gotten to her anyway." He leaned over the desk again. "Here's how this is going down. Neither of the patrolmen who arrived to back you up Friday night saw the woman. They went inside with you and when you told Rogers to check the outside, her car was already gone." He paused, "All of this is in their reports and it is all true."

That didn't make me feel any better. It was my mistake that let her get away and put her in a vulnerable position. I thought for a minute and then said, "Madeline's killer must still have been close by when I got there. Whoever it was saw Hood leave and must have followed her. I think she also knew whoever killed her since there was no sign of forced entry at her house."

"That makes sense. Where could someone park near the place on Lakeshore?"

"Most anywhere on the street. Or in the alley. Or on one of the side streets, Cascade or Piedmont. If you parked in front or on Cascade, you could probably see the house and the driveway where Hood's car was parked."

He stood up, "All right. That's all for now. Go find the Straub kid and let's see what he's got to say about all this. But remember, Makarios. Your ass belongs to me if you screw up again."

CHAPTER TWENTY-TWO

Sean was perched on the edge of officer Haney's desk when I came out of Bauer's office. The way they were leaning into each other and the looks on their faces confirmed my suspicion that there was something up between the two of them. I wouldn't consider Sean to be a chaser but he had been around with a couple of women in the six months we'd been working together. I thought young Officer Haney seemed much too nice a girl to be fooling around with a gambler and boozer like him. But what did I know? I hadn't picked a winner yet. Besides, it was none of my business. I headed for the door and said, "Let's go, Sean." As I passed them, he patted her on the shoulder and followed me to the parking lot.

"We'll talk later." I cut him off before he could start giving me his alibi for Sunday. I was still pissed at him and I wanted to stay hard-assed with him for a while.

"Okay. Where we goin'?"

"Smokin' Joe's. I need to talk with Buddy again. I think he knows more than he told us the other day. I really hate the idea that he lied to us but it's a possibility and I want to be certain."

He settled back in the seat of the patrol car and pretty soon he cleared his throat and said, "Um…could we stop by Sharkey's on the way?"

"What?" I almost lost control when I turned and looked at him. "Are you serious?"

He grinned sheepishly and said, "Yeah. I got the money for Fumbles and I want to give it to him."

I swung the car over to the curb and cut the engine. I couldn't believe what he was telling me. Had this dumbass managed to place a big enough bet on one of yesterday's pro games and hit it for enough to pay Fumbles the two thousand dollars? No way, I thought. First of all, he couldn't have found a book that would handle it for him. Secondly, he's not that lucky. And if that's what he did and if that's why he skipped on his assignment; I'll kill him. I sat for a minute while all this was running through my head and then I said, "OK. Tell me what's goin' on."

"I better start at the beginning."

"That's a damn good idea. Try starting from Saturday night."

"Yeah. After we left Central, I stopped at the Inn on my way home. I was really feeling down and worried about the money for Fumbles. I guess I had two or three fast drinks before Sandy came in."

"Sandy? Who's Sandy?"

"Officer Haney. Her first name is Sandra." He smiled, "Anyway when she came in, she sat down with me and we started talking. I wound up telling her all about my problem with Fumbles and a lot of other things. We had a couple more drinks...or at least I did. I think maybe she had one glass of wine. I don't really remember. When the Inn closed, we went to her place and I guess I passed out. Didn't wake up until way after I was supposed to meet Richards and Davis at Hood's house. I had a terrible headache and didn't think I'd be any good to those guys anyway, so I stayed at Sandy's place with her. Later we went out to my house and I got some clothes and stuff. We went back to her place and ate dinner and talked some more. I told her everything...about my gambling and drinking. I spent last night there, too." He looked at me, "But we didn't do anything. I never touched her." He looked straight at me. "I didn't drink anything yesterday either."

I was amazed. This girl was obviously a good influence on the big Irishman. Maybe he'd finally found someone who could help him straighten out. I honestly hoped so. My hard-ass attitude was beginning to soften a little at the edges. I waited for him to continue.

He looked away and out the side window for a moment and then went on, "Sandy told me her dad was an alcoholic and abandoned her and her mother when she was fifteen." He turned back to me, "Kinda like what happened to me. But without the beatings. She has an occasional drink but doesn't like to see people go overboard…like I do sometimes. She wants me to go to an AA meeting this week." He looked back outside, "But I'm not sure I'm ready to do that yet."

"You know what you're in for if you go, don't you?"

"Yeah. I joined once before. But I didn't last long." He shrugged a little. "Truth is, I like the taste of the stuff."

I understood what he was saying. "I know you do, Sean. I like the taste too. But you don't know enough to quit after a couple. You drink until you get drunk. You're not exactly what's known as a social drinker."

"You're right. But maybe I can just cut back." He sounded hopeful. "With Sandy's help I think that might work for me."

"Sean, it's worth a try. I think it would help you." I put my hand on his shoulder, "But it's going to be tough. You realize that, don't you?"

He looked out through the window again. "I know. I really like this girl, Alex. She's a good girl and a good cop besides."

"I'm not gonna forget that you busted an assignment yesterday but I covered for you and the chief doesn't know what happened. Nothing more will be said. Just don't do it again, you hear?"

"Yeah. I understand."

"One more thing. Where the hell did you get two thousand bucks all of a sudden?"

He grinned foolishly, "Sandy gave it to me this morning." He put his hands up, "I didn't ask her for it. She just gave it to me when we were having breakfast. She says it's a loan and I can pay her back whenever." He looked at me and I swear there were tears in his eyes. "She really has some kind of faith in me, Alex."

I was at a loss for words so I kept my mouth shut and started the car. We went out to the Heights and this time I pulled into the alley behind the old pool hall. When we opened the back door, a half dozen guys flushed like a covey of quail from around a pool table. The dice had barely stopped rolling before the players were crowding past the little bar and out the front door. They left a scattering of dollar bills behind on the dirty green felt. We didn't touch any of it.

Fumbles was up front and stood and just watched as his customers jammed their way through the door and out onto Broadway, scattering in all directions. He came out from behind the bar and walked back to the table where Sean and I waited. I spoke first, "Did you see that, Fumbles? Those guys must have been late for a prayer meeting somewhere." I picked up the dice and examined the spotted cubes as if I'd never seen anything like them before.

He looked at me and grinned. "I'm sure you're right." He looked back at the money on the table. "Looks like they forgot their donations." Fumbles scooped up the crumpled ones and fives and stuffed them into his pants pocket. "I'll make sure this gets into the collection box at St Michaels."

I didn't smile back, "You do that. You might also want to tell those boys to hold their pre-meeting meeting somewhere else while you're at it." I dropped the dice in my pocket.

"Good idea." He turned to Sean, "What can I do for you today, Sergeant Dunphy?"

Sean pulled a roll of bills from his inside jacket pocket and laid them on the pool table. "You can take me off your books." He laughed, "At least for a little while."

Fumbles looked at the money for a few seconds and then picked it up and shoved the wad of bills into his other pocket. Sean said, "Aren't you gonna count it?"

"Nah. If you can't trust a cop, who can you trust?"

I touched Sean on the arm and started for the back door, "Be seeing you, Fumbles." Then I stopped and turned back to him. "Oh, one more thing. You should be a little more careful about how you handle your customers...and where you do it. We wouldn't want to see anyone get hurt over a few dollars, would we?" I waited a moment and then went on, "Am I clear?" Fumbles nodded that he understood.

CHAPTER TWENTY-THREE

We weren't coming for lunch this time, so I drove around to the back of Smokin' Joes and pulled up near the barbeque pit. Buddy was just starting to lay out a half dozen decks of ribs on the grates when I grabbed him from behind, spun him around to face me and hoisted him up until his ass was on the concrete rim of the pit. Buddy is a tall, skinny guy and no match for me. I forced him to lean back over the glowing coals.

"Hey, man. What the hell you doin? Lemme down. You burnin' me." He recognized me then and hollered, "Mistah Alex, lemme go. Ah ain't done nothin'. Lemme go." He was screaming and thrashing around. I held him tight over the coals.

"You lied to me, Buddy. The other day you told me you didn't give the Stroud kid any dope and he then showed up out at Colletti's all coked up on Saturday night. Why'd you lie to me about that?"

He was squirming and trying to pull forward away from the heat but I kept pressing him back. "No, suh. Ah din't lie. He din't get nothin' from me. Lemme go. Mebbe I know where he got that junk."

I pulled him off the edge and let go of his skinny arms. He ran to the outside water tap, cranked it open and held up the hose connected to it, spraying water over his head and down his back. Sean and I watched him carefully but we knew he wasn't going anywhere. He turned the water off after a couple of minutes and wiped his face and head with a wet rag. Then he came back to where we stood by the barbecue pit. Buddy looked at me like a puppy that had been unjustly punished. "You got no call to do me like that, Mistah Alex. Ah ain't never lied to you."

"I'm sorry, Buddy. But we know he got the coke he wanted from somewhere and you're the only one we know that handles that stuff." I took him by his boney shoulders and turned him around and so I could look at his backside. His sauce spattered tee-shirt was still steaming a little but it hadn't caught fire. "I don't think you're burned too badly. You're just a little scorched. I'm pretty sure you're gonna live."

Buddy twisted around and tried to look over his shoulder to see how his pants looked. There was a faint scorch mark across the seat of his jeans but the back of his tee-shirt didn't show any signs of burns. I suspected that he would feel like he had a pretty good sunburn from his time over the coals. I said, "You look all right. Nothing serious. And I am sorry. You're right, I shouldn't have done that to you. I apologize." I waited a minute while he mopped his face with the rag again. "You did say you knew where he got his fix. Who sold it to him?"

He looked around as if he thought someone else might be listening. "You hear of a dude name of Dipsey James? Hangs at that redneck biker bar way out on Getty?"

"I think I heard something about him a while back. Is he a dealer, too?"

"Yeah, he deal some. But not jus' weed like me. He got coke 'n meth and crack and other hard shit, too." He shook his head, "Somebody tol' me he even got H. Man, tha's bad. Ah don' do that stuff. Make a man crazy. Or dead."

"Dead is what you gonna be, you let them ribs burn." Joe was trying hard to keep from laughing. He had come out of the restaurant when he heard Buddy holler and now he was standing by the back door next to the smokers. Buddy jumped back to the pit to tend to the ribs and Joe looked at me. "Never figured you for a police brutality lawsuit, Alex. Do I have to lodge the complaint with Chief Bauer? Or call my attorney?"

"Sorry, Joe. We thought Buddy lied to us and I wanted to scare him a little. Never meant to hurt him. He's not burned and I think we're straight now. Sorry if I upset you, Joe." I put out my hand and we shook.

"I'm all right with it if Buddy is. Are you still looking for the Straub boy, Alex?"

"Yeah. We're working his sister's murder and we still need to find him. No one's seen him since before the girl was killed. You hear anything about him we can use?"

For a minute or so he watched Buddy fuss with the ribs. They were starting to pick up a little char and the smell of the rich sauce that glazed them was beginning to make me forget we hadn't come for lunch. Joe turned back to me and said, "One of Mama's girls, the tall blonde, name of Cynthia, came in last night to pick up an order and meet with her boyfriend for a minute. I heard her tell him that the kid came into Mama's real late Friday and again on Saturday night. She said he was all messed up." We watched Buddy rub his rear end and Joe grinned at me and called to him. "Better get you a block of ice to sit on for a while, Buddy. Your jeans look like you been sittin' in them coals."

I thanked Joe for the tip and told him we'd check it out and see if Peter was still at Mama's. I walked over to Buddy and stuck my hand out. "I am truly sorry, Buddy. No hard feelings?"

He looked me straight in the eye and said, "Naw, Mistah Alex. Ah know you jus' doin' your job. It's all right, man. We good."

We shook hands and I said, "We'll take a good, hard look at this Dipsey James dude. If he's dealing all that hard stuff, we'll make sure that he goes down. Thanks for the tip. You take care, now." I waved at Joe and we climbed into the car. Sean and I agreed to talk to the narcs at Central and pass the information on Dipsey James to them. They could have the glory of the collar. We headed out toward one of the poorer sections of town to see if young Peter Straub might be holed up at the 'Eastside Gentlemen's Club'.

CHAPTER TWENTY-FOUR

On the extreme east side of Muskegon Heights proper is an area appropriately known as 'Eastside'. It could also be called a ghetto or a barrio or a slum. Those three descriptive names all fit. It isn't a very big area, only about six city blocks square. It consists mostly of two and three story apartment buildings built during World War Two to house the workers at the big Continental Aviation plant and the other large plants that blossomed in Muskegon. Most of the buildings contained four, but sometimes six, walkup apartments, two or three up and down with a central inside stairwell and wooden stairs hugging the outside and leading to the minute yard spaces. In bigger cities these buildings would be called tenements. Although still functional, the buildings showed their age. With fairly cheap rents the majority of the apartments housed one or two families each of African-Americans, Asian-Americans or Latinos. The ethnic territories in Eastside were clearly defined and woe be unto the man or boy who strayed onto someone else's turf. Major turf wars weren't all that common but they did happen. I'd been called out several times to help break up small fights that erupted over infringements or disrespect. The side yards of the apartment houses were final resting places for broken vehicles and busted refrigerators and washing machines. The kids played in and out of the old cars and trucks because there were no city sponsored playgrounds in Eastside. It was a totally dangerous and depressing area. With one exception.

In the middle of the block on Summit Avenue, the street that bisected Eastside, sat a two story red brick mansion nearly half a block square. Two of the old apartment buildings had been razed to provide space for the imposing structure which looked as though it belonged on a plantation somewhere in the Deep South. It sat squarely in the middle of what had been two double wide lots and was surrounded by a lush green lawn and well-tended shrubbery. The entire property was enclosed by a six-foot-high brick wall topped with ornate wrought iron fencing. Two eight-foot columns and an iron gate provided entry to the grounds from Summit Avenue.

We pulled up and parked in front of the gate. Sean looked at me and pointed to the house. He said, "You ever been in there?"

"No. Like you, I've been out here in Eastside a bunch on patrol and on calls to break up a fight or to try to arrest someone. But there's never been a problem in there that I know of and this whole block is pretty quiet." I grinned at him and added, "I've never been inside the club. We probably can't afford anything that's in there anyway."

He agreed and we got out of the car. I walked up to the gate and pushed it open. A red brick walk led across the immaculate lawn and ended at a set of wide steps. A young Hispanic man sat on the second step. He wore a reddish-tan suit over a pale green shirt and a yellow tie. The hat that matched the suit was pulled low over his forehead, shading his eyes. Sitting at his side was a large pit-bull the same color as the man's suit. The big dog had a yellow kerchief around his neck. It matched the man's tie. The young man didn't look up as we approached but we knew he was watching us. So was the big dog. The man was peeling an apple with a flick-blade knife that sported a thin blade easily six inches long. As we came up the walk, he cut a small piece from the apple, balanced it on the thin blade and offered it to the dog. The dog took the apple but never moved his eyes from Sean and me. We passed the watching pair and mounted the steps to the wide porch. Neither of them spoke to us.

An African-American man, much larger than the man on the steps, rose from his chair and moved to stand in front of the big oak door with ornate glass panels. I stopped about three feet in front of him. He was about four inches taller than I am and much broader and heavier. His custom tailored dark blue suit probably cost more than I made in a month. It covered a white shirt and red silk tie. I recognized him.

"I know you, man. B J Barnes. Linebacker at the Heights, then at Michigan and then for the Bears. Good to see you again after all this time." I offered my hand and he took it in his massive paw.

He smiled showing a mouth full of teeth the size of dominos, some capped with gold. "I didn't recognize you right off, Makarios. I guess the last time I saw you was in Colorado Springs the day us Wolverines came out there and put a big time ass whupping on you Kaydets boys." He laughed and shook his massive head, "Man, that was ten, 'leven years ago."

"Yeah, I remember that game, B J. I think I've still got a couple of bruises from trying to block you or from you tackling me. That was the senior year for both of us." I laughed, "But you put a few licks on me in high school long before that. As I remember, you had some good years with the Bears after that, didn't you?"

"Yeah, I did. Nine of 'em. But that was enough, so I came home about a year ago." He looked past us at the run-down buildings across the street. His eyes went vacant for a moment and then he refocused on me. "What can I do for you, Alex?"

We showed him our badges and I said, "B J, we need to speak to Miss Brown." I raised both hands and added, "There's no problem with the club, B J; we're just looking for some information and I believe she can help us."

He reached back and rapped once on the ornate oak door. It was opened immediately by an Asian woman who looked about fourteen and was probably three times that. She wore a traditional Vietnamese Ao Dai of pale grey silk embroidered with white egrets. It showed her slight figure to full advantage. I smiled at her and repeated that we needed to speak with Miss Brown.

She frowned and said, "Cannot see. Mama taking bath now."

"I'm sorry, miss. It is really important that we see her."

The girl shrugged, "You follow me. I see if possible." She turned and walked up the hallway.

The Eastside Gentleman's Club is a very plush private club. As we followed the girl down the hall, I looked through the double doors on the right and into a huge room with a bar and a billiard table. There were no pockets in that table. Like it says in Music man, pool is not a gentleman's game. The bar, probably twelve feet long, lined one wall. Four low cocktail tables with comfortable chairs arranged around them were separated just enough to allow quiet, private discussions by the members. Bookshelves and a reading table completed the furnishings of the club room. A stairway at the back of the wide entrance hall led to the rooms upstairs. The girl took us past the club room and around the corner to the door of a suite of rooms that obviously belonged to Miss DeLois Brown, known as 'Mama' to her girls and a lot of other people.

The girl stopped us at the door to the suite. "You wait here. I tell Mama." She disappeared but was back in a minute. "Mama in tub. Cannot see you. Go now."

I said, "Wait. Take this to Miss Brown and tell her we just want to see her for a minute." I handed her my badge and she frowned at it and disappeared into the suite again. And again she was back in a minute or so and this time she gestured for us to follow her. She led us through the beautifully furnished living room, stood aside at the door of the bathroom and waved us inside. The bathroom was spacious and done in soft blues and greens. There was a glass enclosed shower with two different heads, a commode, a bidet and a large black marble jetted tub. And there, lying back in that tub with soap bubbles up to her breasts, was Mama.

An ice-filled champagne bucket with a nearly full bottle rested on a low table along side of the tub. Mama was holding a flute of the bubbly as she lay back in the iridescent bubbles. Ms. DeLois Brown was about forty-five years old but easily could pass for twenty-five. Her skin was flawless and the color of coffee with a shot of Carolans in it. I knew a little of her history. She was born in Muskegon and grew up in Eastside but she split for Las Vegas as soon as she finished high school. It didn't take her long to become one of the more popular show girls on the strip. After twenty years or so in Vegas, she came back to Muskegon with a master's degree in business from UNLV and enough money to build the club. Somehow she got a liquor license and approval to establish the Eastside Gentleman's Club as a private club for members only. It had been flourishing since 1987. She took a sip of the Champagne and smiled up at us. "Sorry to disappoint you boys, but I paid the other nice policemen last Saturday."

I smiled back, "You're joking, of course."

She arched her brows and grinned over the rim of her glass, "Am I?"

I didn't know if she was kidding us or not. To cover my confusion, I moved into the room and retrieved my badge from the edge of the tub. "I hope you are just having some fun with us, Ms. Brown. But we're here to collect Peter Straub. He is here, isn't he?" I decided to get right to the point. I'd worry about whether or not she was paying protection to the police force later.

"Yes, he is. He came in late Saturday night. He's been passed out upstairs since then." She stood up in the tub, water and soap bubbles sliding smoothly down her flawless skin. She smiled at Sean. "Would you hand me that robe, honey. The one over there on the chair." She waved her arm in the general direction of the far wall. I don't think either Sean or I even knew there was a chair in the room. He finally tore his eyes away from the woman and retreated to the chair. He picked up the white terrycloth robe and opened it up for her. She stepped gracefully out of the tub and slipped her arms into the sleeves of the robe, pulling it closely around her and quickly tying the belt. "Thanks, honey." She patted Sean on the shoulder. "Let's go see how young Mr. Straub is doing." She went past me to the door and turned around. "You boys just come along with me. And you can call me Mama."

We snapped out of our stupor and followed her into the hall and toward the stairway that led to the second floor. A tall blonde came down the stairs just as we got to them.

Mama asked her which room Peter was in and she said 'His father's apartment'. Mama said, "There are six apartments up there for the use of our members and guests from out of town. Rudy Straub maintains one all the time. His boys use it sometimes." We went up the stairs and followed her to the door of the room with a brass 'four' on the upper panel. She stopped there and turned to me. "Peter was pretty well out of it when he came in the other night. Had a lot of trouble talking but we got the idea that he just wanted a place to crash. He's been doing that quite a lot the last couple of months. Mostly on weekends." Worry lines creased her forehead and she said, "I like the boy but he can be a real asshole sometimes. We kept him away from the other members the other night and got him right up here. I think he might be mixing his drugs. Maybe meth or heroin with his coke." She frowned and went on, "You know I don't allow that stuff here in the club but I've seen enough of that action to know it can kill you. Cynthia has been checking on him occasionally and he seems to be sleeping most of the time but it's almost like he's in a coma. We thought about hauling his ass to the hospital but I really don't want to be involved." She looked directly at me. "You know what I mean?"

I nodded. "Let us take a look at him. We'll move him to the jail or the hospital. One of the two." I opened the door to room four. "I can't promise to keep you and the club out of it but I'll do my best, Mama."

The apartment was not very large but it was well set up. There was a bed-sitting room and a bath with a tiny kitchen alcove complete with a fridge and a microwave. It looked exactly like a middle grade Las Vegas hotel room. A crash pad. It was furnished with decent pieces of furniture and very clean. Peter Straub lay face down on the bed. He was in his underwear and had pushed a blanket off onto the floor. He appeared to be sleeping soundly, his breath coming in and out noisily. His clothes were folded and stacked neatly on a nearby chair. Three small plastic baggies lay on the floor next to the bed. All three contained small amounts of white powder. I pulled on my latex gloves and indicated that Sean should do the same. I picked up all of the bags. The coke was obvious but the powder in the other two was new to me. Mama looked at it and said "That's Meth. You can snort it just like coke." I put the bags in my jacket pocket.

We rolled Peter over and he swung his arm out and grabbed Sean's lapel. "Saw 'em ....there...office...couch...they were..." He mumbled a few other words we couldn't understand and then let go of Sean's coat and fell back on the bed. I saw that he had thrown up at least once. The bed was covered with the results and the room was full of the stink of urine and vomit. The blonde went to the window and shoved it open. I reached for my cell phone and turned to Mama. "We'll get him out of here now. Thanks for looking out for him." I called dispatch and ordered an ambulance before I stepped back out into the hall. Sean stayed in the room and began to search for anything else Peter might have brought with him. Mama followed me into the hall. I asked, "Where's his car?"

She smiled, "I had it put away. Sometimes this street isn't a very safe place to park a new car at night. B J has the keys."

"Could you have someone bring the car down to Central later, please. They can leave the keys with the desk sergeant." We went down the stairs and had just reached the front door when the EMT's pulled up out front. They unloaded a gurney and came up the walk and onto the porch. B J opened the front door for them and I pointed down the hall, "Upstairs. Room four. Dunphy's up there. The kid is almost comatose. It looks like he might have OD'd."

They went past me without a word. Mama and I started for the porch. I stepped back and walked over to the door to the main club room. I wanted a look at how the other half lived. None of the other girls who lived at the club were there and there were no members in the big room. I guessed it was a slow Monday. I heard mama laugh and then she said, "You thinking about joining our club, Lieutenant?"

I smiled and said, "I doubt that I could afford the dues, Ms. Brown. Besides, I don't think the other members would allow me in. What do you think?"

"You're probably right on both counts. It is a little bit expensive and who can join and who can't is tightly controlled by the board...and me." She smiled, "But we do have guest memberships available now and then."

I knew that a great deal of business and a lot of political activity went on in the big conference room behind the club room. The three or four girls who lived in the house were more for decoration and service help than for sex although that was probably an expensive option. A lot of the membership lived in cities far away from Muskegon. Some as far away as Washington DC. We moved out onto the porch. B J walked away from us and took up a position at the other end. The sharply dressed young man and his dog were still on the second step. Mama was perfectly at ease. I watched her for a moment as she looked out over the rundown neighborhood. "I know you lived in Vegas, Ms. Brown. Why'd you come back here?"

She smiled, "Please. Call me Mama." She waved her arm at the street. "I grew up here. Right here on this lot, in fact. So I wanted to change things a little…give something back. I had the old tenements torn down and built this place on the spot where I grew up. We take care of that little park up the street, too." She pointed to the run-down tenements across the street. "See those? They'll be gone next summer and there'll be another park and a playground for the children over there. It's not much but we do what we can."

The EMTs came down with Peter strapped to the gurney and headed for the ambulance. Sean came down behind them. "Nothing else in the room. There's some clothes in the closet that look like they'd fit Rudy. This was under his pillow." He held out a wad of cash and another plastic bag. Coke again.

I held the roll of cash out to Mama. "Take what you need to cover the cost of the room and cleaning it up." She nodded thanks and peeled two one hundred dollar bills from the wad. I handed the rest of it back to Sean and put the baggie of coke in my pocket with the rest of the dope. "Let's go get him checked in and see if we can get the docs to bring him around so we can talk to him." I took off the latex gloves and held out my hand to Mama, "Thanks for your help, Ms. Brown. It's been an interesting visit." I gave her my card and continued, "Let me know if I can help."

She took my hand and smiled. "Come back anytime. Perhaps we can arrange a guest membership for you." I didn't answer but waved at her and B J as we headed down the walk to our car. The young Hispanic man with the knife was still peeling his apple. He and the pit bull watched us all the way to the gate.

The ambulance was already headed out with lights and siren going full bore. We followed it to Lakeview General Hospital and pulled up near the Emergency entrance. Sean called Central and filed our report as we drove to the hospital. The report would be recorded and transcribed and the stenographers at Central would have it typed up and ready for proofing and signing the next time we came into the squad room. The EMT's took Peter straight into the ER and we waited outside in the hall for a doctor to come out and tell us what was happening. It didn't take long before a young doctor approached us and said, "He's in bad shape. Not really an overdose but we're treating him as though it was. We'll give him the standard anti-drug regimen to start. He's pretty dehydrated and malnourished right now so we'll feed him and give him liquids IV."

"How soon before we can talk to him? It's pretty important." I was anxious to get some information from him and have him explain what he was mumbling about at Mama's.

The doctor shrugged, "Could be anywhere from twelve to twenty-four hours before he's coherent. But even then he might not know what he's saying. He could have some brain damage. Depends on how much of that shit he took, what it was and over what period of time he took it. You got any ideas?"

I said, "He's been known to use coke once in a while but something set him off Friday or Saturday. We're fairly sure he got hold of some meth and may have used 'em both. We think he probably started taking the stuff sometime Friday night and crashed Saturday night or Sunday morning if that helps."

"Yeah. We'll treat him for both drugs and let you know when he starts to withdraw. It won't be pretty. Thanks." He turned and went back to the ER.

My cell phone went off and I dug it out of its little holster. "Makarios."

The chief's voice was low and he growled, "Bauer here. Get your asses back here right now. There are some people in my office that want to talk to you."

CHAPTER TWENTY-FIVE

Sean agreed to stay at the hospital to keep an eye on Peter until I could send someone to relieve him. I headed back to Central with the flashers, weaving in and out of the Monday afternoon traffic. Lakeview General was only a few blocks from downtown, so I made it to the parking lot in less than ten minutes. When I got to the squad room, Officer Haney was at her accustomed desk and I asked her to send someone to relieve Sean. She said she would take care of that and I made my way to the closed door of the chief's office. I knocked and opened the door. The office was crowded.

Richards and Davis stood at one side of the chief's desk while Ken Washburn, the County Attorney, anchored the other side. Two men in dark suits, white shirts and striped ties sat in two of the three chairs facing Bauer's desk. Jennifer Clayton was seated in the third chair.

The chief looked up as I came through the door. "Where's Dunphy?", he growled.

"Babysitting Peter Straub at Lakeview General. We picked the kid up at the Eastside Gentlemen's Club. He's all drugged up and still pretty well out of it so he couldn't talk to us. The doc says it'll be a while before we can get anything out of him. Might even be a day or two, but he's in our custody now." Bauer grunted and waved me into the room. I walked over and stood next to Washburn. Who were the suits and why was Jennifer sitting there?

She looked great in a light grey pants suit with a crisp, frilly-fronted white blouse. I smiled at her but she didn't smile back and avoided eye contact.

Bauer waved toward the men in the chairs and introduced me to the two out-of-towners. "This is Lieutenant Makarios. He's the lead investigator on the Straub girl's murder." He turned to me, "Alex, these gentlemen are FBI Special Agent Frank Duncan from Washington and John Price from the US Attorney General's office. They haven't told us why we are all here since they wanted you in on it too." He paused and studied Jennifer for a moment and then he sighed, "And this young woman is FBI Special Agent Shannon Oliver." He looked at me again. "I think you know her already... but maybe under a different name."

I looked around the room. Richards and Davis looked as lost as I felt. I stared at the woman I knew as Jennifer Clayton. What the hell was going on here? Why were the FBI and the AG's office interested in a small town murder case. Especially since Madeline Straub's death was strictly a local case. How did Jennifer figure into this? Then I realized that she probably had been undercover for some reason and was playing a role during her time in Muskegon. If that was the case, she certainly fooled me. The two suits nodded at me but no one spoke for a minute or so and then I blurted out, "Can someone please tell me what the hell is going on?" I pointed to the FBI guy from DC. "What do you have to do with our murder cases? I don't think we need your help in finding Madeline Straub's killer." I turned to Bauer, "Right, Chief?" The big man nodded and said, "You're right on that but I don't think these people are here about a couple of murders." He picked up his cigar and turned to the man from Washington. "Agent Duncan, suppose you tell us exactly why you are here."

The FBI man stood up and smoothed the jacket of his suit. He was about five nine or ten and in his early fifties by the look of the grey beginning to show in his wavy dark brown hair. He looked like he was about to address a jury. "No, we're not here because of those killings even though Madeline Straub's death overlaps what we are interested in a little bit. But I'll start from the beginning." He looked at all of us in turn and then began, "Last February your Senator Markham, the one who is retiring and whose place Rudy Straub wants to take, came to us with a story about an attempted bribe. He told us that Straub came to his office in January and asked for the senator's endorsement for his campaign. Senator Markham put him off. It seems that the senator doesn't particularly care for Mr. Straub and didn't want to endorse him despite what the party wanted. Markham told us Straub was upset when he left but said he would come back and see the senator again. He did come back a week later and again asked the senator to back him. Markham refused again. He told us that Straub then suggested that if the senator endorsed his candidacy, he could arrange for Markham to get a nice consulting position with the company in Europe that was backing the Altzeit Brewery. He told Markham that the job paid very well and allowed for a lot of travel to Europe, all at company expense. Markham also said Straub mentioned a 'signing' bonus of one hundred thousand dollars if Markham accepted the job. Markham said he flatly refused the offer and told Straub not to come back. A couple of days later the senator came to see us." Duncan stopped and looked around at us. "I realize this is all new to you but have any of you heard any rumors about anything like this?"

I was trying to process the news that a foreign company was backing Rudy. We had all wondered where he got the money to buy and modernize the brewery. Now we knew. Since I didn't doubt for a minute that Rudy would try to bribe the senator, I wondered what else he was capable of doing. None of us said anything and Duncan went on. "O K. We started poking around and looking into Straub. He had not been on our radar before but it didn't take long for us to find a reason to open a full investigation. We learned he was connected with a certain bank in New York that we were watching This particular bank was suspected of laundering money from Europe. The investigation of Straub was passed to Shannon. You should know that she is one of our up and coming agents." He stopped for a minute and smiled at Jennifer or Shannon, or whatever she wanted to be called. I still couldn't believe she had fooled me all along. I was trying to think of something she did or said that should have tipped me off that she was using a phony name and was under cover. But I couldn't think of a single thing that would have alerted me.

Jennifer/Shannon took up the narrative. "We decided that I should go under cover here and try to get close to the Straubs. By leaning on the banker in New York we were able to get me in as Madeline's piano teacher and I was able to convince Rudy that I could help her. Our plan has worked pretty well for the past six months." She stopped and looked at me, "Of course with Madeline's death, it's over now. But during that time, I was able to pick up quite a bit of information about Rudy's background in Germany and Canada. That uncovered the problem of the family's entry into the United States. The family came into this country illegally. They came in through Detroit with fake Canadian passports. Working with the CIA, we also found that Rudy worked for the STASI, the East German Secret Police, when they lived in Berlin That was before the wall came down. His superior was a man named Rutgar Beidecker. The CIA confirmed that Beidecker ran a spy ring in West Germany. We think it's possible Rudy might have worked for him again in Pirmasens, Germany before the family immigrated to Canada. Our counterparts in the CIA also think Rudy may have been sent here as a 'mole', in deep cover, but that is unconfirmed."

Richards interrupted her, "East Germany is long gone. How could he be working for the government of a country that no longer exists?"

Agent Duncan said, "Apparently, many of the former STASI agents were trained by the KGB in Russia and worked for them as well as their local bosses. With the breakup of the German Democratic Republic, what we called East Germany, some of them continued to work for the KGB. The

CIA believes Straub might be one of those." He looked around the room at each of us in turn. "If he were elected to the senate, he could do enormous damage to this country. We and the CIA believe that might be what he was groomed for. We can't let it happen." He added, "By the way, the KGB is now called the SVR…but it's the same nasty people…same nasty methods."

"So how are you going to stop him?" Bauer's cigar was back in his mouth.

"We're planning on arresting him tomorrow on the illegal entry charge." Duncan faced the chief. "The only reason we are letting you in on this is because of the daughter's murder. Shannon thought that since your people have been involved with the family already you could be of help during the arrest and interrogation of Rudy Straub and the rest of the family." He stopped and looked at the other suit who nodded. "You also need to know this: Rudy Straub is not his real name. He was born in Dessau, Germany in 1940 and his real name is Gerhardt Krantz."

I muttered, "Shit." During my time with the Air Force OSI, I had worked on a couple of cases involving STASI or KGB slash SVR operatives in Germany who were trying to recruit airmen to provide information for cash or other favors. I'd been briefed and trained on some of their methods. My fellow agents and I had helped the CIA break up a small spy ring in Berlin in ninety-four. I thought if Straub was a mole, he may have already done some damage.

Shannon/Jennifer spoke up, "Alex, have you narrowed down your list of suspects in the killings?"

Bauer waved his cigar at me and I said, "No. Until we can interview Peter, the whole family stays on our list. We haven't found anyone who had any sort of motive to kill the girl but there might be something within the family. It looks like she was abused from quite a young age and maybe that would be a reason. She was also pregnant when she was killed. There's another possibility. The problem is, we don't know who abused her or who the father of her child might be. She had no known boyfriend that we can find. While we think it might be someone in the family; it also could be an outsider. We're still digging." I looked at Agent Duncan. "When are you planning to make your arrest?"

"We haven't set a firm time yet but we're thinking early afternoon tomorrow. Why?"

"Straub is going to Lansing to attend a fund-raising dinner tomorrow night. You'll have to catch him before he takes off. But there's something else. We'd like to talk to Peter before we beard Straub. When we picked him up, Peter mumbled a few words that lead us to believe he saw someone do something to the girl. It might be important to the case." I shrugged, "But I don't have any idea in hell what it could be or when we'll be able to talk to him."

Shannon/Jennifer said, "We could probably hold off until around one o'clock, but that's the latest. Maybe you can get what you need from Peter by then."

I thought about that for a minute. It all depended on the doc bringing Peter around long enough and early enough for Sean and me to grill him. It would be dicey. I said, "That'll have to do. Can we arrest him or any of the Straub's after they're in your custody, if one of them is connected to the murders?"

Price answered, "Sure. You can arrest any of them anytime we've got them. You seem certain one of them is the killer."

"As I just said, we don't know which one but I'm pretty sure someone in that family killed her. And probably Catherine Hood too. Are you going to arrest them all at once?"

Duncan smiled, "Yes, I'm afraid it's going to be a circus. We'll take the four of them at the house if we can and then pick up Peter at the hospital later."

"How are you going to get all of them at the house at the same time?" Richards' question surprised me.

"Shannon has arranged to meet with them to offer her condolences as a family friend. Just a small get-together as a memorial for the girl. She sent personal notes to the five of them this morning. She'll meet with them at noon."

"Might work." Bauer interjected, "Who do you want there from our side?"

Duncan looked at Shannon/Jennifer. She said, "Alex and his partner should be enough for this."

Well, I thought, maybe she does need me for something. I still couldn't get my head around the undercover thing and I wasn't sure about what to call her. I thought of a few things I'd like to call her but this wasn't the time or place. I wondered if that time and place would ever come. The chief and the FBI guys were working out the logistics and timing of tomorrow's raid but I kept watching Shannon...I had decided to call her that and was repeating it over and over in my mind. It did have a nice ring to it and it certainly fit her along with the green eyes and auburn hair.

The suits were all getting ready to leave and we agreed to meet in the morning at ten to finalize things. I told the chief that I was going back to the hospital to see what was happening and that I'd see him in the morning before the meeting. Everyone was out of the office when I walked through the door into the squad room.

Shannon was waiting for me outside my cube. She smiled and touched my arm, "Come by my place when you get through at the hospital, Alex. It won't matter how late it is. The door will be open."

CHAPTER TWENTY-SIX

When I got back to the hospital, I found Sean and Officer Haynes deep in conversation in the hall outside of Peter Straub's room. I walked up to them and stood there for a full two minutes before they realized I was there. Must be love, I thought. Sean finally looked up and said, "Hi, Alex. The kid's still out but the doc said he thinks he'll be coming around in another hour or two. The stuff they pumped into him to bring him around must have worked quicker than they thought it would."

I turned to Officer Haynes. "Sandy, is it? Guess I'll have to call you that since you seem to have taken over my job of watching out for Sean." She blushed and I went on, "Thanks for coming up here to relieve him but you both didn't have to stay." She blushed again and I said, "Unless you had important things to talk about."

Sean said, "Well, yeah. I guess we did...or do. Anyway, what did I miss? I guess I should have been at the the meeting with you. Is there something we have to do?"

I quickly filled him in on what Agent Duncan had told us and what the plan for the next day was and then I said, "Yeah, we've got some more footwork to do. We need to know what Rudy was up to in Grand Rapids on Friday. Bauer told me that Chief Lyle's people found out he didn't get to the Convention Center until just before the dinner. That was around seven o'clock. He left here early that morning so where'd he spend the day?"

Sean frowned and said, "Maybe that kid that was with him in Bauer's office knows. We should look him up and have a little chat."

"Might work. Find out where he's staying." Sean went down the hall to find a phone book and I turned to Officer Haynes. "No point in you staying here any longer. I'll call Central and have someone else sent out to relieve you."

She smiled and said, "Thanks, Lieutenant. I'll stick around until you and Sean are finished here if it's not going to be too long. I'll leave when the relief shows up."

"We'll be here for a little while yet. As soon as Sean finds our guy, we'll take off. I don't expect Peter will come around this evening. The doc said it would probably be tomorrow morning before we could get anything usable out of him. You can stay or take off, whichever you want."

She said 'thanks' again and went off to find Sean. She had a nice trim figure and looked good in her uniform even if it did include a bulky vest with a radio and sidearm attached to it. I called Central and asked them to send someone out to baby sit.

I went into Peter's room. He was strapped to the bed and had tubes running into each forearm. A funny kind of oxygen mask was clamped to his face and I could see that he was breathing normally and easily. The IV tubes were hung on the usual stanchions and there was a bunch of wires coming out of the right sleeve of the ugly standard hospital gown he was tied into. The wires led to a roll-around cart with three CRTs and a keyboard. I guessed they were monitoring everything about him. I watched him for a few minutes and he didn't move a muscle. That didn't surprise me since his arms and legs were strapped to the bed with padded restraints. He couldn't move if he had wanted to.

A nurse came in and looked at me quizzically. I flashed my badge and asked, "Why is he strapped down like that?"

She shrugged, "Sometimes when they come out of a drug induced coma, they do a lot of thrashing around and we don't want them to hurt themselves...or any of us." She grinned at me for a second and then went to the machines on the cart. She looked at all the CRTs and typed some entries on the keyboard. When she was finished, she turned back to me. "He's looking a lot better. Another ten or twelve hours should have him back among the living and probably coherent." She pointed at him, "What's he done? Something serious?"

"Maybe nothing too bad, but he's a material witness in a murder case and he's been missing since Friday so we couldn't talk to him. We found him like this earlier today. We'll come back and talk to him in the morning." I left the room just as Sean came back.

"Straub's gofer is staying at the Four Star Motel out on Airline Road."

"That dump? I didn't think anyone stayed there for more than two or three hours at a time." I started down the hall. "Let's go see if he's home this evening." Sean turned to Haynes and she kissed him in the cheek. I heard him tell her he'd see her later.

Before the freeway between Muskegon and Grand Rapids was built, the Airline Road was part of US 31, the main highway to points north and south. Now it paralleled the interstate for a few miles and then disappeared like a lot of old highways. The area we were going to was a backwater with a couple of older, rundown motels and a restaurant or two. The Four Star was one of those that managed to stay almost respectable. It was usually clean and mostly trouble free: a road salesman's typical overnight stop. Despite my comment, it was not really a hot bed sort of place. We drove in under the portico and Sean went inside to see where Rod Ashley was staying.

"Unit fourteen. Last one on the first floor." Sean told me as he climbed back into the car. I slowly drove down the line of parked cars to the end room. The Four Star was busy. A slightly beat up '98 Chevy Cavalier was parked in front of number fourteen.

We went to the door and Sean banged on it hard and shouted 'Police. Open up.' After a minute or so, the door opened a crack and Rod Ashley peered out over the flimsy security chain. Sean flashed his badge and told him that we needed to ask him some questions. He mumbled 'Just give me a minute.' and tried to shut the door. The toe of Sean's size twelve kept it from closing all the way. It was still on the chain. Ashley went back into the room and we heard him tell someone 'Get in the bathroom and put your clothes on.' I stood behind Sean and kept quiet. We had decided this was his show and I was going to let him run it.

Ashley came back to the door, unhooked the chain and let us in. The rooms at the Four Star were typical of most second-rate motels. This one was furnished with a double bed and matching nightstands which were complete with the scars of old cigarette burns and the telltale rings from countless glasses. A sagging, stained lounge chair, two straight chairs and a small table completed the furnishings. A bottle of cheap Prosecco wine and two half full glasses were on the table. Ashley stood in the middle of the room nervously looking from one to the other of us and at the door to the bathroom. We didn't speak and he finally asked, "What's going on? What do you want from me?" He was dressed in a pair of running shorts, the kind with a short slit up the side, and flip-flop shower shoes. No shirt covered his skinny whale-belly white hairless chest.

Sean said, "Sit down, Rod. This won't take long" and pointed. Ashley backed up to the foot of the bed and sat. I walked over to the bathroom door and shoved it open. The teen aged boy was just zipping up his khaki cargo pants. He looked up at me with deer-in-the-headlight eyes. He was a good-looking kid with a nice tan. I recognized him as one of the boys who were always around the yacht club during the summer. These kids hung around the dock at the club and ferried people back and forth to the boats that were moored out at the buoys. The kids worked for tips and sometimes got to sail with a member if they didn't want to go out alone. It was a good summer job for a fifteen or sixteen-year-old. I had sometimes done the same thing when I was that age. I beckoned to the kid and he came out of the bathroom struggling to get his shirt on and carrying his shoes and a light jacket. I pointed to one of the chairs by the little table and he sat down. He looked at the door once but I shook my head and he busied himself with putting on his shoes.

Sean pulled out his notebook and made a pretense of looking through a half dozen pages. He was doing his best Colombo imitation, flipping back and forth through the mostly blank book. Rod Ashley looked up at him and asked, "Am I in some kind of trouble?"

Sean took a long look at the boy sitting at the table, smiled and said, "Well, Rod, I think you might be." He looked back at Rudy's gofer, "It all depends on how cooperative you are tonight. You still a student down at Michigan, Rod?" Both of us had seen the university's parking decal on the Cavalier parked out front.

"Not anymore. I finished pre-law last spring." Ashley smiled and puffed up a little.

Sean gave him a disgusted look and flipped a few more pages. "That when you hooked up with Rudy Straub's campaign?"

"I worked for him all spring while I was in school but went full time with the campaign as soon as I finished. My dad helped me get the job." The kid was giving us more information than we were looking for but quite often people do that when they're nervous or guilty.

Sean pursued that. "Who's your dad?"

"Gordon Ashley. He's an attorney in Detroit. He's with Grimm, Ashley and Benoit. It's a very big firm. They do a lot of corporate law."

"Is your dad a big contributor to Straub's campaign?"

"No, I don't think so. He's on the party nominating committee, though. He helped sponsor Mr. Straub. I think they've known each other a long time."

Oh great, I thought. Maybe Straub did buy the nomination after all. Perhaps this kid's job was part of the package. I wondered if his dad would also get a job with that nameless outfit in Europe that was backing Rudy's brewery. But then I thought it more likely that this kid's father's law firm would pick up some serious business.

Sean moved on, "What exactly do you do for Straub?"

Ashley sat up a little straighter and thought for a minute before he answered, "I really work for David Walsh, the campaign manager. He's the one who pays me. But mostly I just run errands and drive for Mr. Straub and see that he gets to his meetings on time. Oh, and I make sure that he has the right materials in his briefcase for the discussions. Things like that." He smiled up at Sean. "Mr. Straub likes the way I do things. He told me."

Sean muttered, "I bet he does." and then asked, "So you drive him around a lot?"

"Yes. We usually use a rental car when we go out of town but I've driven his Mercedes a few times around here." He ducked his head and added, "It's a lot nicer than my old Chevy."

"You and he go out of town much?"

"Sure. Five or six times a month since I've been working for him. He mostly goes to Grand Rapids but there've been some trips to Lansing and Detroit too." He frowned, "I don't go with him when he flies to Washington or New York."

Another search through the empty pages. Sean looked up and asked, "You in Grand Rapids with him last Friday?"

"Sure."

"What time did you get there?"

"Around ten…maybe ten-thirty that morning. We went to to the convention center to meet David…Mr. Walsh…and they talked about Friday night's dinner. Oh, we had a quick lunch in the coffee shop at the hotel next door."

"What time was the dinner scheduled to start?"

"Cocktails were at seven, dinner was at eight and then Mr. Straub had meetings with some of his committee members and a couple of fund raisers. I think it was almost twelve when he was finally finished and we left to come home."

"Do you know when he was notified of his daughter's murder?"

Ashley looked away and then answered, "I don't know exactly. I think it might have been around six thirty or maybe nearer seven o'clock. I think Mrs. Straub called him."

"Were you with him all day?"

Ashley began to look worried and began fidgeting. Shrugging his shoulders and clasping and unclasping his hands. Finally, he responded, "No. Just until right after lunch."

Sean stepped closer to him and leaned down. "Where did Straub go that you didn't go with him?"

Ashley looked at me and then at the kid sitting by the table before he answered. "I drove Mr. Straub downtown and left him at the hotel on the river…you know, the Riverview Suites."

Sean looked at his notebook again. "So you dropped him off at the hotel. What time was that?"

"Maybe a little after one."

"What did you do all afternoon?" He was probing and Ashley fell for it.

"I went back to the conventions center and helped David until it was time to pick up Mr. Straub from the hotel."

"Do you know why he went to the hotel?"

Fidgeting again. Looking everywhere but at Sean or me. I could see him starting to sweat.

"No. I really don't know what he goes there for."

Sean looked over at me and then at the boy in the chair before he turned back to Ashley.

"Do you mean he goes there often?"

"Yes. I mean, I take him to the hotel almost every time we go to Grand Rapids." Ashley was really sweating now.

"What time did you go back to pick him up Friday?"

"It's always the same time. Six o'clock on the dot." He brushed his hair back from his forehead. "He always stays there from around one until six. But I had to wait for him on Friday. We were late to the cocktail party."

"Does Rudy keep a room there or do you arrange one for him?"

"I just drop him off." He wouldn't look at Sean. He was searching the room for a way out. "I don't think he registers at the hotel. I think he meets someone there." More voluntary information.

"Man or woman, Rod? Who does he spend his time with?"

"I don't know" Ashley looked at me and suddenly grinned as if he and I were in on the secret. "But I think it might be a woman. He's usually pretty happy when I come back to pick him up at six."

"How often does this happen?"

"Two…three times a month he would go to the Riverview Suites. About once a month we would go to a different motel. One of those out on Plainfield by the Plaza. He'd meet with a man out there but that never was an all afternoon thing. He always had me park and wait for him while they talked. It was usually only about half an hour."

"How'd you know who he meets there?"

"I saw them in the coffee shop a couple of times when I was parked out front."

"You know who this guy is? Could you recognize him if you saw him again?"

"Yeah. I guess I probably could. But it isn't always the same guy, so I'm not sure." The kid was really sweating and fidgeting now. "Why? Is this important for the campaign? Is Mr. Straub in trouble?"

Sean looked at me and I nodded. We had enough to work with. Rudy would have a lot of explaining to do when we got our crack at him. I beckoned to the boy at the table and pointed to the door. He got up hesitantly and took a small step toward it. I stepped aside and waved him out of the room. He hit the door in a rush and disappeared into the night.

Sean put his notebook away. "You've been very cooperative, Rod. Now I have a couple of suggestions for you. One: you need to quit your job with Rudy Straub, effective immediately. Two: you also need to pack your shit and get out of Muskegon. Tonight. You know we can hang you by the balls for what you were doing here with that kid. But we don't want to hurt the boy." Sean paused a beat for emphasis. "So this is your lucky day. But if either Lieutenant Makarios or I find you in Muskegon again, you're gonna wish you'd never been born. Understand?"

Ashley nodded a couple of times and looked down at the floor. "Yes. I hear you." Then he squared his shoulders and looked up defiantly. "But you can't make me quit Mr. Straub's campaign. Mr. Straub is going to win and likes me. He'll protect me."

Sean reached down and grabbed Ashley by the back of the neck. He hauled him to his feet and snarled, "Listen, you little punk. Rudy Straub's goin' to prison and if you want to go with him, that's fine with us. But you better do what I just told you or that's where you'll end up…and, believe me, a sweet little thing like you won't like it there. Now get the hell out of here." He shoved him back onto the bed and turned away.

I said, "Let's go. We got what we came for." We left the room door open when we went out to the car. I looked back and Rod Ashley was sitting on the end of the bed with his head in his hands. He was crying. We got into the patrol car and headed down Airline and I said, "I'll drop you at your car. I've got someplace to go but I'll see you in the morning at Central. Let's just hold on to this stuff about Straub until the time comes to spring it on him and the feds."

"You think they don't know about what he does in Grand Rapids?"

"We'll find out in the morning at the briefing, I guess. But right now I think we've got an exclusive. Jennifer or Shannon, or whatever her name is, might have tumbled to it while she was working them but I doubt it. It looks like Rudy has a steady squeeze in Grand Rapids if it's a regularly scheduled thing. We'll have to make him give up her name. How long do you think it takes to drive from Grand Rapids to Muskegon?"

"Maybe forty-five minutes…tops. Why?"

"Just thinking. Rudy might have had time to get to Muskegon and back if he skipped his afternoon roll in the hay. That keeps him on the suspect list, but I can't see him for Hood." I thought of something else. "The other meeting worries me a little. Who do you suppose those guys are?"

Sean shrugged. "No idea. Maybe they're Rudy's money men. Bringing him some cash from his backers." He turned to face me, "Or maybe it's someone Rudy's paying off. You don't think the Ashley kid could have killed the girl, do you? He also had all afternoon to come back here and still make it back to Grand Rapids?"

"No. I don't think he has the balls to commit murder...nor would he have a motive. And what about the Hood woman? He couldn't have done her too. That would be cutting it close. Besides, I don't think he's big enough."

"We'll have to make Straub give up the guys he met with as well as his girlfriend." I pulled into the parking lot at Central. We drove into the garage and I hung the patrol car's keys on the board before we walked outside into the cool night. There was a smell of rain in the air.

Peter Straub's new black Charger was parked askew, taking up parts of three marked spaces. B J's little joke. I pointed to Sean's Chevy. "There's your car. Who's that sitting in it?"

He grinned. "It'd better be Sandy. See you in the morning, boss."

I waved him off, got into my Rover and headed for nineteen thirty-three Lakeshore Drive.

CHAPTER TWENTY-SEVEN

I eased into the driveway and parked behind the red Mustang. It had been a long day and I was tired. As much as I wanted to go home and go to bed, I wanted to see what Shannon had to say for herself. There was a light burning in the hall of the old house and I crossed the porch and tried the front door. It was unlocked. Had she really waited up? Why? I was hoping that she hadn't had second thoughts about her invitation and that she really wanted to see me, but I had trouble believing it. I entered the big house and walked down the carpeted hallway. The yellow cop tape still sealed off the two studio doors. When I got to the door of Shannon's apartment, I waited a minute or so, listening intently. I could hear music softly playing from inside. My light knock at her apartment door was answered immediately. The deadbolt snapped as she unlocked it and swung the apartment door open.

Shannon was wearing loose-fitting sweatpants and a University of Virginia sweat shirt. She was barefoot. Her auburn hair was tied back in a ponytail and looked damp as if she had just come from the shower. She wasn't wearing makeup and her face looked freshly scrubbed. She smelled like Ivory soap. I thought again that she was the most beautiful woman I'd ever seen. I felt my heart pounding like a trip hammer and I just knew she could hear it. "Come in, Alex," she said and that was enough for me. I stepped into the apartment and she turned and waved towards the counter bar, "Fix yourself something if you want. I'm having a glass of wine."

"Thank you. It's been a long day and I could use a pick me up." I moved to the counter and saw that she had set out a bowl of ice and a rocks glass. The bottle of Jim Beam was still there. I poured an inch of the bourbon into a glass and added two ice cubes. When I turned around, I saw that Shannon already was holding her glass of white wine so I didn't offer to pour a glass for her. She was curled up at one end of the couch with her long legs tucked under her. She patted the cushion next to her and I moved over and slowly sat down.

She smiled, "I'll bet you've got a ton of questions for me, haven't you?" I thought that had to be the understatement of the year but I just nodded and took a small sip of the whiskey. She went on, "I can't tell you everything, Alex, but here's the gist of it. I work out of FBI headquarters in DC. As Frank told you all this morning, I was assigned to the Straub case around the middle of February and by March we knew the Straub family wasn't what they seemed. Frank and I decided that I should come out here under cover and see what more I could find out. The piano teacher thing worked since I really can play and the teaching part was pretty simple." I sipped the bourbon and waited for her to go on. I could see that it would be easy for her to play the undercover game. She was confident and glib. I was sure she could tell any story she wanted and make you believe it. She sipped her wine before she continued, "I was able to pick up some hints and bits and pieces of the family history from Maddy, Peter and Paul. It was enough to lead us to the fake passport thing and their illegal entry from Canada. Another agency confirmed that Rudy, or Gerhardt, came from East Berlin to Pirmasens, West Germany to work at the Parkbrau brewery. Pirmasens is close to several of our military bases in that part of Germany." She looked closely at me and then added, "But you probably know that, don't you?"

I nodded, "Yeah, I've been to Ramstein and Kaiserslautern…and a couple of other lesser known posts over there. None of them are very far from Pirmasens." I grinned and added, "And I've had my share of Parkbrau

beer. It's pretty good. The stuff that Rudy's brewery puts out is a lot like it."
I paused and then said, "Seriously, do they really think Rudy was in the spy business over there?"

"They don't know for sure if he was doing espionage work while the family lived there but the CIA believes he had SVR contacts in that area and at that time. Anyway, he and the family got visas for Canada and emigrated in '71. They packed up and came into the States through Detroit the next year. We now know they used forged Canadian passports." She took a sip of her wine. "You pretty much know the rest, I think."

She was right. Chief Bauer had filled us in on the Straub's life in Muskegon from '72 on. I didn't want to talk about the case. The questions I wanted to ask were about her personally so I decided to plunge right in. "Thanks. That brings me up to speed on your case and ours so I guess we'll figure out what to do about it at tomorrow morning's briefing." I finished the bourbon, put the empty glass on the coffee table and leaned back against the sofa cushion and relaxed. I looked right into those beautiful green eyes. "Now, please tell me all about Shannon Oliver."

She uncurled from the corner of the couch and sat up, facing me. She reached back and undid her ponytail. Her auburn hair swirled down around her shoulders and she shook it free. I wanted to grab her and kiss her. Before I could move she said, "There's really not a lot to tell. I grew up in Florida and Virginia. Went to the university in Charlottesville and graduated from law school there in '92. I joined the Bureau the next year and went through Quantico and into the field in San Francisco for a couple of years and then back to DC and the headquarters. I've worked cases all over the country from there. Sort of like what you did while you were assigned to the OSI, I think." A tiny smile played around her mouth. "I've read your file."

I didn't think there was very much of interest in my file but I didn't doubt that the FBI would have a copy. I asked, "Is your dad really a judge?"

"Yes, he is. What I told you about my family at the yacht club the other night is true. Dad was appointed to the Southern Judicial District of Texas and he and mom do live in Corpus Christi." She finished her wine and put the glass on the table next to the empty rocks glass. "Last Saturday night I wished that I could tell you who I really am. I didn't want us to start out on a false premise but that's the way it had to be then. Frank sent me the file on you after Maddy was killed so I know a little bit about you…but not much really. That file is pretty thin."

I grinned at her, "There's not a lot to put in it." I stretched my arms out wide. "What you see is what you get."

Shannon got up from the couch in one smooth, swift movement, turned and said. "I'll take it." She walked over to the switch next to the door and turned the living room lights off. The only light in the room came from a small bedside table lamp shining weakly through the bedroom doorway. She came back to the center of the living room, turned to me and smiled. "You've got sixty seconds to get my clothes off, Alex. The time starts now."

I got off the couch and moved to her. She turned her back to me and raised her arms. I slowly pulled her sweatshirt up over her head. She wasn't wearing a bra. I dropped the shirt to the floor and put my arms around her, cupping her full breasts in my hands. I bent and kissed the nape of her neck and then her shoulder and she murmured 'Tick-tock'. I bent further and hooked my thumbs in the waistband of her sweatpants. I pushed down and they dropped into a puddle of fabric on the living room floor. She wasn't wearing underclothes. She stepped out of the pile of cloth and turned to me.

"Made it just in time," she whispered. Then she kissed me, long and hard. I pulled her close and we held on for a minute or so and then she pushed away. We broke apart and she went into the bedroom, calling back over her shoulder, "If you're not in this bed in two minutes, I'm getting dressed again."

I was still wearing my sports jacket but I shucked out of it as I went through the bedroom door. Shannon was lying on the double bed with the sheet pulled up to just below her breasts. There was a chest of drawers just inside the doorway and I put my service pistol, holster and badge there before I peeled off my shirt. I moved to the bedside, dropped my slacks and sat on the edge of the bed to take off my shoes. I heard her laugh and say 'Tick-tock' again. I slipped my undershorts off and said, "I doubt if you've ever seen anything like this."

She sat up in the bed. "How naïve do you think I am?" She laughed again, "Or are you bragging?"

I felt myself blush and managed to stammer, "No…no, not that. I meant this." I swung my left leg and its prosthesis up onto the bed.

CHAPTER TWENTY-EIGHT

S hannon abruptly sat up, the sheet slipping down around her hips. She leaned forward against me and put her arm across my shoulders. I could feel the warmth of her breast pressing against my arm. She pointed to the titanium and plastic prosthesis which served as my left foot and ankle and said, "The report I got from Frank didn't mention this." She put her left hand on my thigh. "I knew you had been medically retired... but that was all the report said. There were no other details in the file he forwarded to me. How did you lose your foot?"

"Well, we kind of ran afoul of an IED on our way out to a contractor site in Iraq. My foot and ankle were crushed and the docs had to take it off."

Her fingers traced the burn scars on my neck and shoulder. "And where did these come from?"

"Same place, same time. Got some hot shrapnel inside my flak jacket. Our Humvee pretty much came apart. One of the crew was killed. A chaplain riding with us was burned pretty badly but survived. I was lucky."

She leaned forward and looked closely at the prosthesis that was attached to what was left of my left leg. It started about nine inches below the knee joint and culminated in an artificial foot that looked almost real... except it didn't have toes. She said, "I had no idea you had that. I've never seen you limp. And you said you run. How does that work?" She reached out and touched the cup that attached the prothesis to my leg. "It doesn't look like any other artificial foot I've ever seen."

I pulled my leg up so she could see it better. "This is a new type. It's really still experimental. It's an advanced type called a Neuro Impulse Driven prosthesis. This particular one is the NID Four. The doctors connected the computer chip in the prosthesis to the nerves in my leg so it responds naturally." I flexed my foot up and down and then sideways. "Did you see the Star Wars movie where Luke got his hand sliced off by Darth Vader?" She nodded, still looking at the prosthesis. "Remember he got a new hand and arm. One that functioned exactly like his natural one. This kinda works like that. I can move my foot by thinking about it or the computer just reacts to what's going on…walking, running…whatever. I don't have to think about that. For a while I had to go back to Seattle every six weeks or so to get it tweaked up. But now they've moved the lab to Johns Hopkins in Baltimore. I'm almost due for another upgrade. This is the fourth model of the NID. Each iteration is an improvement but there are still occasional bugs in the system." I stretched my leg out again. "The only pain I have is in my upper leg sometimes when I get over tired, but I can still run and walk pretty naturally. I made it through the physical training part of POST without any problems." I turned to her so I could look into her eyes. "Everything else about me works the way it's supposed to."

She leaned back, pulled me down on the bed and stretched out beside me. I moved so that I could get my arm under her shoulders and pulled her closer. After a minute or two she rolled up so that we were face to face. We kissed and afterwards she murmured, "I believe I've wanted to do that for the past three days." She wriggled out from under the sheet that was half covering her and I turned so that I could move her up on top of me.

We kissed again and I managed to mumble "Me too."

There was a hunger to our love making but it was unhurried and cooperative; each of us wanting to please the other. I don't know how long it took us to reach that pinnacle of satisfaction we were striving for but we got there together.

It was some time later when we came back to the real world. I would have been content to spend the rest of my life just lying there in that bed with my arms around her, watching her breathe and smile. But that wasn't how the real world expected us to act so we started talking again. Shannon rolled over so her head was on my chest and I absently drew my initials on her back with my forefinger. She wriggled a little and said, "Am I branded now? Marked as yours forever?"

"That would work for me if that's what you want." I waited a moment and then said, "I think I love you."

She lifted her head up a little so she could see my face. "You don't know me well enough yet to say anything like that."

"I know I don't. But I'll learn." I knew we were going way too fast for this to be anything serious but I couldn't help myself. "You need to tell me all about yourself. The truth, not some cover story concocted by the agency." I shook my head. "You had me completely fooled with the Jennifer Clayton thing. What really bothered me was your lack of emotion when the girl was killed. I couldn't get my head around how you could be so cool and detached."

She sat up and moved back in the bed until she was leaning against the headboard. "I almost blew my cover there. That was so unexpected. I was getting some good information on the Straubs and it was a routine undercover assignment up until then. I didn't know whether to tell you who I really was or to continue to play the role. Finally I decided to play it out until I could talk to Frank and see what he wanted me to do. I just tried to keep everything in check and as calm as I could until I heard from him."

"Well, you pulled it off. How about the rest of it? True or false?"

"All true. I'll never lie to you again, Alex. Now it's your turn to fill in the blanks.

Your file said you were married but are now divorced. What happened?"

"Yeah. Cathy was a coed at Colorado State and I was a junior at the Academy when we met. I graduated in June of ninety and we got married in October. We lived in Quantico while I went through OSI training and then I was assigned there permanently. The Office had formed a couple of special teams that could be deployed to help the normal field staff on short notice. I was assigned to one of them and I spent most of my time traveling. Most field offices are pretty small and they get overwhelmed sometimes. We were kept busy augmenting them, especially overseas. It was a real learning experience for me but Cathy did have some trouble with the separations. She decided to get a job and found one at Fort Belvoir. That seemed to take care of the problem. I was on temporary duty in Falluja when I got hurt. I hadn't realized that Cathy's big ambition in life was to be a 'Missus Colonel Somebody' someday and when I was medically released from active duty, she realized that wouldn't happen with me. So while I was in Seattle, she went looking for an eligible replacement. It only took her six weeks to find one. She divorced me before I finished rehab and got fitted for the NID." I pulled Shannon closer and kissed her. "Now you know the whole story."

"Oh, I'm sure there's much more…but I don't think we need to go into all the little details…right now." She kissed me again.

Our love-making this time was even more intense. As before, each of us sought to bring the maximum pleasure to the other and in doing that, we each achieved our own deepest satisfaction. Afterwards we lay silently for a time and then I got up and started gathering my clothes. Shannon watched me with a slight frown. Finally she spoke. "Where are you going in such a rush? I was planning on fixing breakfast for us."

"That would be great, but I need to get over to the hospital and try and interview Peter before the meeting with you and your boss this morning." I sat down on the edge of the bed and then reached for her and pulled her up out of the covers. We held each other for a moment and then I said, "I'd really like to just stay here for the rest of the day." I kissed her and went on, "But that may have to wait until we get this case…or these cases…put away and both of us have some free time." She hugged me hard and then I let her go.

She snuggled back down into the bed clothes. "I hope that's soon." She pulled the sheet up over her breasts and waved her hand at me. "I'll see you later at the meeting." She yawned and stretched like a contented cat and said, "But right now I think I'll take a little nap. 'Bye, Alex."

CHAPTER TWENTY-NINE

All the way back to my apartment I could think of nothing but Shannon and our brief night together. She was an amazing woman and a terrific lover. I didn't know if I was in love or in lust, but I really didn't care. She was smart and beautiful and she made me happy. I wanted her to be part of the rest of my life. And I wanted that to start as soon as I could arrange it.

I thought then about the way I had minimized what had happened to me in Iraq. Sure, it was true that we had only 'run afoul of an IED' but I knew I would never forget the sounds and smells that overwhelmed us that day. It was supposed to be an easy run out to a contractor's site to look at some documents and time sheets relating to the construction of the hospital at the base. We were a small convoy of three Humvees, each carrying two passengers and a crew of three. We left the base early in the morning and were traveling a well patrolled and supposedly safe route. The highway passed through half a dozen small villages. They were mostly just little clusters of mud brick houses and market stalls. I had been over the road before and was pointing out some interesting old ruins at the edge of one of the little villages to Father John, a newly assigned chaplain. He was an Army major, well-educated and interested in the history of the area. We had just decided that the ruins might have been Roman in origin when our world suddenly erupted with a deafening blast. The bad guys had let the first Humvee go over the IED buried in the road and then triggered it as our vehicle passed over it. That was a favorite trick of theirs. They figured the first and third vehicles were only escorts and so they targeted the middle one of the convoy as being the most important. Whatever their reasoning, it worked.

Our Humvee was knocked off the road and into a ditch, rolling over and coming apart in the process. When the doors came off, I was thrown out and part of the machine landed on my left leg, crushing my foot and ankle. The other passenger, Father John, dragged me away from the burning wreck even though he was burned quite badly himself and had a torn-up knee. He tried to go back into the wreck to get the driver but it was too late. The young man died at the scene. The gunner and observer were also injured but both survived..

After someone had put a tourniquet on my leg, we were hauled back to the base in one of the other Humvees. I blacked out at the field hospital while they cleaned me up as well as they could. The next thing I remembered was waking up in the Army hospital in Wiesbaden, Germany. A week or so later they transferred me to Walter Reed hospital in DC where they finished repairing my leg and started me on rehab. One of the doctors who worked on me thought I might be a candidate for an experimental prosthetic procedure so I was shipped to the VA hospital in Seattle where the new type of prosthesis was being developed.

The neurosurgeons, computer geeks and mechanical engineers had been working on the NID prosthesis for several years and had finally achieved a breakthrough. It turned out that I and eight other service members with similar injuries were chosen to be the first to try out the new type. All of us who were chosen had been athletes in college. We were all under thirty years old and generally were in better than average physical condition. Six of us had lower leg amputations and three had lost arms and hands below the elbow. It took several weeks for us to be fitted with the NID and then several more while we learned how to use them. In all, I spent four months in Seattle before I was deemed ready to go out into the world and try to live a normal life. Now it was a matter of going back to the laboratory, which had since been moved to Baltimore, for periodic updates. That was fine with me. In nineteen ninety-six the Air Force temporarily released me from active duty but did not medically retire me. Technically, I waa still a captain and subject to recall at any time. I also had the option to request a return to active duty if I wanted to do that. All this is well and good but I don't receive active duty, retired or disability pay.

When I got back to my apartment I showered and changed clothes. It was almost six o'clock and I hadn't had any sleep since early Monday morning, but I certainly wasn't tired. Somehow, I had gotten over that. I was still too amped up from my night with Shannon. I had a feeling that we were soon going to put the murders of Madeline Straub and Catherine Hood in the closed case files. I had no clue how the FBI would fare with their problem with the Straub family. That was their worry. I fixed a couple of eggs and wolfed them down with a piece of toast before I headed to the hospital.

On the way I called Sean on my cell phone. He was at Sandy's but said he would get to the hospital as soon as he could. I was hoping that Peter would have come out of his drug-induced coma enough to answer our questions coherently. We needed to know what he knew about Madeline's last day.

The hospital was beginning to come to life when I walked through the lobby and took the elevator up to the second floor. I guessed that shift change was around six and there were nurses and doctors coming and going when I got there. A patrolman I didn't recognize was sitting next to the door of Peter's room leafing through the morning paper. I showed him my badge and he told me that doctors had been in and out of the room several times during the night and had left again just before I got there. I told him I'd get someone to relieve him as soon as I could. He looked like he needed a cup of coffee badly so I sent him off to the cafeteria before I went into the room.

Peter was sitting up in the bed and looked much better than he had the last time I saw him. He was still hooked up to a monitor and had a tube in his arm but he was awake. They had taken the restraints off. He looked at me when I walked close to the bed but his eyes weren't really focused. I showed him my badge. He stared at it for a minute and then looked up at me and said, "I think I know you. Didn't you bust me once?"

"Yes, I did, Peter. We met a year or so ago. How do you feel this morning?"

He shrugged and looked at the tube and wires leading out of the arms of his gown, "I don't know. OK, I guess. I'm kind of groggy and my head hurts. What happened to me?" He looked around the room. "Do you know why I'm in here? The doctors and nurses won't tell me anything." He hands were twitching and he was sweating a little. He was having trouble staying focused on me.

"You O D'd on that drug cocktail you were using. How much do you remember?" Sean came into the room before Peter could answer. He moved to the other side of the bed and looked closely at the patient.

"So, you're finally awake and back among the living. For a little while there we thought we were going to lose you, boyo." Sean glanced at me. "You started questioning him yet?"

"Just about to start. Glad you're here." I turned back to Peter. "We have some questions for you and it's very important that you answer them." He nodded as if he understood and I went on, "Peter, let's start with last Friday. We know you had lunch at home with your mother and sister. Do you remember what you did after that?"

"Jesus, what day is today?" He looked around the hospital room in a panic. "How long have I been here?"

Sean said, "It's Tuesday, the first day of October. But that doesn't matter. What we need to know is what you did Friday afternoon." Sean pulled out his notebook and found a blank page which probably wasn't too difficult.

Peter sank back into the pillows supporting him and watched his hands shake for a minute or two. Sean and I waited until he was ready to talk again. "I think I took Maddy to her piano session after lunch. I usually do that on Friday."

"About what time was that?"

He twitched and wiggled some more. "I don't know...probably around two. Maybe two thirty. That's about the time she wants to get there."

"How did Madeline act? Did she seem all right?" I took a wild guess and went on, "Was she upset about something? Or did everything seem normal?"

He thought for a few seconds. "She seemed was a little bit upset but she's been awfully touchy for a week or so." He looked away and then back at us. "Friday, she started crying."

"Why did she do that, Peter? Did you do something or say something to make her cry?"

He turned away from us and tears began to run down his cheeks. "I guess I might have set her off. I told her I knew she and my brother Gerd were lovers...that I knew they were having an affair. I don't think anyone was supposed to know that."

I picked up a pack of hospital tissues from the tray table and handed it to him. "How do you know they were lovers?"

He blew his nose and snuffled a little before he wiped his eyes and said, "I walked in on them in papa's office at the brewery. Maddy and Gerd were on the couch in the office...they were..." He started blubbering again and then burst out, "I couldn't believe my own brother and sister would do something like that."

"We get the idea. When was this?" I looked at Sean and shook my head in disgust.

Peter wiped his nose some more. "A couple of months ago. Back in early July sometime. They didn't know I saw them. I went to the brewery one afternoon to see Gerd. When I went up to the office, I saw them on the couch but I just turned around and got out of there. I never said anything about it but it's really been bugging me last month or so and Friday, I just had to tell her I knew." He looked at the soggy tissue in his hand, dropped it on the bed and pulled another from the box. Then he said, "How could he do something like that with his own sister?" He shook his head violently from side to side. "That's just so wrong."

"You're right. It's very wrong. What did you do after she started to cry? Were you still in your car?"

"Yeah. I think I asked her some questions about her and Gerd but I don't really remember what they were. She just started to cry. She wouldn't answer me when I tried to talk to her.

"What did she do then?"

"She sat there for a few minutes and then she got out of the car and went into the house where the studio is." He sat up and looked at his hands. They were shaking and I could tell he was trying hard to control them. It wasn't working for him.

Sean had been busy scribbling in his notebook and now he asked, "What time was that?"

"I don't know what time it was. Probably a little before three."

"Where did you go after she went into the studio?" I wasn't entirely sure he couldn't have killed her for what he said he had seen her and his older brother do.

"I went out to Smokin' Joe's to see Buddy."

"Why did you do that, Peter? You and Buddy good friends?" Sean needled him a little.

He fidgeted around in the bed for a minute and then shrugged as if he'd decided to give up. "He sells me weed sometimes and I really needed something."

I said, "Really? Is that a fact? Buddy sells drugs?" I looked at Sean. He was grinning but became serious again when Peter glanced at him. "Make a note. Sean. We'll have to check on that. Did you buy any from him?"

"No. He told me he didn't have anything to sell."

"So where'd you get all the stuff we found in your room at Mama's? You had quite a stash of coke and some other shit when we picked you up. A real pharmacy."

"You gonna bust me for dope this time? Am I under arrest?"

"We haven't decided about that yet. You keep cooperating and we'll see what happens." I didn't tell him the FBI was going to gather him up sometime later in the day. "Who sold you the coke and meth, Peter?"

"I know another guy, Dipsey James. He's a dealer out on Getty." He sighed and continued, "I got some stuff from him and then I got high and drove around for a while. Afterwards, I went to Mama's to crash."

"That was on Friday night, right? What did you do Saturday morning when you came down?"

He shrugged, "Got high again. I guess I left Mama's some time in the afternoon and just drove around some more. I think I might have gone down to Grand Haven. I don't know. I do remember I wound up back at Mama's again." He sat up in the bed and looked me straight in the eye. "That's all I remember until I woke up here sometime early this morning."

"You remember having a little run in with Fumbles Cernak out at Colletti's on Saturday night?"

He shook his head. "Who said I was out there? And who told you I had a fight with Fumbles? Did he tell you that?" He slumped down in the bed. "Man, I don't remember any of that shit."

Sean laughed, "We're cops, Peter. We find out a lot of things from a lot of people. And we've got a couple of witnesses that put you out there on Saturday night."

Peter scrunched himself up into the bed covers. He was shaking badly now. His nose was running and he pulled another tissue from the pack and wiped it. He sat up and looked at me and said, "Have you asked Maddy about any of this? Why are you grilling me? Talk to her."

I moved closer and put my hand on his shoulder. "Peter, I really hate to have to tell you this…your sister is dead. She died Friday afternoon after you left her at the piano studio."

He collapsed into the bed again. "How? What the hell happened? She was all right when she left me in the car."

Sean took over. "She was murdered, Peter. Someone strangled her. We don't know who that is yet but we're going to find out very soon."

The look of shock on his face was genuine. He rolled over onto his side and curled up into a fetal position with his hands covering his face. He was shaking uncontrollably. I wanted to ask him a few more questions but I knew it was no use now. He'd gone catatonic. We'd have to wait. Right then a nurse charged in through the door before I could say anything. She was pissed.

"What are you two doing in here? Get out now. This patient is in no condition to be interrogated by you." She grabbed Sean by the arm and pushed him towards the door. "I said get out. The doctor will tell you when you can come back. Now I want you out of here." She was dead serious and we beat a hasty retreat into the hall.

We left him then. I told the patrolman outside to make sure Peter stayed put. We knew the Feds would come and get the kid after they rounded up the rest of the family. Right now we had to go see what the feds were up to and then we definitely needed to talk to Gerd Straub.

CHAPTER THIRTY

We headed back to Central for the ten o'clock meeting with the feds. I was anxious to see Shannon again even though it had only been a couple of hours since I'd left her bed. Had the two of us gone too fast or too far? I didn't have a clue but I didn't care. She had me completely under her spell and I liked it. Before I believed she was a real ice maiden because she was so calm and aloof. Now I realized that was part of her cover. Last night she had been a totally different woman. All I knew for certain is that I wanted to see her again…and soon.

Chief Bauer was standing in the doorway of his office and hollered at us as soon as we came into the squad room. "You guys talk to Peter Straub yet?"

"Yeah, Chief. We saw him early this morning and he had some interesting things to tell us." We went into his office and I gave him the gist of our talk with Peter and then I said, "Based on what he was able to tell us about Gerd and his sister, I think we need to have a serious talk with big brother as soon as we can get hold of him."

"Damn right," he said, "we need to pick the son of a bitch up right now."

I agreed but said, "He should be at the house when the FBI does their thing so they can bring him in along with Rudy and his wife. We can talk to him then." I had forgotten about Paul and now I asked, "Is Paul supposed to be out there? I guess the suits have a warrant for him too." Neither Sean nor I knew where Gerd or Paul might be at the moment. It was still early in the day but he could be at the brewery already. "If we get through with our meeting early enough, maybe we could pick him up at the brewery. I know we didn't want to tip off the rest of the Straubs about the pending raid but if we have him in custody, he can't say anything. Chief, we don't know if he's the killer but he's certainly the number one suspect at this point and I'd like to have him in hand."

The chief nodded. "All right. I guess that's the plan. The feds can bring the rest of them in and we'll sort 'em out then. We can sweat 'em a little to see what happens. I think we might have trouble breaking Rudy or Gerhardt or whatever the hell his name is. If he's been trained by the STASI or SVR, he should be able to resist any interrogation at this level." He grinned and picked up the cigar. "But I'll bet the feds have ways of dealing with that. "He pointed the cigar at me. "And you can put Gerd through the wringer when you find him. If he's been making it with his own sister and that got around, the idea of going to prison just might have been a motive for murder. You got anything else?"

"Just that stuff about Rudy's activity in Grand Rapids that we got out of the Ashley kid. But it's nothing we can act on until we get more info." I was hoping the Grand Rapids police would have something more along that line to help us.

There was a knock at the chief's door and Frank Duncan, the FBI agent, came into the office. Price, the AG guy wasn't with him this time but two other men were. Little spots of moisture speckled their nearly identical dark blue suits. As forecast, it had begun to sprinkle. The three men who came through the door might as well have been wearing uniforms. The only thing different about the way they were dressed was the color of their Windsor-knotted ties. Frank Duncan wore the power-red one. I looked for Shannon, but she was conspicuous by her absence. Chief Bauer looked at them and growled, "You're early. I thought you said the meeting was scheduled for ten o'clock." He gestured at the two newcomers. "Now who else do we have that's come to assist us?"

Duncan made the introductions. "Chief Bauer, this is Dean Wilcox from the Central Intelligence Agency and Tom Larsen from Immigration. Washington decided that they should also be involved in this case so they flew in last night." He paused and then said, "Bauer, there's been a change of plans. The raid on the Straub home has been postponed until we can get some more people up here from our office in Detroit. Washington has decided to make it a full-blown FBI operation." He gestured off-handedly toward Wilcox and Larsen, "With their help of course. We also decided we won't need any of your people after all." I watched the CIA man roll his eyes as Duncan passed on this latest news. Agent Wilcox stood in a very relaxed stance, a little bit behind and to the left of the FBI man. I got the impression that he didn't much care for the officious Mr. Duncan.

"That's bullshit." The chief slammed his fist down on the desk. "All you Washington weenies have done since you got here is screw up our murder investigation. We need to talk to those people now and your diddling around has kept us from doing that. Well, we're not going to fuck with it anymore." He turned to me, "Makarios, you and Dunphy bring Gerd Straub in…now. I don't care where you find him, I want him in here before noon."

"You can't do that, Bauer." Duncan stepped forward.

Bauer glared at him. "The hell I can't. We have jurisdiction here. We're running a double murder investigation and right now Gerd Straub is our prime suspect. We're bringing him in."

"But if you arrest him at the house, you'll tip off the rest of the family. That will blow the whole thing. They may run." Duncan put his hands on the chief's desk and leaned in. "If they get away from us, I'm putting the blame on you for interfering."

"I don't give a shit who you blame. It'll be just too damned bad if the rest of them do run. You and all your people from Detroit can chase 'em. With all the help you're bringing in that shouldn't be a problem for you." The chief leaned back and put his cigar in the big ash tray. He looked at me, "Makarios, why are you still here?"

"We're gone, Chief." Sean and I turned away and started for the door.

"Wait just a minute." Duncan stepped back from the chief's desk and held up his hand. "Bauer, I promise we'll bring them all in as soon as the rest of my people get here." I saw Wilcox turn away. He was smiling and shaking his head. I believe he liked the way the chief was handling Duncan.

Chief Bauer growled, "Where is Ms. Oliver? Is she still going out there today for the little get together? Or have you postponed that, too?" I was extremely interested in Duncan's answer to that question.

"No. That's all been changed. Shannon's been given some other things to take care of."

I wondered what that might be, but I saw Duncan wasn't going to say anything more.

Bauer wasn't happy. "And just when are you planning to bring all the Straubs in? Will it be this afternoon or sometime tonight? Or maybe tomorrow? You know Rudy, or Gerhardt or whoever the hell he is, is supposed to leave for his fund raiser today. If you don't get them when they're all together, there's no telling where they'll scatter to."

Duncan spoke up again, "That can't be helped. We're not ready to move on them like we had originally planned. But I promise you we'll bring them all in, interrogate them and then make them available to you as soon as we're finished. Then you can interview them about the murders. You have my word on it."

Bauer picked up his cigar again and leaned forward over the desk. "That's mighty big of you, Agent Duncan." He spoke softly and fixed his eyes on the FBI man. "But I think we will bring Gerd Straub in right now without any help from your people." He pointed the cigar at Duncan. "And then we'll make him available to you…but not until we're through with him. What you do about the rest of that family is up to you. And I wouldn't take your word if you told me today was Tuesday." He waved the cigar at Sean and me and barked, "You two, get the hell out of here. Bring Gerd Straub in."

CHAPTER THIRTY- ONE

Sean and I left the chief's office and headed for the front door. When we got there, we saw that the little sprinkles of rain that had speckled the nice expensive dark suits of the government men had turned into a full-blown rainstorm. The ice-cold rain was coming down in sheets, blown nearly horizontally by the cold west wind off the big lake. This kind of storm was not unusual in October and November. We Michiganders were used to them. Sean cursed as we looked at the rain swept parking lot, "Damn. This is my good sports jacket and the car's way the hell out there."

"Sit tight," I said. "I'll grab us a couple of slickers." I went back through the squad room to the locker rooms and pulled two yellow slickers off the rack. When I got back to the entryway, the three suits had joined Sean in staring out the door. They were watching the parking lot turn into a small lake. The wind was blowing so hard I expected to see whitecaps form on the puddles. None of Washington men had raincoats and they looked hard at the yellow slickers I was carrying. I handed one to Sean and he shook it out and looked at the big black letters, 'MPD', stenciled on the back and chest of the bright yellow plastic. "Might as well paint a target on these." was his only comment. From the expression on Duncan's face as he watched us pull the slickers on, he probably thought that was a good idea. Wilcox grinned at me and said, "Did you order up this rain just for us, Alex?"

I said, "Nope. And don't try to tell me it doesn't come down like this in Virginia. I spent my time at Quantico just like you did." The Quantico training facilities were used by a number of different organizations, one of which was the USAF. That is where OSI agents are trained.

"I suspect we were probably there about the same time, too." Wilcox smiled. "We might have had a few beers in the same joints. What do you think?"

I laughed and said, "I'm sure we did. Maybe we'll do that again one of these days."

The CIA man nodded, "I'm sure we'll get that chance. I'm looking forward to it."

Duncan continued to scowl and glare at the rain as if that would help. I wished them a nice day, buttoned up my slicker and we made a dash for the car.

Once inside, it only took a minute or two for the windows to steam up. This storm was bringing cold rain down from the northwest. I cranked the defroster up on high and the windshield began to clear. When I could see well enough to drive, we headed out of the parking lot and on to Clay St. The rain came in sudden bursts, driven by the gusty winds of the squall. The wipers were working overtime to keep the windshield clear but weren't having much effect. I hadn't seen a storm come up as quickly or be as violent as this one since I had come back to Muskegon, but squalls like these are not uncommon in western Michigan in the fall. I wondered if Theo had gotten Paul Straub's boat pulled out of the yacht basin yesterday.

"Where do you think Gerd might be at this time of the morning?" Sean's question brought me back to the business at hand.

I glanced at my watch, "I think he should be at the brewery by now. It's closest so we'll give that a shot first. Maybe we won't have to drive out to the Straub's house and screw up Duncan's plans." Frank Duncan had said the raid was off and that Shannon wasn't going to do the sympathy visit so I didn't think nabbing Gerd at the brewery would upset anything they had planned but I really didn't care. We didn't have a clue about how they would run their raid. Sean surmised that it would be with sirens blaring and a caravan of black SUVs like they do it on television. I shuddered at the thought.

The AltZeit Brewery took up nearly a city block and wasn't far from downtown so it didn't take long for us to get there. The rain was still slashing down and we waited in the car for a few minutes, hoping it would let up a little before we made a run from the parking lot to the door marked 'Visitors' on the front of the old red brick building. Straub had changed the name of the brewery when he bought it, 'AltZeit' means 'OldTime' in German and that's pretty much the kind of beer they brewed. Their beers were based on old German-style combinations of hops and barley. They bottled two kinds of beer regularly: a pilsner and a lager. And every October they came out with a limited production of what they called 'AltZeit Festbrau' to celebrate Octoberfest. It was a strong, high alcohol content malt liquor that had to be drunk quickly because it didn't keep well. I liked it.

The rain eased off a little and the wind seemed to be dying down so Sean and I hoofed it for the door of the big building. We crowded inside the waiting room and shook the rain from our slickers. There was no one in the sparsely furnished area. The desk, where the receptionist should have been, faced the door and three uncomfortable-looking plastic chairs were lined up against the outside wall. A low coffee table piled haphazardly with magazines related to the brewing industry completed the furniture. A large window took up most of the wall behind the empty desk. Through it we had a good view of the bottling line in the huge main room of the brewery. We saw three men and a woman, all dressed in white jumpsuit-style coveralls, working in the big room. I punched the buzzer that was prominently displayed on the desk. We heard the raucous clangor of a bell sounding in the big room. All of the people there looked toward the office. One of the men said something to the others and then headed our way.

When he came through the door into the waiting room, he didn't look pleased to see us dripping water all over the worn tile floor. Whatever Rudy had spent on rebuilding and updating the brewery, he hadn't included much in the budget for the reception area. "How can I help you?" was the guy's greeting. 'James' was embroidered over the breast pocket of his white coveralls.

We showed him our badges and I responded. "Police. We need to see Gerd Straub." I didn't see any need to be overly friendly.

James glanced back through the big window, "He's busy right now. We're just starting a bottling run. Can it wait?"

I followed his gaze through the window and saw one of the men in coveralls heading for a set of iron stairs that led up to the second floor. "No, sorry. This is important." I pointed to the man who was now halfway up the stairs. "That's Gerd, isn't it? Is his office on the second floor, James?"

He nodded and we started for the door. He stepped in front of it and held up his hand. "Could you take those slickers off and leave them here, please? That's a clean environment out there around the bottling lines." We shucked out of the dripping yellow raincoats and dropped them on the plastic chairs. The foreman stood aside and we went through the door into the bottling room of the brewery. The brewery building was huge. Some of the old brick structure was one story and served as a warehouse area for everything it took to brew and bottle beer. Other parts were two stories high like the one we were now in. The room we entered housed the bottling lines. Behind the conveyors and spigots of the line we could see the huge stainless-steel kettles where the wort was magically turned into beer. Overhead there was a mass of stainless-steel piping and cable trays that carried water, steam and everything else it took to control the brewing and bottling process. We headed for the metal stairway that went up to the second floor which covered half of the building. When we got to the top we saw that the stairs opened into a wide corridor bisecting the second floor. There was a large laboratory and a suite of offices on the left side of the hall. Both of those had window walls overlooking the main floor. There were two doors that opened onto the other side of the corridor, both sheathed with metal. One was marked 'Maintenance' and the other was labelled 'Storeroom'. We stopped at the paneled wooden door marked with Rudy's name and the word 'Office'. I banged on it and hollered, "Police. We need to talk to you, Gerd. This is Alex Makarios. We're coming in."

CHAPTER THIRTY-TWO

Sean shoved the door open and I went into the office with my hand on my Glock. One quick glance told us this was obviously Rudy's office. The walls were paneled in walnut but little of the expensive paneling showed. The paneling was covered with plaques and pictures of Rudy with politicians and local business people. I recognized some of them but had no clue who the majority of them were. A couch and four low upholstered chairs arranged around a coffee table were placed along one wall. A credenza occupied the same space on the opposite side of the room. I saw that the couch wasn't visible from the hallway outside. In the center of the wall facing the door was a big walnut desk with the window overlooking the first floor and the bottling lines behind it. Gerd Straub sat calmly behind the empty desk with his hands folded on the ornate leather blotter. The white jumpsuit that he had been wearing when we saw him downstairs was draped over one of the chairs by the coffee table and he was wearing a light blue flannel shirt and khaki pants..

I crossed the room and lowered myself into one of the chairs that faced the big desk. He looked at me and I said, "Good morning, Gerd. We've got a few more questions we think you can help us with." He nodded and I pulled my notebook from my pocket and flipped a few pages. "Tell me again where you were last Friday afternoon."

"I was here, at work. Like I told you that night at the house." He unfolded his hands and leaned back in the chair. "You still don't believe me? Go and ask the people downstairs."

"We will, Gerd. But right now we need to know something else." I decided to go for shock value. "How long have you been abusing your sister?"

Gerd's reaction was not what I expected. He raised his hands to his face and burst into tears, his big shoulders shaking with his sobs. Sean and I looked at each other. Gerd wasn't faking. After a couple of minutes, he regained control of himself and pulled a handkerchief from his pocket. He dabbed at his eyes and then looked straight at me. "I have never abused Maddy. I loved her." He wiped his nose and said, "We loved each other."

Sean broke in, "She was your sister, you fucking pervert. We know you screwed her right here in this office." He pointed at the couch. "Right there on that couch. We have a witness."

Gerd turned to face him. "You are wrong. You do not understand. Madeline was not my sister."

"What are you saying? How could she not be your sister?" I needed an answer.

He sat up straighter in the chair and put his hands on the desk again. "Maddy was the daughter of Papa's old boss in East Germany. We brought her with us when we came back from one of our trips." He shook his head, "She was just a baby. Mutti told people she was born while we were over there. Everyone here believed her."

"So for over twenty years your family has covered this up?" It made sense when I remembered that Chief Bauer told us the girl was born in Germany. Bauer said the baby had only been a month or two old when the family came back. Gerd's story was plausible and could be proved with a DNA test. I was sure that analysis, if we could get it, could prove it one way or another. Maybe the FBI guys could arrange that for us. I changed my line of questions. "You say that you and Madeline were in love? What do you mean?"

"Ja. Since she was sixteen or seventeen, we have been in love. But we knew we could never get married and live here. Mutti and Papa told us that. They forbid us to get married." He started sniffling again and turned away, the handkerchief to his eyes. He was silent for a couple of minutes and then turned back to face me. "But now we decided that we would get married anyway. Maddy was pregnant and it is the right thing to do. So we told Papa and Mutti we would go away."

I asked. "Gerd, . When did Madeline find out she was pregnant?"

He looked away, "She went to the doctor in Grand Rapids. Maybe it was two weeks ago. That's why we were going to get married now. So we could have our baby here."

"Did she tell anyone else she was going to have a child?"

"Only Papa and Mutti. We told them a week ago. Last Monday."

"And they were all right with you two running away to get married?'

"Nein. They were very upset. They knew she was not my sister but no one else knew that. Mutti said if we married it would cause a big scandal and would ruin papa's campaign for the senate. They said we must not do it. Mutti said that it would upset all their plans. Papa told Maddy to get an abortion. We told them we would not do that. We wanted our baby." He shrugged. "We left the house then but later we went back. We have no place else to live. For a week now, Papa and Mutti do not speak to us."

"That must have been rough on the two of you. Did your mother tell you what plans your marriage would upset?"

"She told us nothing. We did not care about what they did...or their plans. We were making our own plans for the wedding."

I moved on to our other major problem. "Gerd, we know Madeline was physically abused when she was just a little girl. We need to know who did that to her. The scars she carried on her body tell us someone physically tortured her for a long time. I'm asking you now, did you do that to her?"

"No. It was not me. I would never do that." He looked straight at me and said, "I stopped him when I found out what he was doing to her."

"Who, Gerd? Who did you stop?"

"Paul."

CHAPTER THIRTY-THREE

We sat in silence for a moment. I couldn't believe what Gerd had just said. Sean recovered first. He stood up and stared down at me. "I'll kill that murtherin' bastard." My partner's face was contorted with rage and his fists were clenched. I got up and put my hand on his arm.

"No, Sean. We'll get him…if what Gerd is telling us is true. I promise you…we'll find a way to get him." I turned back to Gerd. "All right. Tell us everything you know about what Paul did to Madeline. I know this is very hard for you but we need to know everything. Start from the beginning."

Gerd got up from behind the desk and began to pace around the room. He stopped and looked at the pictures and certificates covering the walls. Scattered among the politicians and businessmen were a few framed family photos. Most of those were of the Rudy and Karla with Paul or Peter. A couple of them included Madeline. Gerd was not in any of the pictures. We waited until he composed himself and was ready to talk again. I knew we had to get his story absolutely straight. I also knew we'd have to be patient. I encouraged him again, "I know this is painful for you, Gerd, but we have to know the details…everything you know. How did you find out that Paul was abusing Madeline?"

He heaved a great sigh, mopped his face with his handkerchief and came back to stand by the desk. "Maddy told me."

"How long ago was this?"

"Years ago, it was. Maddy was maybe only six or seven. It was the summer after I finished high school." He looked hard at both of us. "You maybe remember me from those times. It was just before I went to the army. One day Maddy showed me some bloody marks on her leg and told me Paul did that to her."

"How did he do that? Did she tell you?"

"Ja. He screwed a bottle cap to an old ping-pong paddle and used it to spank her."

"Why would he do something like that? Why would he spank her?" I was still having a hard time believing all this.

"She told me he was punishing her for not doing what he told her to." Gerd wiped his face again. "Maddy said that he spanked her whenever she wouldn't be quiet or take her nap...things like that. Paul was minding Peter and Madeline that summer. Papa and Mutti were traveling a lot for the brewery. I was working here a little before I went away. Paul was maybe going into the junior year in school and he didn't want to stay at home and watch the little ones." He turned to me, "You remember, Alex. The football team was always practicing out on the beach. He wanted to be out there with the rest of you."

I did remember those summers. The football team couldn't officially practice during the summer but the coaches strongly encouraged us to get together and play touch football on the beach. It was great conditioning and we had access to some of the playbook. That was against the rules, of course. Occasionally one of the coaches would park across the street and watch from his car. That was also against the rules.

"Paul was how old then...sixteen or seventeen?" Paul and I are the same age. We would have been sixteen that summer.

"Ja. He's ten years older than Maddy then." He went back behind the desk and sat down. "But she told me he had been doing that to her for a long time. Sometimes without the paddle…just with a bottle cap. He would put it on her and turn it while he pushed on it."

"Who else knew about this? Did your parents or Peter know?"

"Mutti knew about it for sure. Papa… maybe knew something but Peter didn't know." He looked away, "Peter still doesn't know that Maddy is…was,,, not our real sister. He was also young when we brought her back. Paul knows, of course. He was older, like me."

"And your mother didn't do anything about any of this?" Sean broke in. He had been scribbling in his notebook while Gerd talked. I knew we would have another session about all this and that it would be filmed and properly recorded but Gerd's story might change and Sean's notes were necessary.

Gerd looked at him. "Mutti did not really like Maddy. To her, Maddy was just another girl…she was someone else's daughter."

"How could Rudy not know what Paul was doing?" My question brought Gerd's attention back to me.

"I don't know. But I don't think he knew anything about it. He loved Maddy…spoiled her. He treated her like she was his real daughter. If he knew, I think he would have done something terrible to Paul."

"What did you do when you found out Paul was abusing her?"

"I went to Paul and told him he must stop. I was bigger and older and told him I would hurt him if he did that bottle cap or paddle thing to her again. I think he believed me. Later Maddy told me he had stopped and didn't do it anymore."

"Did you tell your mother or father that you knew about the abuse?"

"Ja. I told Mutti that Maddy had shown me the scars and that I spoke to Paul about it."

"What did she say or do?"

He looked down at his clenched hands. "Nothing. She told me to let it be. She said that it wasn't serious and that Maddy wasn't hurt. She said Paul was just playing…like all boys do.

That seemed to fit with the way the woman had behaved on the night of the girl's murder. Her coldness and lack of emotion was easier for me to accept now that I knew Madeline was not really her daughter. But Gerd's behavior that night still seemed a little cold and uncaring also. I found it hard to understand how a man who professed to love a woman as much as he did could be so casual about her sudden death. I didn't doubt Gerd's story and it seemed to clear him of the two murders. His problem with the FBI and the rest of the suits from Washington was something I didn't even want to think about…nor tell him.

"Gerd, we're going to have to ask you to come down to Central so we can get all this on film and tape. You understand that you are not under arrest or a suspect in either of the murders we're investigating. We just need you to make a formal statement. Strictly voluntarily, of course. That O K with you?"

"Ja, naturlich. I will just tell James and the others that I am leaving now."

CHAPTER THIRTY-FOUR

The squall had passed and the rain had stopped completely but the wind still blew cold from the west. There was a smell of snow in the air. After we retrieved our slickers and put Gerd in the back seat, I drove back across town to Central. Sean took Gerd to one of the interview rooms and I headed for Chief Bauer's office. He was alone when I entered.

"Tell me something good," he growled. "I've heard about enough crap today from those Washington weenies. What's the story on Gerd?"

"Well, I believe he's clean on the murders." Bauer nodded and then I briefed him on what Gerd had told us at the brewery, adding that we had spoken to James, the foreman, and he had corroborated Gerd's alibi of being there until nearly seven on Friday evening. Then I asked, "What do we do about Paul and his abuse of Madeline? Is there anything we can charge him with?"

Bauer thought for a minute or so, chewing on the cigar, before he answered. "I don't see how we can do anything about that. It happened a long time ago and we don't have a complaining witness. Unfortunately, She's dead."

"Yeah. That's what I was afraid of. If Gerd brought it up, it would be only his word against Paul's. Do you think there's a motive for murder there? Maybe the girl threatened to expose Paul. A charge like that certainly wouldn't help his career in this town."

Bauer's face showed a tight little smile, "Or his father's campaign for the Senate."

I thought that over for a little bit, "That would make it a motive for two of the Straubs…or maybe three. Karla Straub seems pretty keen on getting Rudy elected."

"How about Peter? Do you like him for the two murders?"

"No, we think he's off the hook, too. I don't think he has the guts to do something like murder. Also, I'm pretty sure he was coked out by the time Hood was killed. I also believe he loved the girl he thought was his sister. He was awfully shook-up when we told him she was dead. He didn't fake that."

The chief eyed his cigar and then pointed it at me. "But Gerd says she wasn't their sister at all. I guess that jibes with what I knew of the Straubs. I told you they went back to Germany several times. I suppose it all could have happened like Gerd said." He dropped the cigar in the big ash tray. "I think think that the exposure of even that little piece of fraud could cause a scandal that might hamper Rudy's campaign. I suppose a DNA test could prove they weren't the girl's parents. Can Karras do one of those here?"

"I'm sure she can but we'll need samples from Rudy and Karla. I don't think they'd give 'em willingly. I guess Chris could check on who the father of Madeline's child is at the same time." I knew that Chris would keep samples of tissue from the victims for the lab in case they were needed at a trial sometime in the future. Getting samples from the Straubs might require a court order but it could be done.

I said, "There's another loose end here. We still don't know who Rudy was seeing at the hotel in Grand Rapids. We're positive it's a woman. I'd really like to find out who she is before we interrogate him. We also need to know who the other guys he met with are."

Bauer drummed his fingers on the desk and then picked up his cigar. "I'll call Lyles again. They should be able to nail down the guest list at the hotel if we give them the dates of Rudy's visits. We don't have time to go down there and do it ourselves." He chewed on the cigar for a minute and then said, "You'll just have to confront him about the other guys. We don't have enough information to try and trace that lead."

I looked up as Sean came into the office. "How's Gerd doing with the statement?" I asked.

"Everything's all right. Richards is leading him through it and they're filming the session. I gave Richards my notes. Gerd seems to be telling the same story." He turned to the Chief, "Did Alex tell you about that bastard Paul and the bottle caps?"

Bauer nodded, "Yeah. But we probably can't do anything about it now."

"That's what I figured." Sean looked disgusted. "Sometimes the law gets in the way of justice." He turned to me, "But I'm going to find something on that bastard and make him pay for what he did to that girl. One way or another."

Sean and I left the chief's office and headed for the interview room. Just before we went back in I stopped him and said, "We'll figure out what to do about Paul later, Sean. Don't worry, we'll find a way to get him. Let's see how Richards is doing. Then I'll see if Gerd knows anything about the woman or the men Rudy was seeing in Grand Rapids."

CHAPTER THIRTY-FIVE

Richards was just finishing up with Gerd's statement when we entered Interview Room One. Gerd looked absolutely worn out. He sat slumped in the hard chair with his arms resting on the table. His face was pale with deep tiredness lines on his cheeks. I felt sorry for him. Especially since he didn't know that the feds would come for him soon and start the whole interview thing over again. I believed his story and considered him off the hook for both murders but I didn't know what the government would charge him with or what they would do to him. Still, I wasn't quite through with him. There were still a few more questions I had to ask.

I spoke to Richards, "Jim, we'll take it from here if you're through. Can you turn that camera off? I don't think we need to record this part of the interview since it doesn't have anything to do with Madeline's murder." Richards said he had just finished, turned off the video camera, gave Sean's notes back to him and gathered up his own. He left and I sat down at the table facing Gerd. He straightened up a little and asked, "How much longer am I going to be here?"

"Just a little while longer, Gerd. We've just got a couple of things we think you can help us with. Let me ask you this, did you ever go with Rudy when he took his business trips to Grand Rapids?"

"Ja, maybe one or two times a month. But not so much this last year."

"You didn't go with him this year? Not since he's been campaigning?"

"Nein. All that political stuff has nothing to do with the brewery, so I don't go. I can do most of that business on the telephone now but sometimes I go to Detroit or Lansing by myself if I need to." He looked away and continued, "Maddy went with me once to Grand Rapids."

"So you don't know who Rudy goes to see or who he talks to down there?"

"No. Sometimes he tells me if it's somebody I know from before. But I don't ask him about the politics."

"Gerd, does Rudy have a mistress in Grand Rapids?"

The question caught him off guard. He looked around the room and sat up straighter in the chair. After maybe a full minute, he said, "I think… no, I don't know." He shrugged and spread his hands. "Maybe once he did." He looked at me again. "Why do you ask me that kind of a question?"

"Gerd, we know Rudy has been seeing a woman in Grand Rapids a couple of times a month this past summer. We need to know if the woman is a girlfriend or if she could be a business acquaintance or if she's someone connected to his campaign. I thought you might be able to help us."

He looked away and then shook his head and said, "Ach, ja. It is maybe a mistress. He had one before when we lived in Germany."

"Really? Tell us what you know about that."

He settled back in the chair and seemed to be studying something in the far corner of the room. "I told you that Maddy was the daughter of Papa's old boss in East Germany. I think Papa and his boss's wife had an affair when we lived in Berlin. I was young then, maybe only eight years old. I saw them making love one afternoon when they thought I was out of the house. A month or so after that we moved from Berlin to Pirmasens in West Germany and Papa went to work at the brewery. It was a long time later…after we came here…that we went back to Pirmasens and Papa's old boss, Herr Beidecker, from Berlin came to see us. He asked Papa and Mutti to take Maddy and bring her here like she was their own daughter. I think he paid them a lot of money to do this."

"What did your dad and his boss do for a living in East Germany?"

"They both worked for the government there...in Berlin."

"Did they work for the STASI?"

Gerd looked down at his hands folded on the table. "Ja."

"Gerd, do you know what your father's specific job in Berlin was?" We all knew this had nothing to do with the murders, but I was curious. I knew Wilcox would pursue this when they interrogated Rudy but maybe I could point them in the right direction if Gerd could tell us anything about what went on in Germany.

He shrugged. "I don't know very much about it. Like I told you, I was young then and did not pay much attention. He was an inspector of some kind, I think. I remember he was always traveling. Mostly I think he went to other cities in the German Democratic Republic. Sometimes he would bring something back for Paul and me. It was usually a toy or a book. Once he brought back some beautiful Matryoshka dolls for Mutti." He paused and smiled as if he was seeing the dolls again. "I think maybe he went to the Soviet Union on that trip."

"How about after you moved to Pirmasens in seventy-four? Did he still travel a lot?"

"Ja. But then he worked for the brewery. He was a territory manager. He traveled all over West Germany selling the beer. Even sometimes he went to France and England." Gerd's face lost some of its pallor and he said all this with a smile. He was proud of his father's accomplishments.

Richards came back into the interview room and said, "The fibbys brought Rudy and Karla in a few minutes ago. They're in the conference room. Bauer wants all of us to sit in on the interviews."

CHAPTER THIRTY-SIX

We went down the hall to the squad room and the chief's office. He was standing at the doorway and waved at us to join him. He was holding his cigar and pointed it at the conference room and said, "They put the Straubs in there for now. Apparently the FBI and the CIA don't get along too well. Duncan and Wilcox are in my office arguing about who's going to do what and when. Sergeant Davis is babysitting the Straubs." He looked at me. "Did you know Davis speaks German?"

"No, I didn't know that. But that is a damn good thing. If those two speak German while they're getting their stories straight, he'll be able to shut them up...or listen in."

Bauer nodded, "Yeah. That's what I thought. Anyway, we need to separate those two and get 'em to start answering our questions." He looked at me, "Who do you want to tackle first?"

"Let me start with Rudy. He doesn't know that we already are aware of some of his secrets and maybe we can trip him up. But if he's STASI trained; he might go into resistance mode." I had been through the Air Force SERE program during my OSI training and part of that program was concerned with techniques to resist interrogation. I was sure that STASI training in that area would be much more thorough.

Duncan and Wilcox came out of Bauer's office. Neither of them looked happy. Duncan was red-faced and breathing like he'd run a half marathon. Wilcox was frowning and had his hands jammed in his pockets. Bauer grinned at them and said, "Well, boys, where do you want to begin? Or should we just take over and turn them over to you when we're through?"

Duncan snapped. "Don't get cute, Bauer. We can take them out of here right now and you'd never get 'em back." He stopped in front of the chief and looked up into his face. "This is an important case for us and I won't have you screwing it up."

As large a man as he was, the chief seemed to grow bigger as he listened to the FBI man. He went from a cuddly teddy bear to a Yellowstone Park grizzly in about five seconds. Bauer spoke softly, "Duncan, you can take your important case and shove it up your ass. I've already told you we have two murders to solve and those two people in there are the prime suspects at the moment. We are going to interview them now. And when we're through with them, and only then, it will be our pleasure to turn them over to you." He paused, "Do you understand me?"

I glanced at Wilcox. The CIA man's frown had disappeared, and he was smiling as he listened to the chief. He leaned comfortably against the edge of a desk with his arms folded across his chest. He looked like he was enjoying himself at Duncan's expense. I wondered what his thoughts about the interview were; so I asked, "Agent Wilcox, how do you think we should do this? I would think that you might have something to say about it."

He grinned at me and said, "Oh, I do. I know Frank is concerned about the alleged bribery attempt and Agent Price has a problem with their false passports and their illegal entry. My problem is that our boy Gerhardt might be a sleeper agent in deep cover." He smiled at the chief. "But I can wait until you're through with him. I'm sure he's not going anywhere."

Duncan scowled at him and then appeared to wilt. He stepped away from Bauer, shrugged and said, "All right. Do it your way. Just remember, we brought them in so they're federal detainees but you have the right to question them about the murders…but not about anything else."

I spoke up again, "Wait a minute. We've found out that he met with some people regularly in Grand Rapids and we need to know who they were. That may not be part of your investigation but it could be something of interest to Agent Wilcox. And it is relevant to ours since it relates to Rudy's alibi. So we're going to pursue that." I looked at the chief. "Of course, I'll pass on whatever we find out."

Wilcox shrugged again but Duncan looked pissed and said, "That could be related to his campaign and the bribery allegation. That's not relevant to your investigation."

Bauer pointed his cigar at Duncan. "Don't be so damned territorial. If it turns out to be campaign related, we'll let it go. Hell, it could be that the people he sees there are spies for the SVR. Whatever we learn we'll let you know."

Duncan threw his hands up and grumbled, "Go ahead then. Let us know if it bears on what we're thinking."

Bauer asked, "Do you or agent Wilcox want to sit in on the interviews?"

"No. I don't think that would be a good idea. I agree that we've really got three different problems here and I think we should keep them separated as much as possible." I was surprised at Duncan's response but he continued. "I assume the interviews will be filmed and recorded so I think we can stay up to speed and use whatever you might uncover if it would help us. Is that not correct?"

Bauer nodded. "Of course. You can have full access…after we're finished. Everyone okay with that? Good." The big man turned and headed for his office. When he got to the door, he turned and pointed the cigar at us. Then he barked, "Makarios, you and Dunphy take Rudy someplace and get busy."

"Got it, Chief. What do you want to do with Gerd? I think we should let him go home. If these guys want him, they can pick him up again. He's given us all he knows and I don't think they really have anything to charge him with. He was just a kid when they came into the country. That probably applies to Peter too. He was born here and, except for the dope, he's pretty harmless. The narc squad can pick him up anytime they want to for that stuff."

Bauer nodded and turned to Richards. "Go cut Gerd loose. Remind him not to leave town 'cause we might want to talk to him again."

I turned to Sean and said, "Get Rudy and take him to number three. I'll meet you there in a couple of minutes." I grabbed Frank Duncan by the arm and pulled him across the room to my desk. He didn't come very willingly but my grip on his bicep convinced him that it was a good idea if he came along. When we got to my desk, I turned him to face me, "Where is Shannon Oliver right now?" I hadn't released his arm and now I increased my finger pressure. He grimaced and tried to pull my hand away. I knew I was hurting him. It was what I intended. "Answer me, goddammit."

"She's finishing up some loose ends here. I decided we didn't need her on today's operation. That's all you need to know." I relaxed my grip and he pulled his arm free and began massaging it. He stepped back a pace and looked up at me. "We have other things to do here and Shannon is taking care of those. That's all I'm going to tell you. Besides, what she is doing is none of your business."

I very nearly smacked him but I knew I'd be in serious trouble with Bauer if I did. I didn't care about any trouble the FBI could cause me. I'd lost all respect for them because of the way Duncan was handling this case. My frustration grew as I realized that I would get no more information from him or anyone else from his staff.

The files we had created on the Straub family were on my desk and I grabbed them and brushed past Duncan, headed for Interview Room Three.

CHAPTER THIRTY-SEVEN

Sean opened the conference room door and motioned toward Detective Sergeant Davis, his counterpart on Lieutenant Richards' team. Rudy and Karla Straub were seated at the far end of the long conference table; Karla at the head and Rudy on her left. Davis was sitting at the near end of the room, close to the door. He got up when Sean came into the room. Sean spoke quietly. "Have those two been talking?'

"Only to each other. They've been trying to ignore me." Davis grinned and went on, "I think they're a little concerned because the FBI was in on their arrest. I understand that it was the guy from Immigration who led the raid. These two keep talking about Canada and passports. They don't understand why the FBI was involved. Karla does most of the talking. Rudy just sits there listening and nodding now and then."

"Are they speaking English or German?"

"Mostly German. But nothing about the murder of their daughter. They wondered where Paul and Gerd are. They've never mentioned the girl. They also are worried that the FBI will toss their house."

Sean nodded, "Yeah. I think Duncan's team might be doing that right now. He hasn't told us all of their plans. Maybe the Oliver woman is heading that up. I wonder what a search would turn up?" He shrugged, "Well, no matter. I'll take Rudy off your hands for a while now. We're going to start with him." He watched the Straubs for a couple of minutes before he walked down the room and stopped next to Rudy's chair.

Rudy looked up at him and asked, "What are we doing here? Why are we being treated like common criminals? Where is the man from immigration that arrested us? We know our rights. Get Chief Bauer in here so we can straighten this mess out. It's all a big misunderstanding."

"If you say so." Sean knew better so he added, "If you want my opinion, I'd say you and the missus might be in big trouble. Those FBI and ICE guys didn't come all the way out here from Washington to settle a little misunderstanding."

Karla said, "My husband is correct. We have done nothing wrong. Rudy is an important man here. Why are you treating us like criminals?"

"Well, we have some questions we'd like you to answer. Mr. Straub, I'd like you to please come with me now." He turned to Karla and said, "Ma'am, please stay here with Sergeant Davis until we send for you." Rudy didn't move from the chair so Sean took hold of his arm and, remembering this was the man who had called him an "Irish drunk", jerked him to his feet. Sean was none too gentle. He knew he was going to enjoy this.

CHAPTER THIRTY-EIGHT

Interview Room Three was painted an institutional light green and furnished with a scarred wooden table and three metal armchairs. One of the chairs was fitted with rings which served as anchor points for hand cuffs when a prisoner needed to be restrained. A four foot by six foot mirror took up most of the wall facing the table. It was one-way glass, of course. The surface of the table bore the cigarette burns and scars of the many interviews it had been a part of over the years. The furniture had been moved from the old Central building to the new headquarters when it had been declared open for business in nineteen eighty. Many of the scars had accumulated in the twenty-two years Room Three had been in use. There were cup circles and can-circles from spilled coffee and soda on the beat-up table. That told me the place hadn't been cleaned in several days. The room was cold and drab. It wasn't meant to be comfortable.

I removed the cassette from the video recorder. We would let Rudy believe the interview was being recorded but I didn't want this portion to be on tape. When Sean and Rudy came through the door, I was already sitting in the interviewer's chair with the folders spread out in front of me. Sean pushed him around the table to the chair opposite mine.

I said, "Sit down, Rudy. We've got a few questions for you. There are some loose ends in our investigation, and I hope you can help us clear them up." I turned to Sean and asked him to turn on the video recorder. He made a show of doing that and came back to stand at the end of the table.

Rudy sat down heavily and then leaned forward. He clasped his hands on the table and asked. "What am I doing here? Am I under arrest? You have no cause to detain me. I know my rights." A little of his normal bluster came back to him as he sat there. He straightened up in the chair and adjusted his tie and collar. "Get Chief Bauer in here. I want to talk to him right now."

I'd had enough. Between my run-in with Duncan and my normal dislike of Rudy Straub, I'd reached the end of my patience. I snarled at him, "Shut up, Rudy. You'll talk to us and no one else until we're through with you. You're not under arrest yet. We are still investigating the murders of your daughter and Catherine Hood. We've got some questions for you and you're going to answer them if it takes the rest of the week."

He started to get up. "I don't have the time to take this bullshit from you two. I'm a city councilman and I have a campaign for the senate to run."

Sean reached out and shoved him back into the chair. "No, Rudy. Your campaign's finished. The only running you'll be doing is from the nasty big boys in your cell block. Now sit your ass down and answer our questions."

I opened the first folder. I made a show of reading something for a minute and then said, "What's the name of your girlfriend in Grand Rapids? You know, the one you meet at the Riverview Suites hotel every week or so. Or is it a different woman every time? Is she your steady or are you playing the field?"

"What the hell are you talking about?" The bluster was back. Rudy nearly came out of the chair and banged his fist on the table. "I don't have a girlfriend. Anywhere. I'm a married man. And before you ask, Karla and I are getting along just fine." He subsided back into the chair and straightened his jacket.

"Well, if you don't have a girlfriend, I guess maybe you're just having a quickie at the hotel and it is a different one every time. Tell me the name of the pimp you deal with and we'll check it out. Were you with a woman last Friday afternoon?"

"I'll say it again. I don't know what you're thinking. I wasn't there and I don't have a girlfriend."

I smiled at him, "Rudy, we know that's bullshit and we don't have time for it. We have a witness that puts you in the Riverview Suites Hotel with a woman at least two and sometimes three afternoons a month. Who is she, Rudy?"

I sat back and waited for his answer. It took him a couple of minutes. I could almost see the wheels turning in his head as he fought to come up with a story he thought we would believe. Finally, he cleared his throat and said, "A witness, you said? And who the hell would that be? I bet it's that lying little pervert that follows me around and drives for me sometimes? You know you can't trust anything that little shit says."

"How about the Grand Rapids police department and the hotel desk clerk, Rudy? Will they do as witnesses?" I was bluffing. We didn't have anything from either of those sources yet. Rudy didn't know that, of course, and he fell for it. I went on, "We can put you there last Friday. From around one until after six. You were almost late for the cocktail party."

He waited a minute, his eyes flicking around the room and then he mumbled, "She is not my girlfriend." Then he suddenly looked up and said, "What's this got to do with Madelines' murder? That's what we're here to talk about, isn't it?"

"Yes. It cerainly is. Among other things." I checked the folder again. "Now, once more. Who is the woman?"

He puffed up again. "I'm not going to tell you. She doesn't have anything to do with this. Why do you have to know who she is?"

Sean leaned down close to his ear, "She's your alibi, you dumb fuck."

Rudy lunged back as if Sean had bit him. "What the hell do you mean? I don't need an alibi. Madeline was my daughter. How could you possibly think I killed her? Besides you know I was in Grand Rapids until late that evening."

"Rudy, you just lied to me. We know that Madeline was not your daughter."

He slumped in the chair and suddenly lost all his bravado and bluster.

I picked up one of the other folders. "You claim you were there all day. But how do we know that? You were off the grid from one until after six. We think you had plenty of time to come back here, commit murder and get back to Grand Rapids before your cocktail party. So you see, we know you had the opportunity and perhaps a motive. But if you were with a woman in that hotel all afternoon you obviously couldn't have done all that. Tell us the wonan's name so we can ask her if you were with her on Friday."

He thought about that for a couple of minutes while I sat perfectly still. Finally, he gave it up and mumbled, "Her name is Pat...Patricia Walsh."

"Speak up, Rudy. We're recording this."

"Walsh...Patricia Walsh."

I glanced at the folder in my hand, "Isn't that your campaign manager's name?"

"Yes. Pat is his wife."

"How long have you and she been...friendly?"

"Since last spring. March or April, I guess."

"All right. Were you with her Friday afternoon?"

"Yes."

"From when to when?"

"Probably from around one o'clock until six or so."

"Then what did you do?"

"The Ashley kid picked me up and we went to the cocktail party."

"What did Mrs. Walsh do?"

"I don't know. She probably went home to change clothes. She came to the dinner later."

"Does Walsh know you're having an affair with his wife?"

"God, I hope not. David has a terrible temper. I don't know what he'd do if he found out." He shook his head, "He's hard on the campaign workers. Goes into a rage, even over simple little things. I don't know why the party hired him to run my campaign. I didn't have anything to say about it."

I motioned for Sean to activate the video recorder and he put a fresh cassette into the machine and made certain it was aimed at Rudy. We had enough to clear him of the murders and I wanted the rest of this on record for the FBI and CIA people. I shuffled the papers again and asked, "Who is the man you meet at the motel out on Plainfield?"

"I don't know what you are talking about. I meet with no one at such a place."

"Come on, Rudy. Let's not go through this again. Don't lie to us again. We've got you out there every month or so. What do you do there and who's the guy?"

I had expected more resistance from him. If he had been trained to resist interrogation, he had failed the course. I thought maybe he had gotten tired pretending or had decided his undercover role wasn't worth it anymore. Whatever the reason, his bluster was totally gone and he was beginning to sweat. I could see little beads of water beginning to form at the edges of his receding hairline. Again, he thought about his answer for a minute or so and once more, I sat perfectly still. I had been taught that patience is one of the strongest cards in an interrogator's hand.

Finally, he broke the silence, "I do not know their names. It is not always the same man."

"How do you know when and where to meet with them?"

"I am told to go there."

"What do you do with these men whom you don't know?"

"Sometimes I give them an envelope and they sometimes give me another one to bring back here."

"What's in the envelopes?"

"I don't know. I never open them." He looked toward the blinking green light of the videorecorder and then quickly looked down at the table. He said, "I think sometimes it is money. Sometimes maybe there are just papers." Rudy was sweating hard now. He pulled a handkerchief from his pocket and wiped his face and hands. As soon as he stuffed it back into his pocket, I was ready with the next big question.

"Who tells you when to make these trips…and who do you give the envelope to when you get back?"

"Karla."

CHAPTER THIRTY-NINE

The stunned expression on Sean's face probably mirrored mine. We just stood there. We certainly hadn't seen that coming. Rudy dug for his handkerchief and mopped his face again. He had loosened his tie and now he sat slumped in the chair with his hands in his lap. He wore a signet ring of some kind on his left ring finger and he was twisting it around and around as he sat there. He wore his wedding ring European style...on his right hand. Before either of us could say anything the door opened and Dean Wilcox came in. He put his hand on my shoulder and said, "Thanks, Alex. I'll take it from here."

I got up from the interrogator's chair and moved to stand against the wall beside the door. I said, "Did you get all that?" Wilcox nodded without looking back at me and I knew he'd been in the observation room, the cubbyhole about the size of a broom closet on the other side of the mirror. Each of the interview rooms had such a hidey-hole. They were just big enough for two people if they were good friends and not claustrophobic.

Rudy looked at the newcomer for a minute or so and finally said, "Who are you?"

"My name is Dean Wilcox and I work for the U S government. I also have a few questions for you, Mr. Straub. Or should I call you by your real name, Herr Krantz?" Wilcox spoke very softly so that Rudy had to concentrate carefully to hear what he was saying. That is another valuable card in an interrogator's hand.

A look of shock came over Rudy's face. Then, as if he'd suddenly remembered how to handle being interrogated, he straightened up and tightened his tie. He smoothed his hair and then placed his clasped hands on the table. "My name is Rudolf Straub. Whoever you are, you are mistaken. I do not know the name Krantz." A new face and a new attitude. Rudy went to the bluff and bluster mode again. I didn't think it would work with Wilcox.

The CIA man had a couple of folders in his hands and now he opened one of them and appeared to read from it. "You are Gerhardt Krantz. You were born: August 23, 1940 in Dessau, Germany. You attended schools and university in Dessau and went to work for the East German Ministry for State Security, the STASI, in Berlin. You worked there from 1962 until 1970. After that you were reassigned to Pirmasens in West Germany and worked with the STASI and the SVR there until 1972 when you entered the U S illegally through Detroit." Wilcox closed the folder and leaned back in his chair. "Is that about right, Gerhardt, or did I leave out something important?"

Rudy folded like a Geisha girl's fan. His hands began to shake and went for the handkerchief again, but this time it was to wipe the tears from his fat cheeks. He began to cry quietly, not sobbing but just giving in to the idea that he'd been caught. Pretty soon he blew his nose on the now sodden piece of cloth, stuffed it back in his pocket and faced Wilcox.

"Ja, I am Gerhardt Kranz. How did you know?"

Wilcox smiled. "As you Germans say in the movies, 'We have our ways...'. It really doesn't matter how we know, Gerhardt. That fact is that we do know who you are and what you've been doing for the past thirty years.

You have engaged in espionage against the United States. You are a spy and you will be treated as one by the US government."

"Nein! I am not a spy." He threw his hands up in the air. "I was never a spy. I was always just a clerk in Berlin. After that they gave me a job as a courier. That is all I have ever been." He went back to twisting his ring again and broke out with some more sweat. I wondered how much more water he had in him.

I had finally gotten my head around everything I was hearing and realized that the trips that Gerd and the Ashley kid had told us about may have been Rudy's courier runs in Europe and here. It also made sense that Karla was the one calling the shots. Christos! Was she the real sleeper that Wilcox was looking for? Maybe Rudy was just the means to get her into a position of influence and power. Then I had another thought and grabbed Wilcox's shoulder and said, "Dean, stop. We have to talk."

Wilcox turned around. "What's the matter?"

"We might have a problem. Let's go outside for a minute. Sean, turn that thing off until we get back." Sean turned off the video recorder and Wilcox got up and followed me out into the hall.

"Why did you interrupt me? I had him going." The CIA man was not happy with me.

"You weren't with Duncan when they went to the house and picked them up, were you?'

"No. It was just Duncan, Price, Larsen and some of Frank's FBI people. He didn't want me along."

"Did he arrest Straub?"

"I don't think so. I believe Larsen told them they were just being brought in for questioning."

"So they didn't Mirandize him? Read him his rights?"

I could see the light dawning. Wilcox slammed his fist against the wall. "Shit. If they didn't do that, none of what he said can be used."

"Yeah. That was my thought. Let's get to Duncan and see if he did it by the book or if he just winged it. Rudy's a pretty savvy guy and once he realizes what happened, he'll recant everything. We'll never get another word out of him. I really hate to give him time to think about this but we've got to be sure before you go any farther."

He started up the hallway toward the squad room. "Duncan should be in your chief's office. Let's go."

CHAPTER FORTY

Frank Duncan and the other suits from DC were in Bauer's office when we crossed through the squad room. Chief Bauer was sitting behind the massive desk with the ever-present cigar in his meaty hand. He spotted us through the open door and waved us in. "What are you getting from Rudy?' His question was directed at me but Wilcox answered.

"He's given up some good information, but we may not be able to use any of it in court." He turned to the FBI man. "Frank, did you place him and his wife under arrest?" The sharpness of his tone and the expression on his face took Duncan by surprise.

"No. We just told them we were bringing them in for some more questions regarding the murders of their daughter and the Hood woman." He smiled at the chief. "I told them that it was at your request, of course."

Wilcox stepped closer to Duncan. "So you didn't read them their rights? You just picked them up like you were a fucking cab driver?" He turned to Bauer, "Didn't he tell us this was supposed to be an all-out raid...a snatch and search?" He spun around to Duncan again. "We believe these people are SVR agents and you treat 'em like they jaywalked on Western Avenue. What the hell's the matter with you?"

Duncan stammered, "We didn't want to alarm them by tipping our hand to what we were really after. I didn't want to give them time to get their stories coordinated."

Chief Bauer stood up and growled, "Who gave you permission to tell them that you were picking them up at my request? I sure as hell didn't authorize you do use my name."

Duncan realized he was on the hot seat and stammered again. "Uh…I just figured it would go over smoother if they thought we were acting for you…someone they know."

I turned to the chief. "Since they weren't Mirandized, everything we've got so far is no good. Rudy gave up a hell of a lot but soon he's going to realize that we can't use it. I think he'll close up tighter than a freshwater clam and then we won't get anything from either of them." I waved in the general direction of Duncan and Price. "These guys may have really screwed the pooch on this."

Dean Wilcox nodded. "Alex is right. Now we've got to back in there, find a charge we can arrest him on and read him his rights. He'll holler for a lawyer and we won't hear another peep out of him. I'm guessing his wife will do the same." Wilcox looked down at his hands and a look of wonder crossed his face as he realized that his fists were clenched so hard that the blood had left them. He flexed his fingers a couple of times and the color slowly returned.

I faced Duncan. "What have you done about Paul and Peter? Did you bring them in too?"

"No. The youngest boy is still under guard at the hospital and we can't find Paul. We don't have a lead on where he is yet." He paused, "I think he might have left the city."

"That's crap. He would never leave town with all that's going on. He wants to be part of the action and pick up a headline or two. And I'm sure he's been in touch with Rudy and Karla, probably at least on a daily basis… maybe hourly. Besides, he has a law practice to attend to. That's pretty important to him."

"Well, he's not at his office and they don't know where he might have gone. He didn't tell his staff anything when he left."

Chief Bauer sat down and pointed his cigar at Duncan, "Don't worry your pretty little head about Paul. We'll find him. You guys couldn't find in nickel in your own pants pocket. I don't want you trying to bring him in, either. The way you fucked up on Rudy and his wife, I wouldn't let you write a parking ticket in my town." He turned to me again, "Alex, why don't you and Agent Wilcox go back in there and see if you can salvage something from Rudy and then take a run at Karla. I want these murders wrapped up before these FBI guys cause another one. I assume Rudy's clear on those, isn't he? His alibi is good?"

I said, "Yeah, I'm pretty sure he was shacked up at that hotel all afternoon. He couldn't have made it here, killed both Madeline and the Hood woman and made it back to Grand Rapids by the time the Ashley kid picked him up." Then I turned to Wilcox. I didn't know if he had a plan or not. As far as I was concerned we were through with Rudy. We had nothing to hold him on and I was sure Gerd and Peter were in the clear. Karla and Paul might be another story or two and I wanted a crack at them both. "How do you want to proceed with Rudy, Dean?"

He shrugged so I continued, "Let's go back in and you can charge Rudy with entering the country with a false passport. We'll Mirandize him and then we can see what else he'll give up. I'm satisfied that he's not our killer so he belongs to you guys from here on out."

He nodded. "Yeah, that might work." He looked at the man from immigration, "Tom, you've got a warrant for that, haven't you?"

Larsen reached for the briefcase on the floor beside his chair and dug a sheaf of papers out of it. "Here you go."

I said. "All right. You arrest Rudy on that charge and Sean can read him his rights. We can book him into a cell here until you guys want to take him back to wherever." I looked at Dean Wilcox. "Unless you want to continue to question him."

"No. We've got all that stuff on tape and it gives us a good starting point when we get him back to Langley." He hesitated and then grinned. "Or wherever."

Bauer looked at me. "You sure Rudy is clear on the murders and we can turn him over to these guys?"

"Yeah, I'm sure. We can always bring him back if we need him to testify or if something else turns up. I don't think he's going to be walking the streets for a while."

The chief grunted and laid the cigar in the ashtray. "After you finish up with Rudy, put him in a cell and, as long as the CIA doesn't want another crack at him, go see what you can get out of Karla."

We went out in the hall with Tom Larsen. He smiled at us and waggled his briefcase. "I've got a couple of signed blanks in here too if you need them. Just fill in the charges. The judge was very cooperative." We headed back to Room Three.

CHAPTER FORTY-ONE

Rudy was still slumped in the chair looking like his world had fallen apart…which it had. I watched while Larsen told him he was under arrest on suspicion of having entered the US illegally and with false documents. Sean pulled his Miranda card and read him his rights and I asked him if he understood them as read.

"Ja. I know my rights. I am a citizen." He looked at Wilcox. "I will answer no more questions from you. You never told me who you are. I think maybe you are from the FBI. I know you're not from here." He folded his hands on the table then and sat back.

"Fair enough. We'll have plenty of time to get acquainted in the next few months. I told you my name is Dean Wilcox. But I don't work for the FBI; I'm a special agent of the CIA. We will be taking care of you from now on, Gerhardt. Of course, you'll go to trial for the charges Tom just read and there seems to be an alleged attempt to bribe a US Senator that the FBI is interested in. They will be talking to you about that in due time. But I believe the CIA will be keeping you in our custody at Langley. Understood?"

Rudy's face had turned white and his folded hands had developed a tremor while Dean was speaking. I suspected that his previous handlers had told him all about the CIA and what they could or would do to get information from people. I didn't envy him. He didn't say anything further so I went around the table and helped him to his feet.

"Sean, you and Tom take him to booking and then put him in a cell until these people get ready to move him somewhere. Come back when you get through. I want you here for the next set of interviews. We're going to finish the damn murder cases."

They left with Rudy and Dean and I went back to the conference room to get Karla Straub.

CHAPTER FORTY-TWO

Karla Straub was sitting at the end of the conference table as if she were in complete control of the situation. Her expression was that of a queen just waiting for someone to ask what she wanted for lunch. 'Haughty' was the word that came to my mind. Sergeant Davis sat in one of the side chairs just inside the door.

I moved down the room and stopped near the end of the table. "Mrs. Straub. I'm Lieutenant Makarios and this is Special Agent Wilcox. Would you come with us, please? We have a few questions we'd like you to help us with."

She sat perfectly still and gave me the same icy stare I had received at her house on Friday evening. "I know who you are. You asked me rude questions at my house last Friday night. Now what do you want?"

"As you know, we're still investigating the murder of your daughter. There are still a few things to clear up."

"Ask your questions." She still hadn't moved. I could see that she didn't intend to cooperate. I thought it was time to stop being nice.

"No, Mrs. Straub. We're going to do this our way. I want you to come with us now. We will go to Interview Room Three. Please come along." I reached for her arm.

She shrugged away from my hand and stood. "Do not touch me. I know about you policemen and how you treat people. I have dealt with your kind before." She turned and walked toward the door. She didn't look at either of us and said, "Where is my husband? What have you done with him?"

"We'll get to that in a few minutes." I motioned for Sergeant Davis to come along and, as we went back across the squad room, Sean and Tom Larsen joined our little parade. In Room Three, Sean placed a fresh tape in the videorecorder. I waited until he was finished and then told her to sit. She sat down and crossed her arms across her chest; a typical defensive, uncooperative body language pose. Larsen stepped to the end of the table and read the charges. They were the same as those for Rudy. 'Illegal entry with false documentation'. Sean again read the Miranda warning from the card we all carry and I asked her if she understood her rights.

She listened to all of this without changing her expression. When I was through, she said, "This means nothing. I am a citizen of Germany. Your 'rights' mean nothing to me."

"You are not a naturalized US citizen?" I remembered then that Chief Bauer had told us that Rudy and the two boys had been naturalized but for some reason Karla had not gone through the process with them.

"Of course not. Germany is my homeland. I would never give up my citizenship."

"Where you were born doesn't matter. Everyone has rights under our laws and I need you to acknowledge that you understand them. We are recording this interview so please answer me. Mrs Straub, do you understand your rights as read by Sergeant Dunphy?"

She shrugged and answered in German."Ja. Ja. Ich verstehe."

We all knew what she said but I was glad that we had brought Davis along. If she decided to switch to German for her answers in a further effort to be uncooperative, we had an ace in the hole.

"Good. Thank you. What is your full name and date and place of birth?

She looked at me as if I had asked for her bra size and what model it was. "You know who I am. Why should you have to know my Geburtstag? What has that to do with Madeline's murder?"

"As I told you, this interview is being recorded. Please answer the question for the record." I could hear Dean shuffling through his papers. I guessed that he already had the real information.

She gave a small sigh and said, "My name is Karla Straub. I was born February twenty six nineteen forty-six in Berlin, the capitol of the German Democratic Republic." Her voice grew stronger as she said this. She sat up straighter in the chair and her chin came up as she looked me straight in the eye.

"You mean communist East Germany, don't you?" I wanted to take her down a peg if I could. "What was your maiden name?"

"Stolz."

I glanced at Wilcox and he nodded affirmatively. Now I was ready to start.

"Now, let's talk about last Friday. When did you last see Madeline?"

"I told you. She had lunch with Peter and me and then he took her to the piano lesson."

"That was on Friday, right? What did you do after that?"

"I worked in my garden."

I remembered that the garden plot was lying fallow and it looked as though it hadn't been touched in several weeks. "What do you mean when you say 'worked'? What were you doing?"

"Weeding. Digging it up. What all gardeners do in in the fall." She was lying. No one had been digging in that plot.

I shifted gears. "Were you upset when Gerd told you that he and Madeline were going to get married?"

"What are you talking about? That is absolute nonsense. They were brother and sister. They could never marry."

"Karla, you know that isn't true. We know Madeline was not Gerd's sister. We also know she was not your daughter. They were not related so they could marry if they wanted to."

The woman uncrossed her arms and placed her hands in her lap. "You are wrong. Madeline is my daughter. She was born to me when we were in Germany."

"Don't lie to us, Karla. We know Madeline was the daughter of your old boss from Berlin. You and Rudy passed her off as your daughter to get her out of East Germany. Please don't try to lie to us anymore. Just tell us the truth and this will go a lot easier."

Karla was still stone faced and said, "I don't know what you are talking about."

Dean stepped forward and showed me a piece of paper with the name 'Rutgar Beidecker'. He nodded and whispered 'boss'. I didn't want to go much farther down that road into his territory but I prompted Karla again.

"Come on, Karla. We know all about your visit to Germany and that Beidecker came to visit you in Pirmasens. We know that you agreed to bring Madeline home with you. We also know that he paid you to bring her here. Or was he paying you for something else?"

She had slumped back into the chair while I was speaking. I really didn't know if Rudy's boss was also her boss but it had been worth a shot "Now, tell me. Were you angry or just surprised when Gerd and Madeline told you they were going to get married?"

Karla's eyes darted around the room and then settled on the video camera's blinking green eye. Her face settled into its usual stony, closed look. "We were surprised that they had chosen to do such a thing at this crucial time."

"What do you mean by 'crucial'?"

"It is particularly important that Rudy's campaign not be interrupted. He must win in November."

I didn't pursue that line and went back to Gerd and Madeline's problem. "Did you know they were in love and had been having an affair for some time? Several years, perhaps?"

"Ja. We knew."

"Who do you mean by 'we'?"

"Me, Rudy…and Paul."

"Did you also know about Paul's abuse of Madeline when she was a little girl?"

"Ja. Ich weise."

"What did you do to Paul for that? Did you stop him from abusing the girl? Did you punish him in any way?"

"Nein. He was only playing. The girl was not hurt seriously." She tossed her head. "All boys play like that. It is common knowledge."

"Maybe in East Germany, but not here, lady." Sean's voice was rough. "He'll pay for what he did to her." I asked, "Why weren't you pleased when Gerd and Maddy told you she was pregnant and they were going to marry? Don't you want grandchildren?"

"I told you, doing such a thing now would maybe upset Rudy's campaign for the senate."

"You mean if the truth about Madeline's real parents came out? Or if her abuse by your other son came to light? I guess either one of those things would put a crimp in Rudy's plans, wouldn't it?"

She shrugged, "Maybe it would be embarrassing. People would talk. He would maybe lose some votes" She sat up. "It is a close election. We need every vote."

"What did you and Rudy tell Gerd? Did you tell them to go ahead? Or maybe you said for them to wait until after the election." She didn't say anything and waited for a beat and then went on, "But that wouldn't work, would it, Karla? Madeline was pregnant and would soon begin to show. They knew they couldn't wait. Besides, they didn't want to wait. They were in love. Maybe you told them to run away and get married somewhere else. Or maybe you decided that Madeline should just go away permanently. Forever. What did Rudy decide?"

Katla sat straight up in the chair and put her folded hands on the table. Every inch the boss now. "No. You have it all wrong. Rudy decides nothing. He is not good at deciding for the family." She looked straight at me. "I decide what is good or bad for my kinder. I told them to wait. Perhaps the girl would have a miscarriage and then Gerd would not have to marry with her. Perhaps she would run away."

"They were in love, Karla. They wanted to get married. But you knew something like a miscarriage wasn't going to happen, didn't you? You also knew she was not going to run away. I think you decided to handle the situation yourself last Friday. You had ample time and you certainly have a motive. We know Rudy's campaign means everything to your long-term plans.

You couldn't have anything interfere with that, so I think you strangled Madeline. I also think you thought maybe Catherine Hood saw you as you left the studio. Again, you had ample time to kill her and get back to your house. Paul said he called you with the news of Madeline's death but that wasn't true, was it. You already knew she was dead because you strangled her Friday afternoon." We were watching her closely. "Am I right, Karla?"

She seemed to be searching for something as she moved in the chair and examined all parts of the room. After a long two minutes, she settled back and said, "I did not kill that girl. You have made up an absurd fairy story. You have no proof."

I smiled across the table at her. "You did kill her, didn't you? And then you went to Catherine Hood's house and strangled her, too. We have fibers from your gardening gloves and your car was seen at Hood's place." That last part wasn't exactly true, but she didn't know that. Winters' report had said that one of the neighbors saw a car near Catherine Hood's house Friday evening. He was walking his dog but was too far away to identify the make and model of the car. "I think we have enough to get an indictment from the grand jury and bring you to trial."

"I did not kill that woman." She examined her hands and nodded slowly a couple of times, then took a deep breath and said, "Ja. I killed the girl."

I turned to Dean and added, "O K, she's all yours."

Karla sat up quickly. "What is this? What do you mean?"

I got up and Dean moved into the interrogator's chair. "Karla, I'm Special Agent Dean Wilcox. I work for the CIA and I am going to ask you some questions now."

For the first time, I saw fear in her eyes. She began shaking her head from side to side and she muttered 'Nein.' several times before Dean said "Look at me, Karla. Here's what we already know. You and your husband both worked for Rutgar Beidecker at STASI headquarters in Berlin. From there you went to Pirmasens and then to Canada. After that you entered the

United States with false Canadian passports. We believe you are a 'sleeper'; an agent of Russia in deep cover waiting to be ordered to accomplish a specific task. Your husband, Rudy, is also undercover and you work for him and your handler. Is all that correct?" Dean sat back.

She stared at him in disbelief. "I know nothing about any of what you said."

"Don't lie to me, Karla. You are going to Langley with us and face charges under the Espionage Act. Is that understood?"

Karla struggled to find enough room to stand up between the bolted-down chair and the scarred table. "I am a German citizen. You cannot arrest me. I will answer no more questions. Contact my embassy. I will say no more." She sat down again and folded her hands in her lap.

Wilcox spoke quietly, "Karla, you are coming back to Langley with me where we will continue our discussion. Do you understand that?"

She slumped back into the chair and shook her head, "Ja, ich verstahe."

I saw that Dean wasn't ready to give her to me yet and he continued, "But there's no point in lying to me anymore, Karla. Your husband already gave you up. We know he is really Gerhard Krantz. He tried to tell us that he was just a gofer, a courier, for you and your handler. That's not true, is it, Karla? He is the real boss and you work for him, don't you?. If you tell us the truth now maybe we can do something for you on the spy charge."

She sat up slammed her fist down on the table. "Nein. He told you the truth. I do not work for him. He works for me. I have always been his superior. Even in Berlin and Pirmasens." She suddenly realized what she was saying and collapsed back into the chair.

Wilcox said, "You and Gerhardt and Paul and Gerd are going to be guests of the US government for a long time, Karla. Maybe after a while we'll send you back to Germany and let them have a crack at you." He picked up his folder of notes and got up from the table. He turned back to her, "Of course you are going to be tried for two murders first." He grinned at me. "She's yours again if you want her."

I nodded and said, "Karla Straub, I am arresting you for the murders of Madeline Straub and Catherine Hood." I read the Miranda warning to her again and watched as she folded in on herself and slumped in the chair.

She looked up at me. For the first time since Friday, she showed some emotion. There were tears in her eyes. "You must believe me. I did not want to kill Madeline. And I already told you, I did not kill the Hood woman."

"What do you mean? Tell me what happened. It might make things easier for you?"

She leaned forward and place her folded hands on the table. "We did not want Gerd and Madeline to marry now. They talked to us about it a few weeks ago and we had approved. But only if they waited until after Rudy was sworn to the senate. Then she found out she was pregnant, and they no longer wanted to wait. If they got married now, we knew it could have a terrible effect on Rudy's campaign. We had been told that nothing must interfere with his being elected in November. I told her and Gerd that to marry now was unacceptable and that she must get an abortion." She shrugged. "They could always have children later. They refused to even consider that." She rummaged in her coat pocket for a tissue, found one and wiped her eyes. "On last Thursday night they told us that they were marrying now and said they would do it next Saturday. They refused to listen to reason. They left the house then."

"So who made the plans? And who committed the murders?"

Her eyes had lost the hard, stony glitter that I was getting used to and now had softened into the soft pleading look of a puppy. "Please, I didn't want to do it. I had to stop them from ruining Rudy's campaign any way I could. I had no choice. We loved Madeline even though she was not our own child." Her voice sank to barely a whisper, "It was Paul who planned it."

I still wasn't sure I could believe a word of what she was saying and said, "So now you're telling us it was Paul who planned to kill Madeline?"

"Ja. It was his idea."

"When did he do this."

"We discussed it Thursday night but did not decide when we should do it. Friday I was just going out to the garden when he came to the house and told me I must go to the piano studio, get Madeline and bring her to him at his office."

"Yes. And then what was going to happen?"

"He told me he would take her to his boat and kill her. He planned to take her out on the big lake and dump her body there."

"Why didn't you follow that plan?"

Karla straightened up in the chair. She had regained her composure and seemed sure of what she was doing. "When I got to the studio, Peter's car was still in the drive. I parked on the side street and went to the back door of the studio. I had been there before." She paused as if remembering a pleasanter time and then went on. "The door was unlocked and I went in. Maddy was playing something and did not hear me. I looked at her and became angry because she and Gerd had refused to listen to us and were defying me. I knew if they went through with it everything that I…that we had been trained for would be ruined. I could not let that happen. I went up by the piano and saw the cord on the drape. I couldn't help myself. My garden gloves were in the pocket of my coat so I put them on and took the cord from the drape. I wrapped it around Maddy's neck and pulled it tight." She looked down at her hands on the table. "She didn't struggle for very long. I left by the back door but I think the Hood woman saw me."

"Go on. What did you do next?"

"I went to Paul's office and told him what I had done to Maddy and that the Hood woman saw me. He told me to go home and that he would take care of the Hood woman. He said he knew where she lived. He took my car. He was afraid people might recognize his."

I thought, sure, Hood knew Paul and would think he was coming to see her about his sister's murder, so she'd have no problem letting him in.

I asked, "Did you go straight home from his office?"

"Not immediately. I had to call some people to tell them of Maddy's death. It might affect their plans."

Wilcox broke in. "Did you use the phone in Paul's office? Or your cell phone?"

She seemed puzzled by his question for a moment and then answered, "I used the phone there. I did not have my cell phone with me. It was in the car with my gloves."

Dean sat back grinning like the Cheshire cat with a gallon of cream. He looked at me and said, "Got him."

Suddenly I realized what he meant. By using Paul's phone, Karla had implicated him in her espionage or sleeper activities and that call might be traceable to her handlers.

"Are these people…I mean your handler and his friends… from the SVR?" He dropped a pen and a pad of paper on the table. "I want names, Karla. Right now."

I was pissed. He had just interrupted my questions and I felt sure I was going to get Karla to give us everything she knew. But then I realized that finding out about her handler was of prime importance. She took the pen and scribbled three names on the pad and then looked back at me.

I decided we had enough. All we needed now was to find Paul. I pushed the pad back to her. "Please write out what you just told me and sign it."

She took the pen again and wrote swiftly for seven or eight minutes. Then she dropped the pen and stiffened in the chair. The look in her eye became glittery again and her voice hardened as she said, "I do not have to talk to you anymore. I want to speak to my attorney now." She sat back and folded her arms.

CHAPTER FORTY-THREE

Paul Straub; Attorney at Law, man-about-town, sister abuser and now, murderer. That's a resume' that will get you a good job in Washington DC. Sean and I walked out of the interview room shaking our heads. Why would Paul do that? The more I thought about it, the more it made sense. He had two solid motives to get rid of Madeline. His abuse of her when she was a child and Rudy's potential campaign melt down if she and Gerd married now. If Rudy lost the election it would mean Paul's job as Rudy's Chief of Staff would disappear. Yeah, I thought, those two reasons were good enough. Add the fact the Paul was a sadistic bastard to begin with and it made him the obvious first choice.

We got to Chief Bauer's office in record time and gave him the news. It didn't matter whether or not Karla's story was true, we needed to grab Paul and get him in custody. Bauer said, "Where the hell could he be hiding? The suits have been all over his office and apartment since early this morning and they haven't seen a thing. You got any ideas?"

Up until then I had been drawing a blank but I suddenly had a brain storm. "Let me make a phone call. Maybe I've got something." I headed for my desk and picked through the pile of business cards I had tossed haphazardly in the top drawer. I found the one I wanted and dialed the number on my cell phone.

Mama's voice had a slight edge to it. "You must be clairvoyant, lieutenant. I was just about to call you."

"OK. We've got each other now. You first…what's up?"

"My place must be a magnet for the Straub boys. We've got another one here and he's been a little bit of a problem. Can you help us out by taking him off our hands?"

I couldn't believe our luck. I waved at Sean as I told Mama to keep Paul there and that we would be there as quickly as we could. She said that wouldn't be a problem and we hung up. I told the chief we'd found Paul and were going to go get him and we hit the door running.

We pulled up in front of the Eastside Gentlemen's Club and pounded up the brick walk to the front porch. Neither the thin man with the long blade nor his dog was on hand to greet us. Nor was B J anywhere in sight. I banged on the door and announced "Police." The same slim Asian woman opened the door and pointed to the club room on the right of the entrance hall.

I put my hand on my Glock and went into the big room. Mama was sitting on the plush couch behind one of the low cocktail tables with a half-filled champagne flute in her hand. She favored me with a smile, showing her dimples and brilliant white teeth. Sitting to her left in one of the over-stuffed chairs, the leggy blonde named Cynthia was holding a plastic bag filled with ice cubes to the side of her face. Someone had popped her hard and I could see her cheek was swollen and a purplish bruise was beginning to show. The slim Hispanic-American man with the expensive suit and the long, thin knife was perched on the arm of her chair. They were holding hands. I tore my eyes away from this domestic tableau and looked across the room.

Paul Straub was slumped in another of the comfortable chairs. His jacket was unbuttoned and I could see that his shirt had become untucked.

That went with the expensive tie pulled halfway down his chest. He looked as if he was coming off a three-day drunk. I walked over and looked at him closely. From up close, I could see a few small signs of damage. His nose had been bloodied and possibly broken. It was pointing a little off-center. There was also a bruise beginning to show along one cheek bone. He grimaced when he saw me and I could tell he still had all of his teeth.

I turned to the big black man who was leaning against the bar to Paul's right. "What happened, B J?"

B J showed his gold teeth again when he grinned at me. "Alex, I believe Mr. Straub lost his balance and fell down. Reckon he might have hit his face on the edge of that billiard table."

I smiled back at him and said, "Cut the crap, man. Tell me how he got roughed up."

He nodded toward Paul. "Mr. Straub and one of our other gentlemen were having a slight difference of opinion…about some political bullshit, I think…and Mr. Straub got belligerent. He has been here most of the day and I think he has been drinkin' a little…maybe a little too much." B J nodded toward the blonde, "Miss Cynthia stepped between them to calm them down and Mr. Straub pushed her. We don't allow that rough stuff here but before I could reach him, he took a swing at her and hit her in the face. Then he must have slipped. 'Cause he fell down."

I looked at B J's knuckles. No abrasions or redness. His explanation almost seemed reasonable until I saw how tenderly Cynthia was cradling her boyfriend's swollen hand. I figured Paul was lucky. A broken nose was nothing compared to being gutted like a fish by a long, slim knife. Or maybe eaten by a pit bull who liked apples.

I addressed Mama and the group. "Well, it looks as though this little problem has settled itself and you certainly don't need us to quell a disturbance or anything. I believe Sean and I can see that Paul gets home alright.

Are you OK with that, Mama?" She nodded and smiled and I walked over to stand in front of Paul. I said, "Get on your feet, Paul."

He got up slowly and stood swaying slightly. His head came up and he slowly focused on me. "So what are you going to do with me, Makarios? I apologize if I've done anything wrong. I'm sure I can make it right with Mama." He turned toward her, "Isn't that right?" He was reaching for his wallet when Sean grabbed his wrists and snapped the handcuffs on them. "Hey. What the hell are you doing? You don't have to cuff me over this. Get these damn things off."

I spun him around to face me. "Paul Straub, you are under arrest for the murder of Catherine Hood."

His face went white and his knees buckled. He hit the floor before either Sean or I could grab him. He was making no effort to get up so I pulled my Miranda card, leaned down over him and read the minimal warning. "You have the right to remain silent. Anything you say can and will be used against you in a court of law. You have the right to speak to an attorney and to have an attorney present during any questioning. If you cannot afford an attorney, one will be provided for you at government expense." Paul still was making no effort to get up from the floor. I finished up with, "Do you understand your rights?" There was no acknowledgement.

Sean prodded him in the ribs with his toe, not too gently, and Paul mumbled "Yes".

I thanked B J and Mama winked at me. We perp walked Paul out to the car and headed out.

CHAPTER FORTY-FOUR

When we got Paul to Central, we booked him and put him a holding cell. There were a couple of empty cells on either side of him. He hadn't said a word on the ride from Mama's nor during the brief booking process. I wanted to talk to Chief Bauer before we started to interrogate Paul. I also wanted him sober. We knew he had killed Catherine Hood, but I wanted his confession.

The chief was smiling when Sean and I entered the office. None of the people from Washington were with him. He stood and reached over the desk to shake our hands. "Good job, both of you. Now you just have to wrap up the loose ends."

I retrieved my hand from his massive paw and resisted the urge to flex my fingers. "Thanks, Chief, but we're not quite through. As you said, there are some loose ends. We should be able to wrap it up when I get Paul into Room Three. He pretty much fell apart when I told him why he was being arrested. I think that was almost a confession, but we need the words from him."

Sean nodded, "We'll get 'em if I have to beat the son of a bitch bloody."

Bauer shook his head. "Don't touch him, Dunphy. When he's convicted, he'll be put away for life. And life down in Jackson won't be very pleasant for a guy like Paul Straub. It seems like a fitting punishment for abuse and murder. Now go get the confession."

We retrieved Paul from his cell. Richards and Davis came with us and the room seemed a little bit overcrowded, but I wanted plenty of witnesses. Sean loaded another fresh tape into the video recorder and I sat down across from Paul at the old scarred table.

"Paul, you know the drill. All we need from you is a written statement of how and why you killed Catherine Hood. There's a pad and pen so you can begin anytime you're ready."

He looked at me as if I were insane. "Why would I do something like that?"

Sean's voice had a murderous edge of rage to it. "Yeah. That's what we want to know. Why would you kill that woman? But I've got another question. Why would you torture your sister when she was just a baby? Tell us that, Mr. Straub." He was standing just to my left and Paul looked up at him with real fear in his eyes.

"What are you talking about? I never did anything like that."

"Really? Your mother and brother disagree. They say you did abuse Madeline. With a beer cap on a ping-pong paddle. I bet it was effective in getting her to do what you wanted. Did you enjoy it?" Sean moved a step closer and Paul recoiled back into the chair. I got up and put my hand on Sean's arm. I pushed him back a little. He was trembling with anger and I was afraid he would crack.

"Come on, Paul. Karla has already told us you killed the Hood women. Just tell us how and why and we'll be through here. You told us you were in your office Friday morning but that was a lie, wasn't it? You were at the house with Rudy and Karla. That's when the three of you decided that Madeline had to die and cooked up the plan to kill her. You didn't stay for lunch with her and Gerd. So what did you do?"

"No, that's not right. I was at the office Friday." He seemed to wilt a little. "We discussed the problem of Gerd and Maddy on Thursday night. But nothing was decided."

"Tell me what you did Friday afternoon."

He folded his hands on the table and started shaking his head from side to side. "Alex, what's going to happen to me?"

"Don't 'Alex', 'ol buddy' me. I'm not your friend,Paul. And you're the hot-shot lawyer so you know exactly what's going to happen. You're going away for a long, long time. Now, why did you all decide to kill Madeline? Tell me, dammit, or I'll turn Sean loose."

He glanced at Sean and then looked down at the table and began talking. "Karla was afraid that a lot of negative stuff would come out if Gerd and Madeline got married. The campaign is very tight and it wouldn't take much to throw it to Carlyle. She said we had to stop them. They had refused to wait or consider any other alternatives."

"Like aborting the baby?"

"Yeah. I had told Momma that I could arrange an abortion if they would agree." He looked up into the corner of the room. "I'd done that before."

"So you knew Madeline was pregnant when you decided to kill her?" He nodded and I went on, "But that didn't matter, did it? You didn't care at all about this girl who was supposedly your sister, a girl you had grown up in the same house with and a girl you had sadistically tortured when she was just a toddler." I turned away from him in disgust.

Tears were slowly running down his cheeks now. "I'm sorry...so sorry. If there had been any other way. But Momma and Rudy said this was the only way to be sure Rudy would win the election and claim the senate seat. We would go to Washington. That was all important to them."

"Did they tell you why? Or did you already know?"

"Momma told me Friday morning. Rudy promised me that I would be taken care of by them and their bosses when we got to Washington."

"OK. I'll let Dean Wilcox figure that one out. Why did you go to the house on Friday?"

"I came up with a plan. I went to tell Mama to bring Maddy to my office so we could talk to her. I wanted to try one more time to change her mind about marrying Gerd. But if she didn't come around, I was prepared to get rid of her." He looked down at his hands and flexed them a couple of times. "My boat was still in the water and I figured I could take her out on the lake and dump the body." He looked back up at me and smiled. "But Mama took care of that for us. God, what she did was stupid."

"That covers Madeline. Tell us about Catherine Hood. Your mother told us she thought she was seen at the studio?"

"When Mama told me that, I went to the studio but you and all the other cops were there. I was going to tell Jennifer that I had come to collect Maddy after her lesson, but I got cold feet. I didn't see Hood's car, but I knew where she lived so I drove to her place."

That was all my fault, I thought. If I'd kept her at the crime scene, she might still be alive. I was never going to live that mistake down nor forget it.

Paul went on without prompting. He was like a penitent unburdening his sins to his priest. He couldn't stop now if he wanted to. "I waited maybe a half hour and then went to the door. She and I had met so she let me in and I was able to get close enough to knock her out. Then I choked her. I didn't want to just leave her in the living room where anyone might find her. Then I found the freezer in the garage. I put her in there and went out to the house to meet mother."

"When did you telephone Jennifer Clayton?"

"Oh. I called her from the car. Asked her for a date and she told me about Madeline. I called Momma at my office and told her to go home. I got there just before she did. We got there just a few minutes before you did."

"When did you tell Rudy?"

"Momma called him at the dinner in Grand Rapids while you were talking to Gerd and me."

I looked at the other guys in the room. "Anyone else want to ask questions?" A lot of headshakes answered me. "Come on, Paul. Let's put you back in your cell for the night."

"Can I get a lawyer? And maybe get bailed out? I don't want to stay here all night."

"Too bad, but I think you're out of luck. You can call your attorney but there won't be a bail hearing until sometime tomorrow, so you're stuck with us. By the way, everything you told us will be transcribed and ready for your signature in the morning. It was also recorded. Don't even think about recanting."

Sean grabbed him by the arm and the four of us escorted him back to the holding cells.

Agents Duncan and Wilcox were in the Chief's office when we all trooped in. Bauer looked at me with a question in his eyes. I nodded, "He confessed. In detail. I'm pretty sure it'll stand up in court." I turned to Wilcox, "Where are the other two?"

Duncan jumped in, "I'm taking them to Washington for safe keeping."

Wilcox said, "What the agent means is that they will be in the custody of the CIA for the next several months. I understand that Karla is accused of murder and that her husband is at least an accessory to that so we will make them available to any court in Michigan that needs them. Is that satisfactory?"

Bauer grunted, "Perfectly. It's a pleasure doing business with a man who keeps his word." He shook hands with Wilcox and pointedly ignored Duncan. Wilcox and I shook hands and he said, "Congratulations. We're going to get out of here now. Look me up the next time you're in the DC area and we'll swap a war story or two."

"I'll do that...and thanks for your help. Maybe I can do something for you some day."

He gave me a funny look and mumbled, "Maybe you can." before they went out of the office.

Chief Bauer looked at the four of us. "Reports on the desk by noon tomorrow. I'll see you all sometime in the morning. Get out of here."

Sean and I were the last two out the door and again we heard Bull Bauer say, "Good job."

We walked over to our cube and collapsed into our chairs. Richards and Davis were already headed for the outside door and Sean looked as if he would soon follow them. I said, "Hit the road, Sean. There's nothing that can't wait until tomorrow. We can put our report together in the morning."

He nodded and got up. "Thanks. It's been a long day. I'll be at Sandy's place if you need me. See you later."

I watched him as he left. He was right. It had been a long day and I was beat. My leg was throbbing painfully. I knew I would have to have it looked at soon by the people at Johns Hopkins. I was ready to call it a day, but I needed to make one more stop before I went home. Outside in the parking lot I stopped a moment to look at the stars. It was turning colder and they shone with icy brilliance in the clear night sky. I climbed into the Rover and headed once more to nineteen thirty-three Lakeshore Drive.

CHAPTER FORTY-FIVE

The big house on Lakeshore Drive was dark except for a light burning in the hallway. The front door was not locked, and I went into the hall. Yellow cop tape still crisscrossed the door to the studio where Medline Straub had been murdered. I walked slowly down the carpeted hall and opened the door to the small office that Catherine Hood had used. A desk and a chair were all that remained. I went on to the second office. It, too, was empty except for the desk and chair Jennifer/Shannon had used.

I stepped to the door to her apartment. Should I knock? Would she be there? I had tried to call her a dozen times and had never gotten a response. I didn't know if she was still in Muskegon or if she had left already. I knocked on the door. There was no sound from inside the apartment. I tried the doorknob. This door was also unlocked and I pushed it open.

Shannon's apartment was empty. There was no sign that anyone had ever lived there. The apartment had been cleaned. There was a faint smell of disinfectant or some other household cleaner in the stale air. The furniture was all there, arranged as if to showcase the place to a potential new renter. There were no bottles or glasses on the marble-topped room divider. Shannon's New Yorker prints were gone from the wall over the couch. But the big monochrome of the Asian fisherwoman still hung on the opposite wall. There was an envelope stuck in the corner of the ornate wooden frame. It was addressed to me.

The note inside was short…'Please take the painting. Enjoy. S.'

There was a second envelope lying on the coffee table. It was also addressed to me.

I sat down on the couch and opened it. This note was also short:

"Alex,

I have to go. There are some reasons.

My job is one. You are another.

Too fast, too soon…perhaps.

I hope we will meet again.

I'd like that.

Shannon"